GENESIS

GARDEN OF EVIL SERIES

EDEN – BOOK 1
EXODUS – BOOK 2
GENESIS – BOOK 3
ELYSIUM – BOOK 4

Shade Owens & Ash S-J
www.shadeowens.com

Edited by Nikki Busch
www.nikkibuschediting.com

RED RAVEN PUBLISHING

ISBN: 978-1-990271-08-3

PROLOGUE

There's so much blood.

She looks like a doll, lying still with her neck covered in puncture wounds and blotchy marks. Any minute now, they'll darken to an inky, orange-speckled purple like the Andromeda galaxy.

She did this to herself.

My breath, slow and calculated, reminds me that I'm alive.

I'm alive, and she isn't.

And I know exactly who to pin this on.

CHAPTER 1 – EVE

The rain barely looks like rain at all.

It lands against my window, crystalized droplets soaking through the filth on the other side of the iron bars. It's only a matter of time before it turns to snow.

I reach by my bedside table, pluck a match out of a matchbox, and light my plain wax candle. We have hundreds of these in the basement somewhere. The air is so moist that the cold runs through my skin and into my bones.

I hate this time of year—the gloomy, lifeless period between fall and winter.

How is Freyda doing, anyway? And what about Gabriel? It's been a week since they left, and I can't seem to shake this anxiety. It's as if a metal ball is sitting at the bottom of my stomach. The women of Eden are becoming restless, too. I'm uncertain whether this has to do with the dreary weather we've been having, or whether they're also anxious to leave Eden—that's the plan, after all. That's the reason Freyda left with Gabriel—to find a new shelter to call our home.

Although I still don't trust him, he's our one hope. I can't afford to send women out in search of some promised land while this man, Gabriel, speaks of a high-security space that might allow us to regain some form of electricity.

Area 82, he calls it.

I have to trust that what he says is true, or at the very least, that Freyda trusts him. If I begin to doubt this mission, I'll worry about Freyda, and I can't allow myself to do that.

The moment we reach safety, he'll be imprisoned. It doesn't matter if he helps us. In the end, he's still a man, and men cannot be trusted, especially not in Eden—in a haven full of women.

A gentle tap echoes through my room and I avert my eyes to the door. It slowly creaks open, and a frizzy-haired head appears.

It's Nola.

What does she want?

I haven't been able to look her in the eyes after what I overheard her saying—after catching her warning my sweet little Lucy about me. She's doing everything she can to turn my godchild against me.

I won't stand for it.

She must sense my hatred. She walks in resembling a child caught doing something wrong. With slouched shoulders and a bowed head, she looks up at me with big honey-brown eyes. Her hair is even more damaged-looking than usual today, no doubt from all the rain we've been having.

I part my lips to speak, but nothing comes out.

I'm afraid that if I start speaking, I'll start to yell. But I can't do that. I need to remain calm—I need to be the leader Eden needs me to be.

"H-hi, Eve," she stammers.

I want to say hello, but even that is too much for me right now. So instead, I stare at her, waiting for her to explain herself—waiting for her to justify why she's disturbing me in the privacy of my bedroom at this hour.

The sun has already started to set, which means curfew will take effect any minute.

What could possibly be so important right now?

"I'm sorry to bother you." She locks her fingers together in front of her belly. "Under normal circumstances I wouldn't come in at this hour, Eve, you know that—"

"Spit it out," I say coldly, and her eyes widen a little. I've never spoken to her this way, nor anyone in Eden for that matter. But right now, Nola is my enemy and the idea of being kind to her pains me.

"A few women say they can hear someone over the wall," she says.

"Over the—" I stand up and tug at the bottom of my white overcoat. "Over the wall?"

She nods quickly. "There are a few women calling out. They keep saying your name." She shifts her weight on one leg, unlocks her fingers, and adds, "It isn't my decision, Eve, but I think they want inside."

I fight the urge to glower at her. It most definitely isn't her decision.

She shifts her weight again, looking uncomfortable this time, and adds, "What would you like me to do?"

I almost say, "You can leave," but I don't. If there truly are women on the other side of the wall, they're here because they've come seeking shelter inside of Eden. I can't deny them that. In most cases, Freyda would be the one to stand by my side as I allow women into Eden, but she's not here.

I lean over and blow out my candle, turn to Nola, and say, "Follow me."

She remains only a few feet away from me as I make my way to the front gates. The hallways are quiet, as they often are around this time, with the exception of children's high-pitched voices coming from the various divisions. They're most likely being tucked into bed by their mothers or guardians. Several of the children here don't have mothers—at least, not anymore—which is why so many women have stepped up and now care for children other than their own.

I walk to the security panel at the front entrance and enter my security code. With any luck, Area 82 will possess more electrical power than this penitentiary. I'm grateful to my engineers and electricians who managed to operate certain pieces of equipment using solar panels found in the prison's basement, but it isn't enough.

It has been almost six years since America collapsed, and the residual effects of the EMP attack remain. Every few weeks, Freyda turns on our analog radio and listens for survivors outside of Eden's walls. Though most of America remains a wasteland, colonies of survivors have begun forming across the states.

Nola flinches when the metallic door makes a loud clicking noise, followed by a beep. The door opens with a swoosh, and I step out into the entrance of the prison. Old sofas still decorate the lobby—assumedly a space that was once used for visitors to wait. Beside me, a reception desk is hidden behind bulletproof glass, though it's so filthy that the interior desk is hard to see. Next to the farthest sofa of the room is a vending machine with its entire right side missing. When we first arrived in Eden, women tore at it until they were able to retrieve what was inside.

I make my way to the front door and unlock the three metallic bolts, then with a swing of my upper body, push the door wide open. A cool gust of wind comes blowing in with thick droplets of water, soaking my pants in an instant.

It feels cold against my skin. I hate that feeling, especially since Eden doesn't have any form of heating system. Even my specialists weren't able to connect the furnace to the solar panel, and I'm assuming it has something to do with the prison's heating system being operated by gas, which we no longer have.

Perhaps Area 82 will have better heating equipment.

I can't complain, though. Winters in Eden almost never drop any lower than 20 degrees. It isn't pleasant—quite honestly it's uncomfortable—but it's survivable, especially when surrounded by concrete walls.

"They're at the front gates?" I ask, turning to Nola.

She gives me a brief nod and wipes rainwater from her face. "That's what Carla and Rosetta said. They said they heard voices—"

When I stop looking at her, she goes silent, most likely realizing that I don't know who Carla and Rosetta are, nor do I care. I walk toward the front gates and climb the ladder to the watchtower beside it.

As I climb, I look down at my red heels that look shinier than ever with water coating them, realizing I would have been better off climbing this barefoot. When I reach the top at last, I lean the upper half of my body over the concrete wall. It irritates me to do so since I'm going to have a difficult time washing the filth from my overcoat, but I need to see who's standing down there.

Several sets of eyes roll up at me, squinting as the rain sprinkles on their faces.

Then, as if seeing God himself through stormy clouds, one woman lights up and starts waving her arms over her head. She shouts words I can't hear through the rain, but it's obvious that she's begging for me to let them in. She looks middle-aged with her weathered skin and gray roots—a strong woman who's endured years of hardship.

Although she's the one waving and shouting at me, she isn't the one I'm looking at. Behind her are three men, and beside her, a young boy no older than two years old.

I pull away behind the wall, my fists clenched on either side of me.

Does this woman not know who I am? Does she not know about Eden? Men are forbidden, yet, here she stands, surrounded by four males. With anger, I grab the wet iron railing and make my way down the ladder.

I hate being put in a position like this—a position in which I decide who lives and who dies.

"What's going on?" Nola asks as I march toward her. "Are we opening up?"

I walk past her, my shoulder brushing against her, and without looking back, I say, "No, we aren't."

CHAPTER 2 – GABRIEL

"How much farther?" Miller asks, resting her hands on her knees. Her short curly brown hair lands over her eyebrows, and her dark glossy eyes roll up toward me.

She looks like crap.

Not ugly in any way... just tired. Like she's ready to collapse any minute. Her eyes are bloodshot, and she seems skinnier than she was six days ago, which is saying a lot. She was already pretty damn skinny to begin with. The kind of skinny that reminds me of one of those insects... A praying mantis, I think they're called.

"Only a few more hours," I say.

We passed the town of Shalotville and now we're getting close to Fayville, an abandoned little village that probably doesn't look much different than it did before the apocalypse. During my Black Marine days, we used to walk from Area 82 to Fayville to train. It actually became government property a few years before all of this. We'd set up decoys and targets and go at it all day long.

I miss my training days... before things got real. Before I started...

Freyda side-glances me and bites down, her jaw

muscles popping out. I can tell she's aching, but she'd never admit it. She's barely said a word these last few days. It's like she's reserving the bit of energy she has to keep walking instead of talking.

I wish Dakota had that mentality. She hasn't shut up since we saw the jet fly overhead. All she keeps talking about day and night is knot speed, advanced flight controls, and something about Silver Snake engines. I have no idea what that is, but I'm assuming it's something powerful. It's like watching a geek enter a comic convention. She knows everything about planes, and she feels the need to talk about things that don't make sense to the rest of us.

"Think anyone's living under there?" Jada asks. She looks almost as tired as Miller, only it isn't as obvious. Her skin is a beautiful dark brown instead of a pale chalky color. She points toward an overpass bridge that sits over what looks like an old highway.

It isn't the first overpass we see, and it won't be the last. At least this one isn't torn down halfway through. The concrete seems to be holding up, and above it, dozens of cars are lined up haphazardly on the road.

I'm getting tired of seeing beat-up old cars. It's damn frustrating. All it does is make me want to drive. Even if I managed to get a car to start up, I'd never get a clean road to drive on. I'd get stuck behind some beaten old car or in tall grass. There's no winning.

"Under that?" I ask, eyeing her and then the overpass. "Maybe. But it's better we don't find out."

Dakota sneers and points a short finger at Fayville. "But you want to cross through that?"

Without looking at her, I say, "We can either cut through it, or we can walk around it and add an extra few hours to our walk. Up to you."

She doesn't say anything, and neither does anyone else. I'm sure they're tired as heck now and all they want to do is get this over with, even if it means risking running into someone. But I find it hard to imagine that anyone would hide out in Fayville, especially since no one lived there before any of this happened.

I kick my combat boots through the long grass and press a hand over my forehead to block out the sun. A loud cricket comes flying out making a high-pitched vibrating noise.

I used to hate insects, but now, every time I see one, it gives me hope. If they can survive this hellhole, so can we.

"After Fayville, there's only a few miles left before we reach Area 82."

"Wish that plane had stopped for us," Miller breathes.

"You nuts?" Dakota chimes in. "That was a fuckin' fighter jet! A jet that size needs a runway that's at least six thousand feet. It isn't some helicopter. It can't just hover its way down to us."

"Well, technically—" I start.

Dakota flicks her wrist at me. "Yeah, yeah," she says, and although no one else knows what she's talking about, I do.

VTOLs.

That's short for vertical takeoff and landing. The first fixed-wing VTOL jet aircraft was called the Short

SC. 1. Its first flight was in the 1950 somethings. That's the extent of the knowledge I learned in training when it comes to aircraft, and it stuck with me. The military guys started calling one of our soldiers, Daniel Stockholm, SC. All because he was the shortest guy in training. Maybe I should call Dakota SC... She's the shortest one of us all.

"What?" Freyda says with impatience. "Some inside joke you two have?" She lets a sharp breath out through her nostrils and stares at both of us. For days, she's been quiet, and I bet she's about ready to rip someone's head off.

"I like my aircrafts old-school," Dakota says. "Not the fancy VTOL bullshit. They're basically drones. They fly themselves. What's the point of being a pilot if you don't even have to sit in the damn thing?"

"You're telling me that plane we saw could have been empty?" Freyda asks. With her hands on her waist and mismatched eyes narrowing on Dakota, she looks a bit more worried than pissed off now.

Dakota shrugs and keeps her mouth sealed shut, though it looks like she'd much rather be yelling at someone. Why does she always look so angry? I swear, when she's mad—which is always—the freckles on her face pulsate. Then again, that's likely because she's breathing so damn hard.

"Yeah, it's possible," I say. "Really possible."

"As in most likely?" Miller asks.

I give her a nod. I hate to admit that what these women thought was human life flying overhead was probably a robot.

Freyda rolls her eyes, so I cut in before everyone

gets upset. "Even if it was empty, there would've been someone flying it somewhere."

"Yeah, Gabe's right," Dakota says, and I'm not so sure I like the sound of *Gabe*. She's talking about me like we're best buds. "Those things don't control themselves."

"You think it's being controlled from Area 82?" Miller asks. She misses her step and falls against Jada's shoulder.

"Whoa, you okay?" Jada asks.

"Y-yeah," Miller stutters. "Need to rest soon."

A cool breeze sweeps through the grass, making a soft whistling sound, and the sun starts to disappear behind some of Fayville's buildings. The city isn't big by any means, but it isn't small, either. The sooner we cut through it, the sooner we can scout Area 82 before setting camp for the night.

If the sun sets while we're still crossing, we're going to have to camp out in Fayville.

I'm about to explain that to Freyda and her women when a nasty sound erupts from a nearby field. At first, it sounds like coyotes fighting over a fresh carcass. The growling is ferocious, monster-like, but it's the high-pitched yelping that makes me realize something's wrong. It's the heart-wrenching sound of an animal being hurt.

Freyda pulls her pistol out of her holster, a motion she's likely done thousands of times on the job, and darts toward the sound. I instinctively charge with her, my long legs bringing me to the front. I see the jumble of fur before I understand what's going on.

Foxes?

Coyotes?

But then I catch a glimpse of a face. They're shepherds, a pack of them, and they're mauling something alive. Fur and blood shoot up, and the yelping is so pronounced now that it overpowers the growling and barking of its attackers. It sounds like something's being skinned alive. I'm about to yell something, hoping that my voice will scare them off, when gunfire explodes behind me and the shepherds scatter. They quickly regroup and run toward a small pine-treed forest.

"What is it?" Dakota shouts in a panic.

Everyone runs toward the wounded animal. At first, I think it's a rabbit. It has a gray coat, but it's the size of a dog. I take two steps closer and realize it *is* a dog. It whimpers, its white-patched paws kicking the grass around its body like it's trying to run away. There's blood everywhere, making the yellow grass look a filthy brown. I'm scared to get any closer. What if the poor thing's been torn open?

Freyda raises her gun and points it at its head. It's like the dog suddenly knows what's coming. It stops squirming its contorted body and rolls its blue eyes her way.

"What're you doing?" I snap.

I don't mean to sound so aggressive, but we don't even know the extent of this poor thing's injuries.

"Putting it out of its misery," she says. "What's it look like I'm doing?"

"Put the gun down," I growl, my voice a deep rumble.

Dakota pulls her chin back and makes an ugly

face—a look that says, *Who are you and where's Gabriel?*

I don't even give her the time to drop the gun. I put my back to it and move toward the dog, my shoulders slouched and my knees bent.

"Hey, hey," I say, my voice soft.

It whimpers and throws its head back like it's trying to slither away without the use of its legs.

"Not gonna hurt you, buddy," I say. But then I realize it doesn't have a penis. "Sweet girl," I correct.

I drop onto my knees and inch my way toward her. She's so scared it breaks my heart. I can imagine exactly what she's thinking: her life is about to end, and she's scared out of her mind. All she wants to do is get away from me.

Her white belly is covered in a rusted red color, but there doesn't seem to be any damage. At least nothing external. No big bites or openings. It looks like they went after her legs. They're all bloody, and her back right paw looks completely raw. I think I see muscle, but it's so hard to tell with all of the blood.

"The worst is her back leg," I say.

"Poor thing," Dakota says behind me.

"What're you going to do?" Freyda asks. "Nurse her back to health? For God's sake, Gabriel, we barely have enough resources for ourselves."

If I open my mouth to talk, I'll no doubt come across as an asshole, so I ignore her. Freyda's only thinking with her head, and I admire her for that. She's right, we don't have many resources, and trying to take care of a dog with the bit of food we have seems pretty stupid.

But what am I supposed to do? Kill it? I can't. It's an innocent creature.

"It's okay, sweet girl," I try. I crawl a bit closer and though she's still panicking, she isn't trying to get away as much as she was before. "Not gonna hurt you, okay?" I slowly reach a hand toward her face, full well expecting her to bite me, but I need to let her smell me. I need her to realize I'm not a threat.

Her dry nose touches the tips of my fingers, and then she starts kissing them. Her tongue is warm and soft, and the kissing becomes aggressive. It's like she's begging me to not hurt her.

"It's okay," I whisper again, and this time, I pet her gently on the head. The yelping becomes more of a sad whimper. It seems to soothe her. Her ears fall flat against the sides of her head and she closes her eyes.

I turn to Freyda with a proud smile on my face, but she doesn't look impressed. She crosses her arms over her puffed chest and walks the other way, kicking her boots through the tall grass.

"Think you can help her?" Miller asks. She crouches beside me, and when she realizes the dog isn't reacting, reaches a gentle hand to scratch the back of her neck.

"I have to try," I say. "Here, hold this." I pull my bag off my back and it makes a thump as it lands in the grass.

Miller drags it away from the dog and lets it sit by Jada's feet.

With my hands, I tear my T-shirt in half and pull it off my chest.

"What're you doing?" Dakota asks, but it comes

out more like an accusation.

I don't bother saying anything. I wrap my fingers around the dog's leg, careful not to stress her out, and bandage her wound with my shirt. Instead of biting me, she starts licking my hand over and over again like she knows I'm trying to help her.

"It's okay," I whisper.

I can feel Freyda's hateful glare from here. Chances are she thinks I'm wasting everyone's time.

I'm sure there's a reason she's turned out to be so cold, but I'd be willing to bet that before the war happened, she wasn't like this. I can't hold it against her.

I scoop the dog up into my arms and she lets out a little cry but still doesn't try to bite. She seems to be less than a year old.

What happened? Did someone not have enough food to share and decide to leave her behind? Wouldn't surprise me. It's happened many times before. In most cases, though, the dogs are dead when I find them. Either that or completely feral.

Jada's dark face pops up beside me, her lips pulled back into a giant smile.

"Hi, sweetie," she says.

She looks like she hasn't seen a dog in years. Maybe she hasn't.

"Can you hurry up?" Freyda says, a hand on her waist. "What's the plan, now, Gabriel? Are we stopping here for the night so you can nurse your dog back to health?"

What's her problem? I'm trying to save an animal's life and she's acting like I asked her to walk another three days.

I shake my head, not knowing what to respond. I walk past her with the puppy in my arms. Its fuzzy fur tickles my chest, and the heat of her body calms me. How was I supposed to leave her behind? Her pleading eyes roll up at me, and I can't help but smile.

She's such a beautiful dog.

It's obvious life hasn't treated her fairly.

Without putting much thought into it, a name pops into my head and comes rolling off my tongue.

"Justice."

"What?" Dakota asks.

"Her name," I say, smirking. "Justice."

Dakota scoffs, but Miller and Jada seem to like it. I look up at Freyda, but she rolls her eyes and starts marching toward Fayville.

A cool breeze brushes against my back, and I hold Justice a little bit closer, the tiny hairs of her head brushing against my chin. She has puppy breath, something that smells a bit like warm kibble, though she isn't exactly a puppy. Maybe eight months old. I can't say I dislike the smell; it reminds me of my *abuelo's* golden retriever, Tortuga. He named her "turtle" in Spanish because she was unusually slow, even as a puppy. She'd walk her way over to play, even though her entire wavy-haired butt shook from side to side with excitement.

I miss that dog.

I let my chin rest on Justice's head, and her warmth comforts me.

"Come on," I say and quicken my pace a bit. Jada and the others follow close by as I catch up to Freyda.

We pass by an old saloon some of the military guys once used as a break area during training. They'd brought their own beers and let them sit in a bucket at the back. They were never cold, but cool enough to drink on a hot summer day.

I don't much like the look of it now. A wooden panel sits overhead of the protruding balcony, and it reads, Sand Storm, a name I never understood. But somehow, it suits it. Most of the roads in this town are all made of sand and pebblestone, and if it weren't for all the bullet holes and bomb residue throughout, it might have actually been a charming place.

But now, it looks like something out of a haunted western movie. The saloon's hinged door creaks from side to side as we walk by, and my heart races. What if someone's inside? What if we're walking straight into danger? I can't help but think the same thing for Area 82, but at the same time, if someone is intelligent enough to bring technology back, I doubt they're going to hunt us down like animals.

Hopefully, they'll listen.

They have to. It's our only hope.

"Fuck!" Freyda shouts, and I almost drop Justice to reach for my gun.

But then I see her kicking her boot sideways, trying to fling something off from underneath its sole.

"Goddamn dog shit," she says.

I'm about to laugh, but I can already tell she's in a bad mood. So instead, I shut my mouth and keep moving. Behind me, Miller lets out a muffled laugh, but she grunts when someone either punches her or jabs her in the ribs.

I pull Justice even closer to me, holding her body with firm hands, and I start jogging down Fayville's main road. My anxiety's setting in, and I don't want to black out again. I need to feel cool air hitting my face... like I'm moving toward something and not a sitting duck for someone to attack.

Brushing past Freyda, I'm like a giant stomping its way through a crowd of civilians as my heavy boots slap the ground. The others start jogging too, no doubt thinking that hurrying out of here before it gets completely dark is the best option.

I keep expecting to hear a gunshot go off, or someone let out a pained cry. Every time Dakota lets out one of her bubbly, smoker-sounding coughs, I flinch.

I fucking hate this.

Maybe this feeling will go away, eventually.

At last, we break through the end of Fayville and it's like coming out of a haunted house. A wave of relief washes over me, and I can breathe again.

"Holy shit," Dakota says, coughing one last time into the elbow of her arm. She pats her oversized cargo vest and stares straight ahead at a sight I've come to think of as home, even though I hate everything about it.

The first fence is made of twenty-foot-high chain link and it runs all the way around Area 82. I wouldn't even know how long it is, and I'd be scared to know how much a job like that cost the government. But that's only the beginning of it. Behind the fence is a paved road, which is where most federal vehicles used to park. A few of them remain now—black, chrome-trimmed SUVs with twenty-five-inch wheels. They're beasts, and I remember being mesmerized by them when I first came to Area 82 on the shuttle bus with James.

He'd stared at me wide-eyed, his coiffed orange hair looking yellow with the sun pouring through the bus window, and said something along the lines of, "Holy shit, it's real."

That's what we were all thinking about this place... That it was real.

"Looks locked," Dakota says, taking a heavy step forward.

I raise a closed fist, not realizing that Dakota doesn't understand military signals. She keeps walking, so I hiss, "Wait," in the darkness.

It's dangerous to walk right up to the gates. Not only that, but it's too damn dark to see much.

The moon sits up high in the sky, and thousands upon thousands of stars light up the dark space around it. Widespread lighting comes from Area 82's dome-like building, illuminating the yard around it. It's artificial lighting, too, which makes the windows look like bright white squares. That also means they have full electricity in there.

The Dome, or the main building, is 8.4 million square feet in size. I have no idea how I remember this, but I do recall being told that it was bigger than something called the West Edmonton Mall. Apparently, that thing sat around 5.3 million square feet before half of it burned down in 2051.

I wonder if the new mall is still up... I wonder if Canada's okay and if they weren't affected by our major fuckup.

Staring at the Dome, I remember the time I spent here as a Black Marine, undergoing intense training almost every hour of every day. And the speeches... God, I hated those. Hated how they'd play videos for hours, making us watch some of the most gruesome and horrendous things to get exactly what they wanted... to brainwash us.

The Dome itself is protected by another iron gate that stands twelve feet tall. It seems a bit insane to have so much protection around it when the Dome itself is constructed of heavy metal, cement, and bulletproof glass. But it's a top-secret military facility, after all. Inside are some of the most dangerous and advanced weapons this world has. It's no wonder they wanted it to be impenetrable.

The Dome's front gates sit approximately fifty feet away from the chain-link fence so that only a few vehicles can get in at a time. I guess this was another safety feature of theirs.

Glaring through the darkness, I hope to catch a glimpse of someone walking by a window, but no one passes. There's no telling how many people are in the Dome. And who knows? Maybe they're sleeping.

Around the Dome itself, between the chain-link and iron fencing, are several dozen aircrafts sitting still, looking like ancient artifacts. At least to me, because I haven't seen them in forever (aside from the one that flew right over our heads). But right now, it's too dark to tell whether they're filthy or squeaky clean. I'm hoping they're clean. If they are, that means they're being used.

I turn around and hand Justice to Miller, who grabs her with a grin on her face. I then take a step toward Area 82 and Freyda follows me.

"No, wait here," I say.

She scoffs. "What makes you think it's safe for you to go alone?"

This seems like a dumb question, but I realize she's trying to protect me. It's ironic... that's all I want to do for her.

"Well, if it isn't safe, I'd rather be alone," I say.

She seems taken aback by this like she wasn't expecting me to say something nice.

"Please," I try again. "Just wait here. We don't know who's in there. It could be all men in there, and I'm not putting you in that danger. I need you guys to keep an eye out for me."

"Guys?" Dakota says. It's a bit dark to see her features, but from where I'm standing, it looks like she's scowling at me. "Do I look like a guy—"

Miller smacks her on the arm. "Don't get started with your feminist bullshit. We're in the middle of something here that could potentially get us killed, and you're gonna give Gabriel shit for using the wrong gender terminology? Come on, Dakota. It's a saying. Grow up. Everyone says *guys* to generalize a group of people."

"Not everyone," Jada says. "Think about it—we use guys to include both men and women, but God forbid we say *women* or *girls* to incorporate the two genders... Holy shit. Men would freak."

"Two genders?" Freyda says. "If you guys want to start pointing fingers, I can take this argument to a whole new level."

Dakota slaps her forehead.

No one else says anything, so I take this as my cue to get out of there before the argument gets heated. As I walk away from them, I can't help but think if I'd said *ladies*, would Dakota have gotten upset about that, too? I don't understand why everyone's so uptight about everything. Maybe it's hatred. Maybe the world did this to us... Everyone's so angry that it comes out on other people. Or, maybe all of the injustices have led to this.

If I had the power to create a new world and new personalities, I'd make it so that people reacted based on someone else's *intention*. That way, if someone had a good intention, you wouldn't pick apart their words to make them feel like shit. You wouldn't sit there and assume they meant something awful. You'd feel their intention. The truth is we don't always mean what we say, how we say it. And we also say things based on our own personal experiences in this life.

And this whole gender and sexuality debate? How about we all live the way we want, how we want, without being judged or having fingers pointed at us? Why do people have the need to put others in boxes and then judge their boxes?

It's what's inside that matters.

Words are only words, and so are labels. In the end, I think we all want the same thing: love.

No decent human being deserves to be treated like shit for who they are on the inside or the outside.

No one.

Is that so fucking hard?

I realize I've totally gone off in my own head again. Out of nowhere, I'm standing at the front gates of the chain-link fencing. A huge locking mechanism protects the latch, and it looks electronic. I'm sure it's hardwired to the inside of the Dome, so I wouldn't be able to unlock it if I wanted to.

But I don't even have time to think about how I *might* be able to get around it. All of a sudden, something loud clicks, and I'm blinded by a dozen floodlights pointing down at me.

CHAPTER 3 – LUCY

Emily looks much better than she did two weeks ago, especially now that she isn't confined to her hospital bed. But I can tell she still isn't feeling like her usual self. She sits with slouched shoulders and eyes looking empty of all life.

"You okay?" I ask.

She turns to me with the weight of her body on one hand, causing her bed to make a creaking noise. Pulling her legs up and pressing them against her chest, she drops her chin on her knees and gives me a shrug. It's the kind of shrug that says, *No, I'm not okay, but I have no reason to complain.*

I cringe when she turns her head to the side and lets out a loud barking cough.

I hate that sound.

Every time she coughs, I'm reminded of *sick* Emily—Emily that only a few days ago lay helpless in the Medical Unit in Dr. Lewis's care. She couldn't have asked for a better doctor, though. Dr. Lewis is the only reason she's alive.

I feel bad for Emily. Recovering from pneumonia is hard enough, but she's also been so down lately. It's not like her. For the most part, Emily is all smiles and ready for some next big adventure. I guess the sickness is getting her down, too.

Either that, or it's the weather.

It's been pretty cold out and the sun hasn't been around much. I gaze past her feathery, braided hair that looks like it hasn't been touched in two weeks and up through the Plexiglas of her cell window. It's snowing outside, but that's not what I'm looking at.

The iron bars are caked with dust and cobwebs. She can't even blame her bad cleaning habits on the pneumonia. Her room is never clean, and it's rare that she brings her bedding out to Mrs. Appleton for cleaning.

Maybe Eve's OCD rubbed off on me when I was young. My room is pretty much always meticulously clean. I grind my teeth at the thought of Eve. I don't hate her, but it's clearer than ever now that she can't be trusted.

She's lost her mind.

Emily lets out another loud bark and I flinch at the sound.

"Sorry," she mumbles, wiping saliva from the corner of her mouth.

I lean away from her and wipe my hands on my knees as if this will somehow protect me from catching her germs. "You sure you aren't contagious?"

She shakes her head. "Dr. Lewis said I was past the cont—" Another hoarse cough comes blasting out of her lungs. "Sorry. She said I wasn't contagious anymore. She also said I should expect a bit of anger from some people in Eden in the coming weeks."

I almost laugh, but I realize this isn't a joke. How

on Earth could anyone be angry at sweet little Emily? It's not like she asked to be sick, and it isn't her fault the bug's been spreading in Eden. No one knows where it started.

"This isn't your fault," I say. I want to place a comforting hand on her back, but I don't want to touch her. I'm being paranoid, but in Eden, without proper medical care, everyone is better safe than sorry.

She shakes her head and forces a smile. "It's not about sharing my germs. It's about the antibiotics Dr. Lewis gave me."

"That was Dr. Lewis's decision," I say, "not yours."

She doesn't seem convinced, and I don't blame her. Dr. Lewis has time and time again refused to treat women with antibiotics because of our limited supply, resulting in countless deaths. But she has a pretty strict rule when it comes to treating with antibiotics. She doesn't give antibiotics to anyone over 18. A lot of mothers are quick to defend Dr. Lewis's decision, but a lot of others aren't. They say things like, "Many young women's lives could have been spared if she'd only given them the right medication." They're probably referring to their daughters aged nineteen, twenty, and twenty-one.

I'm not sure how many pills Dr. Lewis has left, but it isn't much. When I was visiting Emily, she showed me bottles that were expired and said they were useful up to a decade after that date. That's how desperate Eden is right now. We're using expired antibiotics. I can't help but wonder what's going to happen when we have none at all.

Emily lets out a bubbly sigh. "So? What've I missed over the last few days? Did you hear anything?" She smirks at me, looking like complete crap with her bright red nose and sunken eyes. "Any big secrets I should know about?"

Suddenly, the image of Eve flashes in my mind, her posture hunched in front of the mirror. She's shouting at herself, looking possessed by some demonic force.

Blinking these thoughts away, I swallow hard and keep my mouth shut. They aren't thoughts I want to share with Emily or with anyone for that matter. Eve is still the leader of Eden, and if I start accusing her of being crazy, everyone is going to turn on me. Or, if they believe me, I'll start a war inside Eden. Either way, the outcome isn't good. Especially not now... Especially not when everything is about to change.

"What is it?" Emily blurts. She inches closer to me, her eyes wide and her runny nose bright-looking like a cherry tomato. "You know something."

Quickly glancing in front of her cell, I ensure no one's lurking nearby. The kids are assumedly in class right now since the corridor of Division Five is quiet. I saw Mrs. Greensmith take a few students outside earlier, but it wasn't long before she came back in. It must be cold.

I turn my attention back to Emily's crusted brown eyes and clear my throat. "We're leaving Eden."

Her jaw drops wide open and she leans in even closer, almost like she'll understand better if my voice carries inside her mouth. Her perfectly aligned bottom teeth are shiny with saliva.

"When?" she asks. "Where? How do you know

this?"

"I overheard it," I say, smirking.

Emily is the only reason I even have this information. She brought me to the storage space connected to the Theater Room. That's where I overheard it, and she knows it.

Her lips stretch into a childish grin and she points at me. "You went spying on your own!"

"Keep your voice down," I hiss. "The adults all know about it, but the kids don't know yet."

"Well that's dumb," she says. "What's the big secret?"

I shrug. "Too much excitement, maybe. Eve wants everyone to stay calm."

Emily rubs her chin but turns away fast and starts hacking into her elbow. The coughing becomes so out of control that she can't even get a word out. Instead, she raises a finger in the air—the kind that says, *Give me a second*—all the while turning beet red in the face.

"You okay?" I ask.

But she can't answer. She coughs a few more times until the sound of phlegm loosening vibrates from her chest. She grimaces up at me with a sour taste on her face, and I do the same.

"Sorry," she mumbles, then spits a glob of mucus into a ceramic bowl by her bed.

"All I know," I continue, trying not to look at the ceramic bowl," is that Gabriel, that man who was in Eden, is taking Freyda and a few others to some new place. I think they're going to see if it's suitable for us, and then they'll come back to take us all there."

"Well I don't know how they expect to migrate

hundreds of people with winter approaching," she says. "You honestly think everyone in Eden is able to walk that long? I mean, it doesn't—"

"You can't do this!" comes a panicked shriek.

I glance at Emily, then back toward where the sound came from. What's going on?

She jolts into an upright position. "It came from the main hall."

"Let go of me!" the grating voice continues.

Then, countless other voices start talking over one.

Emily and I run down the corridor of Division Five to find the main hall filled with women swarmed at the center like seagulls around a piece of bread. I can't see what's going on with all the bodies pressed against one another, but every few seconds, someone shouts something.

"This is for the safety of our children!"

"You have no right to lock me up—"

"Enough!"

Everyone immediately goes quiet, and from Eden's main entrance comes Eve, her pantsuit looking whiter than freshly fallen snow. Her heels tick loudly as she moves forward, the sound bouncing off every inch of the main hall's walls.

"Eve, please," the woman begs.

What's wrong with her? She looks like death. Is she sick? Her skin has a yellow tint, and her black bangs form a flat line over her sunken angular eyes. She stares at Eve as if her life depends on it.

What's going on?

Eve stops walking when the woman starts

coughing, and at the same time, dozens of other women step away from her with their hands over their mouths and noses. The two women who are holding the sick one wear masks over their faces—medical masks, likely something Dr. Lewis would have given them—and medical gloves, too.

Eve flicks a finger in the air, and without any emotion at all, says, "Bring her to M-4. The room is empty."

The woman starts kicking the air and shouting things like, "You have no right! I'm not a prisoner!"

As she's dragged across the hall, women part ways, creating a path like the ocean split by Moses. Why is she so upset? She's sick. She shouldn't be around other people. It's so selfish of her to be arguing it. I watch Eve as she stares at the woman, looking completely disgusted with her wrinkled chin and pouting lips.

For the first time, I don't see her as a monster. I don't see her as Eden's dictator who forces women to do things they don't want. She's doing the right thing by locking that woman up.

Maybe that's what Mavis was going on about. She'd said that anything Eve did, no matter how drastic, was for Eden's well-being. In the end, regardless of her methods, all she wanted was to keep her women safe.

But then, I think back to the other night when I saw her in her room talking to herself. She's lost her mind. Right now, she may be doing the right thing, but within a matter of seconds, she could be doing something totally dangerous.

She catches me looking at her and I swallow hard. She doesn't smile or wave at me. Instead, she stares at me as if I were nothing more than a fixture on a wall. It's like she's empty again when only a few days ago, she was full of life and joy.

That's what scares me.

She flips between two personalities, and I never know which one she has until she looks at me. When Aunty Eve came out the other day, she looked at me as if I were her most cherished possession. Now, she's looking at me like I'm as useless as a broken plate.

She raises her chin a little, her eyes never leaving mine, and the sides of her jaw pop out. Is she angry with me? Resentful? When I caught her talking to herself, she was angry with Nola.

I haven't had the guts to say anything to Nola. I'm afraid she'll think I'm making it up. But I have to warn her. She needs to know her life could be in danger.

I swallow hard, and though I want to look away, I can't. It's as if I'm searching for something, anything, to let me know that Aunty Eve is hidden in there somewhere. Even if she's too deep to see right now, I need to know she's there.

But I can't find Aunty Eve in there.

In fact, I can't even find Eve, either.

CHAPTER 4 – EVE

Why is she staring at me in such a way?

It's as if she knows something I don't. Did she truly mean what she said when she spoke to Nola about me behind my back? When she confessed to not caring about me at all?

Fucking little bitch.

My eyes begin to water, and I can't determine whether it's coming from a place of anger, hatred, or heartbreak.

My sweet Lucy. How could you possibly believe a stranger over me? I wish I could ask her—speak to her directly, but all I can do is look at her. It's apparent she's become uncomfortable with the duration of my stare, so I turn on my heels and begin walking back toward my room.

"Eve, Eve!" someone shouts.

Rapid footsteps scurry behind me, and I'm like a mother being harassed by her children. Is it too much to ask to be left alone? Left to fall into a pit of darkness, haunted by thoughts of Freyda and Lucy? Haunted by feelings of loneliness?

Clenching my fists, my fingernails digging into my palms, I turn around. Mrs. Lavish, one of Eden's best

Cooks, limps toward me with a contorted body.

"Eve," she repeats as if I'm still walking and she's unable to catch up.

Is she here to complain about the group of survivors outside of Eden's walls? I haven't changed my mind, nor will I. Eden is under enough stress as it is—I can't allow an external threat inside my walls.

"Eve?"

I nearly snap and say, *What do you want?* but instead, I hold it inside.

Mrs. Lavish is a gentle soul; she reminds me of a small neighborhood's elderly woman, the kind who cares for several cats, even those that aren't her own—the kind of woman who never has any visitors and to compensate, strolls across her front lawn several times a day, pretending to call out to her felines so she can socialize with a passing neighbor. Mrs. Lavish enjoys socializing so much that some women will go out of their way to avoid her if they're not in a talkative mood.

"What is it?" I say through gritted teeth.

The poor woman is already out of breath. "Contamination," she breathes. "We... We need to decontaminate. I can't be cooking food like this, Eve." She then hesitates, as if only now realizing how much I despise being talked to in such a manner. We are not *buddies*, nor are we friends. She clears her throat. "I-I'm sure you already have this under control." She bows her head so low it looks like she's about to tip over and fall flat on her face. "Please let me know if I can be of any help."

I give her a brief nod, one that says, *Thank you and*

goodbye.

Although I'm in no mood to take charge right now, that's precisely what these women need. I can still hear them bickering in the main hall, saying things like, "Maybe you ought to be locked up with Eun-ji!"

And, "Don't even start. I heard you coughing last night!"

"I have allergies!"

I pinch the bridge of my nose and inhale a long breath, my chest expanding so much so that my back cracks. I feel like I'm surrounded by children all the time—assigned the task of managing a daycare without any form of monetary compensation.

These women are mothers, grandmothers, even.

Is it so hard to be an adult? I'm younger than most of them, yet I still seem to be the only one maintaining order around here. I turn on my heels and return to where I stood only moments ago, my gaze fixated on the crowd of frantic women before me. At that moment, they resemble nothing more than a pack of uncivilized chimpanzees, poking and prodding at each other and shouting accusations behind pointed fingers.

"Ladies, ladies," I say, forcing *charming* Eve to come out.

Right now, it's harder than ever; forcing the muscles of my face to contort into a meaningless smile feels worse than a full day of physical labor. But I have to do it—I need these women to continue to see me as their loving and sympathetic leader.

"I understand how scary this is right now," I say. "No one is being *imprisoned*, so please don't view it this way."

"Isn't being locked up the same thing?" one woman shouts.

I only see the redness of her hairline for a brief moment before the women around her nudge her in the ribs, and she cowers behind them.

"You women are highly intelligent," I say, squinting my eyes in a loving way. "That's the reason you're all here. You understand what it means to survive, which means you understand why we are using the isolation units to contain the virus. Let me remind you what happened the first year we came here." Women lower their heads and others break eye contact. They remember, but I need to voice it. "How many women died? Children, even? All because illness spread around Eden within a matter of days. We have been lucky these last few years, suffering from nothing more than common colds and gastro." Women cling onto their daughters as if the words themselves are contagious. "A virus has returned, and this time, it isn't as forgiving. It's aggressive, and it's spreading quickly. One child almost died last week, and two women, as we speak, are in Dr. Lewis's care."

A woman in the back begins sobbing, and I can only assume she's friends with one of the dying women. I don't mention this—I don't tell them that, as per Dr. Lewis's analysis, their prognoses aren't looking good. She came to me last night, a delicate knock on my bedroom door. When I told her to come in, she did so, but not in her typical medical attire. She'd slipped into a pair of beige cotton pants and a white T-shirt, explaining that her medical outfit needed to be washed every evening after treating anyone with this bug.

* * * * * *

"It's not looking good, Eve," Dr. Lewis says.

At first, I don't understand what she's talking about. I've been so preoccupied thinking about Freyda and Gabriel and this Area 82 he promises that I've completely forgotten about the threat Eden faces within its very walls.

"It appears to be an influenza virus—"

I glower at her, though I know it isn't her fault. "Influenza? As in, the flu? Ezri, how is that even possible? We haven't allowed anyone into Eden these last few weeks other than Gabriel, who didn't appear sick at all."

"He could have been carrying the virus," she says, "but I'm more inclined to believe this is influenza A, which means it could have spread from an animal."

I scoff and lean forward on my desk, my elbows flat on the wood. "You're telling me that some dumb—" But I cut myself short. I don't want to revert to my eighteen-year-old self. "You're telling me an animal, like a bird, could have carried this into Eden."

She nods matter-of-factly as if she's answered this question countless times before.

I let out a sigh and drop my forehead into my palms. How is this happening? Why is it one problem after another? Not only do we need to relocate the women in Eden due to limited resources, we now have a pandemic situation inside our walls.

And what if Gabriel and Freyda return shortly? We can't relocate women who are sick.

"Might I offer a suggestion?" Dr. Lewis says.

I don't answer her, but instead, stare at her, which is a translation for, *Keep talking.*

"We have a dozen empty rooms in the Medical Unit. They have lockable latches on the outside, and even toilets on the inside."

"They sound like prison cells," I say.

She smirks, her teeth resembling shiny pieces of mozzarella cheese in comparison to her dark skin. "A bit. The walls are padded, and the beds are more comfortable."

"Were they psychiatric units?" I ask. "For the insane?"

"Patients suffering from psychosis," she corrects, and I can't help but roll my eyes.

"No one cares about political correctness anymore, Ezri."

She smiles again, and continues. "The point is, I think we should begin isolating those who carry the illness. At least until we can contain it." She chews on her bottom lip and stares at me. "*If* we can."

"If?" I blurt. "What do you mean, *if?*"

"The influenza virus tends to spread incredibly fast; it can spread up to six feet the moment an infected individual sneezes or coughs."

This is bad.

I've heard women coughing around Eden for the last few days, which means they have been sharing their germs with the walls, door handles, the floors.

"What's the final outcome?" I ask, though I'm afraid to hear what she might say.

"It depends," she says. "Some women will get over

it within a week, as they've surely done countless times before in our old world. There's no medicine I can give them. The women need to rest most of all. For some, it will be an unpleasant flu. For others, like the two women in my care right now, it could mean death."

My eyes nearly pop out of my head. "They've died?"

She shakes her Afro and casts her eyes to the floor. "Not yet."

* * * * * *

"Eve?"

"Is she okay?"

I glance up, realizing I've been staring absentmindedly at the main hall's floor tiles for the last few minutes.

"I understand the things you've heard," I continue, "about the isolation units. Inside, you will be provided with food, water, and comfort. If this virus is not isolated and continues to spread throughout all of Eden, it could mean the lives of many. It could mean the lives of your children."

Women nod, and it's apparent by their slanted eyebrows and large, doughy eyes that they're worried, and they understand what I'm saying. Surely, they do not want to be the cause of someone else's death.

"If you have been experiencing any flu-like symptoms, I urge you to go see Dr. Lewis. If you cough or sneeze, please, cover your mouth. Do not allow your children to touch their eyes, their noses, or mouths, and remember to always use the sanitizer stations located throughout Eden."

I hate to promote the sanitizer dispensers, especially being that we are running low, but I have no choice. If I want my women to survive long enough to see Area 82, I'm going to have to allow them to deplete whatever resources we have.

I catch a glimpse of Lucy's velvety red hair as she exits the main hall, followed by who I can only assume is Emily. Why is she spending her time around that girl when a few days ago, she was bedridden in Dr. Lewis's care? She shouldn't be exposing herself to those germs.

Women begin forming a line toward Dr. Lewis's office. Several of them have red, snotty noses, while others do not appear sick at all but are most likely taking necessary precautions after my speech.

"Come on, honey, this is important," one mother says, bending forward to reach her daughter at eye level. "The doctor will make you all better, okay?"

I should feel empathy—heartache, even. I should be afraid for the lives of these children, but right now, all I can think about is my Lucy. It's as if nothing else in the world matters beyond her.

These thoughts are foolish—I'm well aware that the lives within Eden are important to me, otherwise, I wouldn't be standing where I am today; I wouldn't be the ruler of Eden, fighting to keep everyone within these walls safe.

Deep down, I care, but on the surface, I feel like a machine; emotionless in that regard. It's as if my emotions have been siphoned and stored within a glass bottle—a bottle reserved for very few individuals in my life.

Some days, though I admit these are few and far between, I wonder what Eden would be like with someone else in charge. Would it be a better place? Or, have I done the impossible? Have I created a haven no one else could have dreamed of ever creating?

The latter pleases me, so I decide to focus on that.

Without me, these women are nothing.

Elevating my chin, a sense of pride and accomplishment fills me in an instant. Despite how I feel in this moment—despite not feeling any form of attachment toward these women—I will not allow something I've built to come crumbling to pieces.

I brush past a young couple holding hands, and they gaze at me as if I were the CEO of a multibillion-dollar industry. One of them wipes her nose and sniffles, while the other, ignoring my warning, wraps her arm around her lover's shoulder and kisses her grimy forehead.

I turn away, repulsed—not by their affection for one another, but by their exchange of germs. This is precisely what I worried would happen. Women, especially mothers, will comfort those in need, regardless of the danger it puts them in.

This has to stop. Instead of returning to my office, I turn in the opposite direction and march toward Division Three, which will lead me to Mavis and Perula's Herb Shack.

Eden will survive, no matter the price.

CHAPTER 5 – GABRIEL

I blink hard, trying to get the bright light out of my face. Voices are yelling at me, but I can't tell where they're coming from.

"On your knees!"

"Hands in the air!"

Who's shouting? I raise two hands over my head and kneel in the dirt when another clicking noise fills the air. This time, it sounds electronic, high-pitched, and it's followed by the sound of something heavy being unlocked.

Are they opening the gates?

Then, I hear another sound, and a knot forms in my stomach.

It's the sound of guns being cocked.

Not pistols, or shitty little handguns, but energized weapons that only Area 82 would carry. Obviously, these people know what they're doing. I hope to God I didn't bring Freyda and the others to an all-male military base.

That's why I wanted them to stay behind.

I can't risk it.

But then, a husky voice carries louder than all the others, and I look up to find her standing there, two firm hands planted on her weapon belt. She's wearing a typical black and green uniform, which makes her stand out seeing as all her soldiers seem to be wearing BIO-8 Skins: skin-textured armor that literally covers a soldier from head to toe with a click of a button. I used to have one, too. It was onyx gray, and every time I put it on, it was cool on the skin, like silicone, and didn't interfere with anything. It was like wearing a layer of air.

The woman's hair, a dirty blond that looks blanched under all of these blazing fluorescent lights, is pulled back into a tight, greasy ponytail. She searches me like I'm an ex-con... Like she's trying to figure out how many people I've killed.

I can tell she's in charge before she even opens her mouth, and I can also tell that whatever comes out of it is going to be loud and authoritative.

"State your name."

"Rodriguez," I say, not surprised by her tone. "Gabriel Rodriguez."

"Where are you traveling from?" she asks. "Are you alone?"

Am I alone? If I said no, would they spare the women's lives? Or, would they take me inside and leave them behind? I hesitate, my eyes stupidly darting sideways as if pulled by a mind of their own.

Fuck.

Why did I look over there?

"What're you hiding, Rodriguez?"

She takes a step forward, energy rifle held firmly in her hands.

"I asked you a question," she says, but it sounds

more like an order.

She's about half the size of all the men around her, but I can tell this woman's got everything under control. They respect her, and they won't hesitate to launch an energy blast through my skull if I don't make it clear that I'm not here for any trouble.

"I'm coming from Eden," I say. Hopefully, this will satisfy her.

Her blond brows come close together and one nostril goes up like she caught a whiff of something rank.

"Eden?" she scoffs. "You expect me to believe that a man set foot inside of Eden?"

So she knows what Eden is.

"I asked you a question, Rodriguez. Are you alone, or do you have any followers?"

I flinch when she jabs her gun in the air, shadows forming all over her face.

"Wait!"

Jesus Christ, Freyda.

She runs up beside me, her shoes kicking through the dirt, and kneels by my side with both hands in the air.

"What the fuck is this?" the leader says.

This time, instead of taking a step toward us, she takes a cautious step back and raises her gun, her bright her eye staring down the long barrel.

"He's not lying!" Freyda's voice cracks as she waves two hands in the air. "We traveled from Eden. We came here because Gabriel promised us safety... H-h-he promised all of us safety. He said there was technology here. We're running out of resources in

Eden, and…"

"Avi?" comes Yael's voice.

I turn my head to spot her emerging from the darkness, fearlessly jogging toward the blond woman and her small army of soldiers. What the hell is she doing? She's going to get herself killed. The sound of metal against armor echoes around us as the soldiers prepare to fire.

"Yael?"

Who said that? I swing my head back toward the soldiers, trying to figure out who spoke Yael's name. I don't have to stare long to figure out who it was. He lowers his gun and steps out of rank.

He stops beside his superior and leans down to whisper something in her ear.

"At ease," she says, and everyone lowers their guns.

At the same time, Yael throws herself into the arms of this man. It automatically feels like the air got lighter. Like I can breathe without worrying about a bullet splitting my skull in half.

I look at Freyda, who shrugs, arms still in the air.

Can we take them down now? Do I still have to stay on my knees?

Not wanting to piss off the leader, I don't move. Instead, I watch Yael press her face against the man's and kiss his cheek.

He's tall, taller than her, which is saying a lot. His hair, a dark curly mess, matches his beard that looks like it hasn't been trimmed in months. I can't determine the color of his eyes with the brightness blinding me, but they look light in color. A bit like

Yael's, now that I think of it. Across his chest is a black BIO-8 Skin, and through it, his muscles bulge.

"Oh, brother," Yael says, wrapping her arms around his neck again.

She stands on the tips of her toes to reach him, and he digs his face into the curve of her neck.

"I thought… I thought you were dead," she says.

The leader clears her throat like she's about to vomit if she has to watch another minute of this mushy reunion. Avi, Yael's brother, stiffens his stance and takes a step away from his sister, obviously also not wanting to piss off the leader.

"They aren't lying," Yael says, more to her brother than the leader.

The leader glances toward us, then back at Avi, who gives her a brief nod as if to say, *Whatever Yael says is true.*

She lets out a long sigh and swings her energy gun to her back, a clicking sound locking it into place. "How many more of you are there?" she asks, and at the same time, Jada and Dakota come walking out slowly with hands above their heads. Miller follows close behind with Justice still in her arms.

The soldiers get antsy, gripping their guns over and over again even though they were ordered to back down.

I hate that sound. I also hate this place, but it's our best shot at survival. It's the combination of my surroundings, the familiar smell of long grass and hay that seems to linger around no matter how much jet fuel evaporates into the air, and the sound of guns being manipulated that makes me remember some of the horrible shit I went through here.

* * * * * *

"Get ready, boys!"

I hate Master Sergeant Brown.

He seems amused by this in some sick twisted way that only he understands. From where I'm standing, I don't see the point in this drill. Well, I do, but I don't agree with it.

He's extremely unprofessional, too. He almost never uses military terminology. Instead, he makes grotesque remarks that make me want to turn my gun on him, instead of on the targets.

I readjust my shooting ear muffs and side-glance James. I shouldn't have looked at him. These days, he makes me sick to my stomach. He and Master Sergeant Brown deserve each other, that's for sure. He grins from ear to ear, his face so close to mine that I can actually see specks of orange in his freckles instead of a bunch of brown dots. It's like he's ready to show Master Sergeant what he's made of, which isn't something to be proud of.

The other thing that bothers me most about this drill is how realistic the targets look. As I'm thinking about that, one of them comes running out into the city streets, arms flailing above her head. She isn't real, but the holograph is so vivid that I feel like I'm literally standing ten feet away from an innocent, frantic woman. At first, it looks like she's begging for a cab driver to let her into his car, but when she runs past it, I realize that isn't at all the case.

She's wearing a blue skirt that reaches down to her knees, and shiny modest heels that are no doubt meant to signify she's an office worker. Her button-up shirt, a baby blue color only one tone lighter than her skirt, draws the eye in with its flashy pink buttons. That's obviously meant to be a distraction, because above her head, in her right fist, she's holding a grenade.

It's our job to see this, and not an innocent woman frantically running down the street.

I'm too busy staring at the holograph and James beats me to it. He fires his gun, an imitation version that if shot in real life, would fire a solid burst of pure compressed energy strong enough to burn a hole in a typical, non-Area 82 wall. Although it may be simulated, the woman's head literally explodes.

Blood and brain matter flies toward us and I jerk my head sideways to avoid getting hit in the eyes, even though it isn't real.

"Yeah!" James yells in his rugged voice.

He sounds like a fucking idiot. What's he trying to prove? That he can shoot down any woman he aims his gun at?

"Well done, Walsh," says Master Sergeant Brown. He gives James a big thumbs-up. "You saw a threat and you took the bitch down."

I cringe. How can someone in such a high position say something like that?

Goddamn asshole.

Then, the scene in front of us dissipates into thousands, if not millions of little pixels, and white walls appear, but only for a second, before the new scene sets in. I can't tell where it is, but it kind of looks like some underground rebellion facility. Could be industrial. It looks a bit like an abandoned warehouse with its filthy windows and gray exterior. Through one of those windows, several women are gathered around a circular table, carving knives and filling guns with bullets. At least, that's what it looks like.

They don't seem to know we're standing right outside the building, though. Is the plan to move in and take them all out? Blow up the windows?

The guy to my left shifts his weight, obviously as confused as I am.

Then, two women come walking down the sidewalk with baby strollers. Is this some kind of sick joke? Why are they including babies in the holographs? The two women walk quickly with bowed hooded heads. The moment they reach the building's front doors, they stop walking and the taller of the two hammers a solid fist on the door.

There's a rhythm to her knock, which means she's requesting access.

The moment the door opens up, the guy to my left fires only two shots, and straight at the baby strollers.

I'm about to angrily rotate the entire upper half of my body and give him a piece of my mind when both the strollers go up in flames and cause an explosion so big that the entire shooting range shakes under our feet and the scene's industrial doors fly off their handles. Along with it come bone fragments and muscle tissue of the woman who opened the doors for the undercover mothers.

I instinctively raise a forearm to block the body parts and James scoffs at me.

"It isn't real, dipshit."

Clenching my teeth, I fight the urge to shove my gun's barrel up his tight, privileged ass. I can't believe we used to be friends... I can't believe how much this place has changed him.

But I don't do anything. The last thing I want is to find myself dragged out of Area 82 by a bunch of men in fancy black suits. Everyone knows that soldiers who aren't cut out for the program disappear... Forever.

"Good job, Lee," says Master Sergeant Brown. He claps his two oversized hands together. "You set your emotions aside and located the hidden threat. Now, eyes on the prize!" and he points his thick sausage finger toward the bloody scene.

James is already firing shots before I have the chance to raise my gun, and the next thing I know, the scene's changed, and we're standing inside the industrial building. The image spreads on either side of our shooting station and up on the ceiling, making us feel like we're standing at that precise location.

One woman jumps from her chair, and the sound of metal screeching against concrete floor resonates exactly from where she's standing. I won't pretend to understand how they went about making everything look, sound, and feel so damn realistic because I'm no expert in altered reality. All I know is that it bothers me.

I can sense Master Sergeant's eyes on me, which means he's starting to wonder why I'm not taking any shots.

So, for now, I block out Mama's disapproving voice and promise myself that when this is all over, I'll make her proud again. And with a quiet mind, I start firing shots through the women's chests while reminding myself that it's nothing more than a *game*.

* * * * * *

"Is he deaf?"

Freyda kicks my knee and my eyes pop open to find the leader glaring down at me. I wish they'd turn those damn lights off. They're giving me a headache.

"Get up," she orders.

Freyda and the other women are standing beside her, arms crossed over their chests. I'm sure they aren't too impressed with me. This isn't the first time I've disappeared into my head, and now, I'm making an idiot of myself by remaining in the dirt, arms above my head.

How long have I been kneeling here?

The leader, now standing with legs far apart and shoulders drawn back like she's prepared to go on a mission, throws her pointed chin out at me. "Get up. You're taking us to Eden."

I plant one boot in the dirt and stand up. "Taking you?" I say.

"Freyda here tells me Eve Malum is in Eden," she says like she's purposely evading my question.

Eve's name rolls off her tongue like she's said it countless times before. Does she know Eve personally? Or, has she heard of her? It seems like everyone's heard about Eve. And if Freyda had the time to explain to this leader that Eve Malum is running Eden, how long have I been sitting here in a daze, making a complete fool of myself?

Besides, what does her knowing Eve have to do

with me taking them?

I take a step toward her, but not too close. Her men puff out their chests and stare at me like a bunch of robots, or better yet, trained police dogs. I'm beginning to feel like the outsider in all of this. Is it because I'm a man? Am I automatically guilty until proven innocent, while the women remain innocent until proven guilty?

While I don't like the feeling, I swallow my sensitivity and remind myself that this woman probably has many protocols when it comes to outsiders. And being that I'm twice her size, and larger than most of the men here, it would only make sense that I prove my worth before being accepted as one of them.

"How many more of you are there?" I ask, and Freyda's glare tells me I should have kept my mouth shut. I must be coming across as too inquisitive, which is often taken as a red flag. Why would someone like me need information like that?

The leader catches Freyda's death stare and smiles. The curve at the corner of her lips looks out of place. It's like she stuck a sticker over her lips to give her new ones that look a bit less disgusted.

"It's okay," the leader says, the invisible sticker on her face now falling off. "You're obviously ex-military. So long as you prove your worth, you're welcome inside of Elysium."

I'm assuming she's referring to Area 82, but I don't ask her. It's also not a good idea to question her on where they came up with the name Elysium or what it even means. If I'm going to make friends rather than enemies with these people, I'm going to keep my mouth shut and do as told.

"Ever been in a Blue Falcon?" she asks me.

I'm about to say, "Blue Falcon?" when Dakota jumps out from behind Freyda, her face lit up so much you'd think she found a pack of cigarettes. She grins and slaps two hands together. I realize a Blue Falcon is a plane before Dakota even opens her mouth to talk. The only thing she gets that excited about is planes.

"Sixty-two or sixty-three?" Dakota asks, craning her neck to meet the leader's eyes. "D series?"

The leader, visibly impressed by Dakota's knowledge of aircraft, crosses two solid arms over her padded chest and cocks an eyebrow.

"Sixty-six, F-series."

Dakota's jaw drops so low you'd think it unhinged from her skull.

This time, the leader smirks and lets out a faint laugh. It sounds like a forced cough brought on by a tiny bit of dust. The kind of a cough that makes you wonder why the person even bothered coughing in the first place.

"Rodriguez," she says, eyes still on Dakota.

All of my military training comes back to me. I stiffen my posture, legs at shoulder's width and hands hanging at my sides like two solid pieces of wood. I've done it countless times before, prepared to obey any command.

"Freyda says you led them here, which means you can lead the way back. I'm going to require coordinates for Eden's approximate location."

I offer a brief nod. "Yes, ma'am."

"Call me Vrin," she corrects, and my stomach sinks.

CHAPTER 6 – LUCY

Emily's sleeping with her back facing her cell's iron bars, her shoulders moving up and down with every labored breath she takes. Although tempted to go inside and try to console her, I don't. What if she's contagious? Dr. Lewis said she isn't, but now, with the way Eve's locking everyone up, I don't want to take that chance.

I'm sure Emily will understand.

"Elsa, get back here!" someone shouts, and at the same time, little Elsa storms past me and out the back door into Division Five's courtyard.

May, her older sister, who seems to always be chasing after her, stomps down the hallway and rolls her eyes at me—it's a look that says, *Here we go again.* I feel awful for May and Elsa. They've been here since the beginning without their mom and May's been forced to take over the role of parental guardian, which sucks because she's only thirteen.

I'm tempted to go out and help her, but she's done this many times before, and she'll catch Elsa like she always does—by the arm, with Elsa kicking and screaming and saying that she doesn't want to do her homework.

Without giving it too much thought, I make my way toward the main hall and down Division Three's corridor. Today feels like a holiday but in a negative sense. Everyone is standing in the main hall, panicked voices carrying over one another. There's no laughter or joy. Instead, everyone's miserable and trying to place blame on someone else for the bug that's spreading around Eden.

Bugs don't often scare me all that much. So far, my immune system's done a good job of protecting me. But at the same time, things have never been this bad.

"I heard Eve's runnin' out of beds," someone whispers.

"What if this wipes us all out?"

"Ruth," someone hisses, and the sound of skin slapping skin echoes in the hall. "You can't think like that!"

"Ouch!"

"Oh, quit being such a baby."

I tune them out and rush down the corridor as if moving quickly through the air will prevent me from catching the germs. It's pretty bad when even breathing feels like something you shouldn't be doing. Why are all the women standing around like a bunch of sheep, anyway? Eve asked them to go outside because there's less risk of germs spreading.

It doesn't seem to matter what Eve said, though. The women are complaining that it's way too cold out there, and although they're right, they're being a bit stupid in my opinion. Why would anyone want to be trapped indoors, where bacteria sit on surfaces for hours if not days? Well, that's what Dr. Lewis told me.

I kick the door open and a cold gust of wind squeezes its way past my lips, into my mouth and the back of my throat. It feels like an ice cube going down, so I swallow hard and plow my way through the cold wind, arms wrapped tightly around myself.

Hopefully, Mavis and Perula's Herb Shack is toasty. Most of the time it is, thanks to the glass roof that lets all the sun inside. Pearl, Freyda's beautiful horse, seems content roaming the courtyard without anyone nearby. She's chewing away at the grass and standing so still it's a wonder she isn't getting cold.

Without knocking on the Herb Shack's thick wooden door, I swing it open, startling both Mavis and Perula with my rowdy entrance. Perula's glasses nearly fly off her face, so I'm assuming she was on the verge of falling asleep in her rocking chair with the book she has in her hands. Either that, or she *was* asleep.

Mavis looks pissed off like she always does, head bowed low and eyes so narrow they resemble two perfectly drawn pencil lines.

"Always blafenin' and stomperin' around, you kids," she says, wiping soup or potion off her face. It's green, with bits and pieces of yellow root.

My lips start stretching into a smile and I'm about to burst out laughing. Although I didn't see what happened, I know exactly what happened, I made her jump so much that she flung her spatula out of her cauldron and into the air.

I can picture it as if I *did* see it: a big jerk of the shoulders, eyeballs bulging out, and a grimace so ugly she must have looked deformed as the liquid splashed on her face.

I can't hold it in anymore, so I let out a laugh and slap a hand on my belly. It's peeving her off, but I don't even care. I can't help myself.

Perula smirks and side-glances her sister, obviously amused by how much fun I'm having.

Mavis, on the other hand, doesn't understand empathy. An entire room of people could be laughing so hard they're in tears, and her lips and eyebrows would remain as flat as a sheet of cardboard.

"Something funny, monkeroo?" she snarls.

If I keep this up, she might explode on me like she did last time, so I clear the smile from my face. It's warmer in here than it is outside, and it's most likely free of germs. So, if I want to stay safe, I'd better stay on her good side, which seems to be near impossible these days.

"Are you here to help us, child?" Perula asks, observing me from behind her dangling glasses. She closes her book and lays it gently atop a wool blanket on her lap.

"Help?" I ask. "With what?"

It came across as arrogant and entitled, which wasn't at all what I intended. The whole point of becoming a Healer was to learn from Mavis and Perula so that I can use my learned knowledge to help the women of Eden.

And what have I been doing with my time? Checking up on Eve and chasing after conspiracy theories. But they aren't simply theories. Eve's dangerous, and I know I'm supposed to be focusing on my career path as a Healer, but what good is it if I'm a

Healer and Eden falls apart? Surely, I'm overdramatizing everything in my head right now, so I clear my throat and say, "Of course that's why I'm here. What can I help with?"

"Well, what are you waiting for?" Mavis blurts, her voice sounding like a plate being dropped on a kitchen floor. "Get over here and help me cut up garlic."

"Garlic?" I say. The smell hits me out of nowhere. "Oh God." I shove two fingers flat against my nostrils. "How much garlic do you have here? And what's it for?"

Mavis curls a lip over her thick front teeth like she's about to call me an idiot in her own twisted way when Perula gently and fortunately cuts her off. "Believe it or not, Lucy, garlic has been used for centuries as a natural antibiotic. In fact"—she points at the Herb Shack's webbed ceiling like she's about to lecture me on the entire history of garlic—"in the seventeen hundreds, garlic was even used to ward off the plague." That last word slips off her tongue as if capable of infecting people with it—slow and dreary. "Dr. Lewis isn't a strong believer in holistic medicine, but I think it's safe to say that she'll be willing to try just about anything at this point."

I stare at the garlic—pinkish balls attached to long white stems that turn green at the ends, sort of like green onions. Underneath the balls are little strings covered in earth, which I'm assuming are its roots. I've never seen fresh garlic before—only those little beige half-moon looking things that Mom used to chop up and sprinkle in some of the dishes she'd make.

"Good for your heart," she'd say when I'd complain

about it.

I'm about to ask Mavis how I go about cutting them but choose to observe her doing it instead. She snatches a handful of them and glares at me when she catches me watching, sort of like an exhausted nanny forced to take on the responsibilities of a child's alcoholic parent.

Letting out a long breath, she says, "You peel this off first. But don't you go throwin' out the scape!"

"Scape?"

Her eyelids go flat and she breathes out sharply again, this time, through her flared nostrils. "The green stuff. We can use it. So don't be wastin' it, you hear?" She points the tip of her knife at me for emphasis, and I nod. "Now, after this is gone, pull the pieces apart. One piece at a floppidy doppin' time. Like that... See? Ah, perfect."

A proud smile creeps on her face and I can't help but stare. Mavis never smiles, at least not genuinely like this. Right now, she's acting like she performed a successful heart transplant. Her dark eyes shoot sideways at me and the skin of her face droops in an instant. It's like she's afraid or ashamed to demonstrate any form of true happiness. The only laughter that ever comes out of her mouth is usually triggered by petty insults or a drug-induced state of mind.

Poor Mavis.

Looking away, I start peeling the crinkly skin off the garlic cloves, and, as she instructed, I pry them apart. Though I'd never admit it because Mavis is such a grump, I'm enjoying myself. This reminds me of my time baking muffins with Grandma. She'd set me up on a stool and get me to butter the muffin trays while she mixed the batter together.

The one difference is Grandma talked to me. Mavis is quiet, but it's a nice quiet. Not that I'd ever compare Mavis to an animal, but it's a bit like the feeling one gets when they've made progress with an abused rescue animal. Well, from what I've seen online on my H-Cap. Though I've never been through it, I can assume that this is how someone might feel when a feral cat they rescued lets someone pet them for the first time or when a beaten dog accepts a treat. I click and tear at the garlic while she does the same, and every few minutes, I glance sideways at her, thankful that she's letting me stand so close.

We're actually doing something together.

It's nice.

If I voice it, she'll tell me to shut the ugly hole in my face, or that I'm doing a bad job at splitting the cloves and to go outside to find something better to do. So instead, I enjoy the moment and smile on the inside.

I look up at Perula and she winks at me. I'm about to smile at her when something interrupts us—something loud and incredibly disturbing. It's the sound of a woman hollering at the top of her lungs, her voice cutting every few seconds between loud sobs.

That kind of scream that comes out of someone for a *really* bad reason.

I run outside in time to see her collapsing to her knees, tugging at her long auburn hair and pounding at her thighs. Five or six women rush around her, grabbing anything they can to prevent her from hurting herself.

She cries so hard her voice goes hoarse.

On the verge of crying at the sight, I swallow hard.

I know exactly what happened.

Someone died.

CHAPTER 7 – EVE

Nola and a young woman walk about Eden, spraying what I can only assume is one of Mavis and Perula's disinfectant concoctions. It smells of lemon and herbs, though I wouldn't be able to identify what they've put in there. I'm told they are preparing an antibiotic mix. With any luck they'll bring it to me quickly.

Nola shoots mist on every doorknob using one of the cafeteria's industrial cleaning bottles—something we emptied a long time ago—while the woman behind her scrubs at the moist surface with a beaten gray rag.

The woman rubs hard, looking frail and malnourished. The task doesn't appear easy for her, but her determination crushes any weakness she may have.

I can't be certain that the disinfectant works, though Mavis has time and time again attempted to convince me that it is "as good as supermarket fizzle," whatever that's supposed to mean.

I refasten the blue surgical mask around my face—something I feel guilty for even wearing seeing as the supply is limited. Dr. Lewis, however, insisted that I wear one, as my survival is crucial to Eden's survival.

While I agree this is true, I receive looks of resentment and hostility, making me want to tear the mask off. These women are not supposed to despise me—they're supposed to love me. Why can't they see that all I'm trying to do is guarantee their survival?

"I don't think Dr. Lewis even gave her any antibiotics."

"'Course she didn't. Ireela is... *was*," the whisper corrects, "eighteen years old. Everyone knows Dr. Lewis doesn't give antibiotics at that age."

Where is that coming from, and what is everyone whispering about? Keeping my back against the wall, I move down the main hall and toward Division Three, careful not to touch anything with my hands. If Dr. Lewis can't get a hold on this, Mavis and Perula are Eden's only hope.

When I reach the end of Division Three's corridor and step outside, however, I'm greeted by a sight so shocking I find myself holding my breath.

What's happened?

Why is this woman crying on her knees? A small crowd has formed around her—motherly women with rounded backs and concerned looks on their faces as they try to console her with gentle touches and soft words. I lock eyes with Lucy, who appears to be coming out of her Herb Shack. She looks as confused as I am with her fingers locked together and her arms dangling in an awkward fashion in front of her like she doesn't know what to do with herself.

Her steps are so calculated it's as if she's crossing an invisible minefield filled with triggers capable of worsening this woman's heartache with one wrong step.

I move forward, prepared to question the women to find out what's going on when one of them stands up and stretches her seemingly achy back.

"Loretta's a mess," the woman says.

I know Loretta, and I also know the woman who just stood up, though her name sits at the tip of my tongue. She takes a step toward me, and I step back right away, not wanting her skin anywhere near mine.

Her name's Beatrice, or Beatry, I now remember. In my mind, I call her Beatry as I stare at her bagged eyes, her slouched stance, and her gossipy-looking lips flapping up and down. She's speaking so fast, and I'm partially deafened by Loretta's cries, that I can't make out what she's trying to tell me. She takes another step forward, maybe realizing that I can't hear her, and I grimace.

"You remember Ireela?" she says, her rancid breath making me want to push her at arm's length.

Ireela... I know her—a promising young woman full of fiery ambition and an incredible sense of self-discipline. She graduated two years ago and chose her career path in Mechanics. Every time her name escapes the mouths of women around Eden, it is surrounded by positive words of love and positivity. She is destined for great things.

What's going on? I stare at Beatry and then at Loretta, her mother, who is bellowing toward the sky as if she's lost someone she cares deeply about.

Oh God.

My stomach sinks like a bag of sand in water and I find myself rushing toward Loretta.

Not Ireela.

Don't let it be Ireela.

Loretta's bloodshot eyes roll toward me when she hears me approach, and everyone follows her stare. For a moment, the sobbing stops, and we're left standing around in silence as a cool autumn breeze sweeps through grass, bringing along with it hundreds of red, orange, and yellow leaves. They form a small pile around Loretta's knees, almost as if trying to comfort her.

Her stare turns into a glare so rapidly that I don't have the time to process what's going on.

"You!" she spews, and in one quick movement, lunges to her feet and straight for me.

She screams at the top of her lungs, shiny saliva coating her bottom lip and pooling around its corners. At the same time, three women grab her around the waist and chest to prevent her from attacking me.

I'm too shocked to even back away. Instead, I stand there, Loretta's yellow fingernails mere inches from my face as she claws the air like a caged feral cat trying to attack the person responsible for its imprisonment.

Why is she exuding so much anger? So much hatred? I catch a glimpse of Lucy in the background—she's come a bit closer, but it's obvious that the attempted attack has frightened her. She doesn't move, and instead, watches in awe from a distance.

"You—" Loretta shouts, swinging once more across the air in front of my face.

With her lips pulled back over her upper teeth and

features deformed so much, I've nearly forgotten who she is. She takes a swing sideways in an attempt to free herself and hits Beatry between the eyes.

"Ah!" Beatry cries, releasing Loretta to place two hands on her injured forehead.

Loretta gains traction in the grass and lunges forward once more, her claws now grazing the tip of my nose.

Still, I don't back away. Should I be frightened? Or, should I return the anger? How dare she turn on me, Eve Malum, as if I were responsible for the death of her child? Despite *wanting* to be angry, I can't feel anything. This is the first time one of my women has turned against me, and I can't quite figure out how to feel.

* * * * * *

"Do you ever talk about them?" Freyda asks as if she expects me to pour my guts out to her—to tell her how I feel and how my feelings are affecting my ability to rule over Eden. How does my family have anything to do with my ability to lead the women of this garden?

She leans back in the leather chair across from my desk, chin elevated, and nostrils flared as she lets out a peaceful breath.

"You're a ticking timebomb, Eve," she says. If I weren't glowering at her, she would kick her feet up onto my desk. But something tells me my stare has reminded her of her position, and of mine.

She straightens her posture, the back of her chair springing in an upright position, and she clears her throat. "I mean no disrespect, Eve. All I'm saying is that if you keep holding everything inside, you're going to snap at some point... Trust me. Pain, whether physical, emotional, or psychological, has a way of bringing the worst out in people."

I scoff and dig my fingernail into the groove on my desk I've been clawing at for days. The thought of Mila and my mother bring along with it a dark cloud so large I can no longer see the sun, which is precisely why I don't allow such thoughts to enter my mind; the truth is, they *are* a distraction—pollution capable of tarnishing my ability to lead.

My nail bends backward when I press hard into the wood, and a sense of relief washes over me. I look at Freyda, who seems to be expecting me to say something that will comfort her, and force a quivering smile.

"Feelings are a weakness, Freyda. The sooner you learn that, the sooner you'll become of value to me."

* * * * * *

"Stop!" Lucy shouts.

She runs through the grass, clenched fists swinging on either side of her body.

I reach for my face, where warm blood spills across the bridge of my nose onto my cheek. Loretta, not yet satisfied with the amount of pain she's caused me, shouts one more time and swings with a solid fist, no doubt hoping to inflict more damage than a scratch this time.

All of a sudden, every woman in Division Three—a total of six or seven—jump into the altercation, pulling Loretta away from me.

"Stop it!" Lucy shouts again.

Why is she defending me? After everything she's said—why would she care? She doesn't care about me.

It isn't true.

She does care about you.

This is proof.

If she didn't care, she wouldn't be getting involved.

I watch Lucy as she enters the fight in a panic, and in an instant, I don't care about Loretta's threatening shouts or weaponized arms. To my surprise, Lucy places herself in front of Loretta's attacks. While the act is noble, it is useless—the women of the division slowly pull Loretta down into the grass, eliminating the threat.

"Loretta, calm down!"

"Hold still!"

"Don't tell me to fucking calm down!" comes Loretta's voice. She kicks and squirms and throws a fist in the air any time she manages to free an arm from someone's grip. "That bitch—that fucking bitch!"

I don't understand what's going on. Why is she blaming me?

"Eighteen years old..." Loretta cries. "She was eighteen fuckin' years old! What kind of... What k-k-kind of monster prevents an eighteen-year-old f-f-from getting... From receiving fucking antibiotics." She kicks again, hitting a poor middle-aged woman right in the ribs. The woman stands up and stumbles away with a hand over her belly, clearly injured by the hard blow. "She was... She was eighteen! She turned eighteen last week!" she turns her head to the side, and all at once, the anger dissipates, and she starts sobbing against a woman's shoulder.

Without looking back at me, Lucy returns to the Herb Shack. I stretch a hand out toward her, but I don't say anything. Instead, I watch Loretta as she continues to sob, at last understanding why she's put the blame on me—I'm the one responsible for Eden, which means I am also responsible for Dr. Lewis.

Although the decision to deny antibiotics to any woman over the age of eighteen was Dr. Lewis's idea, I'm still the one who approved it. Had I stepped in when Ireela was sick—had I forced Dr. Lewis's hand to prescribe her antibiotics—perhaps Ireela would still be here. Instead, I was busy hiding away, mulling over the depressing thought of Lucy despising me, and worrying about Freyda.

What have I done?

Eve Malum, ruler of Eden, would have never allowed her own emotions to get in the way of her rulership.

Feelings are a weakness, I remind myself.

No matter how many times I repeat this line in my head, it won't change the fact that Ireela is dead. It also won't change the fact that every woman surrounding Loretta is looking at me in a way they've never done before.

Their foreheads are full of frown rolls and their lips sealed tight. Their eyes, dark holes in their faces, stare into me as if I were some vile, poisonous woman not fit to lead them.

CHAPTER 8 – GABRIEL

"You, sit," Vrin says, pointing at me and then toward one of the hundreds of gray cloth seats at the center of the plane. They run along the sides, too, with black straps hanging and waiting to be used as seat belts. "And hold onto your dog."

I pull Justice close to my chest and plant a soft kiss on her forehead, right between her eyes. Poor thing's exhausted. There are so many voices around her that she's having a hard time keeping her eyes closed.

If I were to estimate, I'd say there are about a thousand seats in here. Maybe more. They're all squished together in tight rows, and all I keep picturing is soldiers wearing metal hats, camouflage clothing, and military boots.

All I see when I look at this plane is me, somewhere in the corner, getting ready for takeoff before my mission in North Korea. Although this plane is three times the size of the one I flew in, it's similar. The walls, curved metal without any windows and instead, fluorescent lights overhead, make me feel like I'm standing in a spaceship. It's meticulously clean. So clean that I could lick the floor and not catch a single speck of dust.

"Can you believe this?" Freyda asks. She looks like a kid about to get on a rollercoaster for the first time in their life.

I can believe this, and I do believe it, but I don't say anything. I pull my seat belt from the seat and fasten it around both me and Justice. I'm not trying to be an asshole by not responding. This isn't about the fact that she's been less than nice with me today. I'm not being passive-aggressive, either. I'm scared if I open my mouth to say something, I'll throw up.

Why am I so anxious?

Closing my eyes, I lean my head against the headrest as Vrin marches around the plane, telling her soldiers where to sit and what to do. Yael follows her brother, Avi, farther back in the plane, talking more than I've ever heard her talk before with that thick Hebrew accent of hers. I can't imagine how long they've been separated, but it's apparent time apart hasn't changed their relationship.

Dakota drops into the seat beside me and I crack one eye open to look at her.

"Holy fuckin' jet balls," she says, slapping her knees. "I can't believe I'm sitting inside an F-series Blue Falcon! This thing is... This thing's fuckin' epic. I would've given up my entire life's savings to fly one of these. Hey, you think they'll let me? Fly, I mean? You think the pilot'll let me copilot?"

Justice lets out a whimper. She must be hungry. Either that or she has *to go*. I hope she doesn't pee on me. I pet the top of her apple-shaped head. Maybe she's anxious like me.

"I mean, that'd be a dream come true." Dakota lets

out a donkey-like noise. It's a mix between a grunt and a whine like she's frustrated and excited at the same time.

"What's going on here?" comes Vrin's voice.

Dakota stares at the floor like she's been caught drawing in class.

Freyda sticks a thumb out toward Dakota. "Dakota here's a pilot. You in need of a copilot up there?"

Dakota, clearly embarrassed by Freyda's request, glances up at Vrin. It's almost like she's reverted to her adolescent years. Maybe it has something to do with the plane and Vrin and all the soldiers. Maybe's she's feeling intimidated and out of her league in this thing.

Vrin sucks on her front teeth, inspecting Dakota from head to toe as if trying to decide whether she's worthy of setting foot in a Blue Falcon cockpit.

"You got your license on you? Your medical papers?" Vrin asks.

Dakota pulls her face back and flares her nostrils. "What? How would I possibly have—"

With a dismissive wave, Vrin lets out a soft laugh. "We're always looking for pilots. Come on, I'll take you to the front."

Dakota balls two tight fists by her face and bears all her yellow-stained teeth. I wait for a loud, high-pitched squeal to come out, but she doesn't make a sound. Despite Dakota's bitchy attitude with me, I'm happy for her. She seems so excited, and after what she's been through, losing her daughter, she deserves happiness again.

Everyone deserves happiness, even if they're complete assholes. Maybe if they were happier, they'd be lesser assholes.

Dakota unclips her seat belt and gets up with a swing of her upper body. Vrin, still smiling, turns away and leads her toward the front of the plane. Unlike Eve, Vrin's smile looks genuine. She's hard, which is good, in my opinion, but there's a human side to her that seems to shine through every now and then. And I've only known the woman for a few hours.

The fact that she's working with men also says a lot about her. She isn't holding on to the old ideology that men and women can't coexist. Or that one sex is better than the other.

It's obvious she's using gender strengths, rather than focusing on the subtle differences that set us apart. I'm curious to get back to Area 82, or Elysium, as Vrin called it. Are there many women? And if so, what sorts of tasks has Vrin assigned to them? No doubt she has female soldiers, too. I get the feeling Vrin's a fair leader.

I think of Eve and wonder how that'll play over when we get to Eden. She doesn't strike me as the kind of woman who's willing to resign from her position and take orders from someone else, whether that be Vrin or someone higher up waiting inside of Area 82.

Closing my eyes again, I try to relax my body. The men farther back in the plane are bickering back and forth. Without a doubt, they're excited about the prospect of an all-female colony. They aren't vulgar, though, nor are they disrespectful. Not like Adam and his goons. If anything, it's more like listening to innocent teenage boys talk about their crushes. Most of them are young, too. That leads me to believe that Vrin's been polishing teenage boys into respectable soldiers.

Their voices carry throughout the plane, full of excitement and nervousness.

But that sound disappears, at least from my ears, when the plane's engines turn on. The deep rumbling vibrates under my boots and in my chair. It's a subtle vibration, but it's enough to get my heart going. They're doing their checks, and it's only a matter of time before we take off.

Jesus Christ.

What's wrong with me? I was never like this. I've been in planes hundreds of times before. I've traveled the world. I've jumped out of fucking helicopters. But right now, all I want to do is find the nearest exit door and run off the plane before we're airborne.

"What's wrong with you?" Freyda asks.

How long has she been staring at me? She watches my face, my white-knuckled hands around the armrests, and my face again. "You don't look so good."

"I'm fine," I grumble.

I'm not fine. I want to throw up. And the more anxious I feel, the more pissed off I get because I shouldn't be feeling this way. I'm a brave guy. I'm not afraid of confrontation. Not afraid of guns. Not afraid to tell someone to shove their head up their ass if I have to. But right now, I feel like a kid, and all I can think about is Mama. If she were here right now, she'd slap a hand on my knee and say something along the lines of "Oh, Gabriel, *mi amor*. Do not be afraid. God is here with you. Okay? My sweet Gabriel."

Then, if I didn't calm down, her feisty side would come out and her second slap wouldn't be as comforting. "Be a man, Gabriel. Is only a plane."

I smile to myself. Mama always had a way of comforting me without babying me. She'd offer a few sweet words of consolation, and if that didn't work, she'd tell me to toughen up. I suppose that's why I turned out the way I did: a weird balance of sensitivity and toughness.

I think that's who Mama wanted me to be. She wanted me to be like my papa.

"Gabriel?"

Freyda's still staring at me. I part my lips to lie to her again, to tell her I'm fine when the plane's propellers kick into full gear and the vibration gets so hard my entire seat shakes and my head bounces against my headrest.

* * * * * *

"Commencing takeoff," comes the pilot's voice over the plane speakers.

James nudges me in the ribs, the freckled skin of his face pulled back with so much excitement it looks like he's about to pop. I don't even bother trying to smile at him. James isn't the person I thought he was, and even looking at him makes me sick to my stomach. All I see now is a man capable of shooting a child in the face if it means protecting his country.

He's done it. Well, in our training. There was no hesitation, no guilt, no remorse. I have no doubt he'd be able to do it in real life without so much as blinking. They've turned him into a killing machine. They've turned all these men into killing machines. If it weren't for the sound of everyone's breaths around me, I'd think I were surrounded by nothing more than robots.

When the plane takes off, my stomach doesn't sink. It used to when I first joined the forces, but not anymore. I've flown so much over the last few years that flying feels no different than driving. The difference is we get to where we're going a hell of a lot faster.

I know why James is so excited. Project GENESIS. Something about a new beginning. There's one problem though: it feels like an ending to me. Killing a bunch of our own people isn't a way to start fresh. Doesn't he see that? Doesn't he realize that defending our country by fighting back against rioting women isn't the way to solve this? There's a reason those women are rioting. Why the fuck isn't the government trying to make peace instead of trying to shut them up?

I try not to focus on it too much because the veins on my temples will start to throb. Mama always told me she could tell when I was angry. She'd point a finger at my face and tell me to calm down. I never understood how she knew, but one day, she finally admitted that my veins were what gave me away. That they'd get huge, bulge out, and sometimes even pulsate.

I've been around James long enough for him to know me a bit. He might know about it, he might not. But if he does, I can't risk him knowing I'm not as excited as he is. I need to play the part if I plan to ever make it back to my mama alive.

"Holy shit," someone says.

Now that we're airborne, most soldiers have unclipped their seat belts. Two of them are standing by the large, rectangular-shaped window on the west side of the plane. There's barely any windows on this thing. In fact, I think that one and the one across from it are the only ones for us to look out of. So when someone gets worked up, it isn't hard to know where the voice came from. It's clear they're seeing something that's worth talking about.

Two other guys get up from their seats, their heavy boots slapping the plane's metal floor as they rush to the quickly forming crowd.

"Are those the Breeding Grounds?" someone asks.

Someone slaps the guy. I'm assuming it's his friend. The one who opened his mouth retreats, his head sinking into his shoulders. I know why he looks embarrassed, and I know why his friend slapped him.

The *Breeding Grounds*, a top-secret project, is something we learned about in Area 82 only once. We weren't even supposed to know about it, but one of the Black Marine commanders snapped when he lost his promotion to a younger man and let it spill. Word about the Breeding Grounds spread around faster than herpes at a frat party. After that, the commander disappeared.

Hours after the outburst, we were met with individually and sworn to secrecy.

So the fact that this guy opened his big mouth about it means he has a death wish.

The project is disgusting. Apparently, over the last

year, the military has been collecting Jane Does from across America. Women on the street, drug addicts, survivors of abuse. Basically, any woman without a family who will go looking for her, or at the very least, with a family who wouldn't be surprised that she went *missing*.

And the name of the project is pretty self-explanatory. They're forcing women to reproduce. They're using them like cattle. And when the product develops into a female fetus, they abort them. So in other words, women are being used as sex slaves to produce more males. I didn't get all of the details, but that's what I heard being whispered around Area 82 before we were all forced to keep our mouths shut.

The thought of it makes me sick to my stomach, and I've done everything I can to forget about the project. But, it isn't something you forget. In fact, it's something I've been thinking about taking to the news the second I get out of here. I'll be killed, I'm sure of it. Or, worse, the news would shut me up. But people need to know, somehow. I can't even imagine what those women are going through, and when I think about it, I want to sink into a hole and die. This world isn't a place I want to live in.

The man who opened his trap cowers away and returns to his seat. Maybe he's hoping none of the other lieutenants or commanders on board heard him. Then, after a moment of suspenseful silence, a bunch of soldiers jump to their feet and rush to the window.

Although I don't want to see it, I have to. I need to be able to describe the place and describe its approximate whereabouts. So I get up and shove my way through until I'm able to catch a glimpse of it before it's too far out of sight.

The facility is huge. Not as big as Area 82, but big enough to house thousands of women. Around it is a massive forest, and around that, more fencing, planes, and military vehicles. It reminds me of a prison with its thick concrete walls and its oversized yards. There are two of them. Yards, I mean. One of them looks to be full of women walking around in a sand pit, some of them being handled by men and others fighting like in prison.

The other yard, though, faces north of the facility. It looks much greener and peaceful. Although I can't see from this height, if I were to guess, I'd say that the women in this yard are the pregnant ones. Everything's nicer, which is no doubt done to get maximum results.

"I'd do anything to work there," breathes one of the men beside me.

I should shut my mouth, but I can't. Without thinking, I grab him by the collar of his shirt and pin him against the plane's interior wall, hitting a few other guys with my elbows in the process. His face puffs up like a Cheeto, and he stares at me with bulging eyes.

"What're you?" I say. "A fucking rapist?"

"R-r-relax," he tries, but he swallows hard and slobbers on my arm.

I'm probably crushing his trachea.

Good.

Fucking piece of shit pig.

"Hands off!" someone shouts.

The voice is authoritative, which means it's one of the commanders. I let the guy go, but I want to tear his face off with my bare hands.

"What's going on, here?" growls the commander. He's standing tall, his shaved head looking wet under the plane's fluorescent lighting.

I stiffen. "Nothing, sir."

The man I held seconds ago clears his throat. "N-nothing, sir. Having a little fun is all."

The commander looks at me and then at the other guy, his jaw muscles popping out. It's obvious he doesn't have the time, nor the patience, to deal with our little fight.

"You're soldiers," he says. "You don't get to have fun. Now act like adults and sit the fuck back down. There's nothing to see here."

When no one moves, he barks, "Now!" and everyone rushes back to their seats.

* * * * * *

At first, it feels like an annoying tap. The kind of tap you feel on your lap when a kid wants something, and they keep hitting you over, and over again. But then it turns into a hard hit. Hard enough to leave a bruise.

"The heck is wrong with you?" Freyda snaps.

Vrin is standing right in front of me with military-sleeved arms crossed over her chest and combat boots spread at shoulder's width. She looks fierce, but at the same time, worried. Is she worried about me?

"Where'd you serve?" she asks.

I glance sideways at Freyda. How long have I been lost in my thoughts again? Should I be opening my mouth, or is this some sort of trap?

Vrin doesn't look like she's setting me up, though. It seems like she genuinely wants to know about my past. She bows her head forward, shadows forming under her brows, and waits for me to speak up.

"D-different areas," I say, avoiding the topic. I'm not supposed to talk about my missions. It's a breach.

She scoffs, which tells me she knows why I'm evading the subject.

"This is a new world, Gabriel. Forget what you were told to say or not to say in the old world. No one's here to get you in trouble. I only want to know what your background is."

I clear my throat. "I was a Black Marine before all of this, and before that, well... Japan, during the trade crisis. Ukraine—" But I cut myself short, remembering that Ukraine doesn't exist anymore, and I correct myself. "Russia. North Korea—"

"North Korea?" she says. "2051?"

I nod.

She nods along with me, looking defeated. We share a moment of silence that only we seem to understand. Freyda shifts in her seat and leans in toward me. "What? What's going on?"

"We have someone in Elysium who can help you," Vrin says.

Why's she being so nice to me? Not long ago, I was guilty until proven innocent. It's not like I've done anything to warrant being treated fairly. At least not yet. And what's she talking about? Help me with what?

"Your thoughts," she says. "Your flashbacks. Your blackouts."

"You have PTSD?" Freyda says, her features softening at once.

I grind my teeth. I'm not an idiot. What I'm going through is because of everything I've seen. But if I tell myself I have PTSD, I'm giving it power. Okay, so maybe I am an idiot. I know it doesn't work that way. But I don't want to need help.

I scratch Justice between the eyes and rub my finger over her soft ear. It feels like warm cotton pulled out of a dryer.

"You don't have to talk about it," Vrin says. "I don't. But I can assure you it won't get any better. You might think you're fine, and then something triggers you."

I don't say anything. To be honest, I don't know what to say. I feel weak and vulnerable, which doesn't sit well with me. Why is it getting worse, anyway? Is she right? Am I being triggered? Is it because I made my way back to Area 82? That's when it seemed to get really bad.

"Anyways, we can talk about this later. Get up."

I glance up at her. What's going on?

"Pilot needs you at the front. You're the one guiding us."

CHAPTER 9 – LUCY

"What's goin' on out there?" Mavis says, her nose pressed up against the window. The oil of her skin leaves a round smudge in the dust, which is likely the closest thing to cleaning she's ever done.

"It's Loretta's daughter," I say. "Ireela."

It's like everyone knows Ireela. Well, *knew*. I wonder where she is. Her body, I mean. And how did this happen? I saw her two days ago. She had a cough and dark bags under her eyes, but Emily looked a lot sicker than her. I feel nauseated. I should be used to death by now, but I'm not. All I keep thinking about is how one day, Ireela was breathing and enjoying life, and now, she's nowhere to be seen.

Her body, maybe. But not *her*. The best I can do is hope that there is an afterlife. I need to believe; if I don't, I don't know what I'll do with myself. I have to believe that when my turn comes around, my mom will be waiting for me.

Mavis squints and with her thick, potion-stained hand, wipes a bigger smudge on the window. "D'she croak?"

"Mavis!" Perula exclaims.

I'm tempted to tell her off, too, but Mavis doesn't

think before she talks. She isn't saying it to be rude or thoughtless—words sometimes come out of her mouth without going through a filtration process.

"Yeah, she *passed*," I say.

Mavis pulls away from the window solemnly and shakes her head. "Another one bites the dust."

I don't even bother rolling my eyes at her insensitivity. Slowly, I'm getting accustomed to it.

"Ireela was a sweet young woman," Perula says.

Are we already reminiscing? Are we going to hold hands and talk about what a great girl she was? I can't do that. Not now. Not while I can't stop thinking about Mom. If we start talking about dead people, I'm scared I'll start crying, and the last thing I want to do is cry in front of Mavis.

Perula, I think, would be sweet about it. Mavis would no doubt tell me that I'm dehydrating myself and to suck it up—literally. Or, she'd tell me to collect my tears and use them to salt my food.

"Do you know what happened?" Perula asks. "Was it the flu?"

I shrug. How am I supposed to know? What doesn't make sense to me is that Emily looked like she was on the verge of dying, and she made it out. Was it the antibiotics? Is that what Loretta was referring to? Since Ireela turned eighteen last week, Dr. Lewis refused to give her anything. While I find it harsh that she would do something like that, I can understand. Dr. Lewis has rules to stick to, and if she starts bending the rules, they'll eventually break.

Perula's still staring at me like I have the answer she's looking for.

I peer through the window where Mavis left a big smudge. "Yeah, probably the flu." It still doesn't make sense to me that someone would die within a matter of days when others—some with even weaker immune systems—are fighting the bug off. "Maybe she had a heart condition," I add, trying to wrap my head around it.

Mavis pulls her spatula out of her cauldron and licks it. She winces as if she took a lick of pure lemon, shakes her head, and throws the spatula back into the mixture. "Ain't no telling here in Eden, eh? One day you're fine, the next day you're gone. 'Member Mrs. Pepper?" She throws her pointed chin out at Perula.

Perula, who seems to know what Mavis is talking about, blows out an irritated breath. "Her name wasn't Mrs. Pepper."

"She liked peppers!" Mavis says, smacking something hard on the wooden table.

My shoulders jerk forward and I glare through the window, even though all I want to do is turn around and give Mavis a look that says, *I hate you.*

"Her name was *Mrs. Peabody*," Perula says, clearly offended by Mavis's lack of empathy.

"Pee? Or pea?" Mavis asks, and this time, she throws her head back and laughs so hard I can see a large dark hole in the back of her mouth where molars used to sit.

It doesn't make sense to me how a grown woman such as Mavis can be so immature and insensitive at a time like this. A woman lost her daughter and she's grieving right outside the Herb Shack. We can hear her through the walls, which means she can probably hear Mavis laughing, too.

Has Mavis not lost anyone she cares about? It's not like her or Perula tell me anything about their pasts, other than what they used to do for a living. Did they have children? Grandchildren? Parents? Aunts and uncles?

The only rational explanation for Mavis's thoughtless outbursts and cruel-sounding words would be that she has, in fact, suffered a great deal. Maybe she wears a protective shell to avoid feeling any more pain.

Is that what Eve's doing? I shake these thoughts away. I love Eve, I truly do, but I can't downplay what happened—I can't pretend like she isn't mentally unwell and unfit to lead Eden. Even if my Aunt Eve still lives somewhere deep inside of Eve, I can't become emotional about it. The lives of hundreds of women are at risk.

I need to do something about it. Then, the thought of Nola creeps into my mind. Where is she? She almost always visits me at least one time per day, but I haven't seen her today. She must be offering her nurse expertise and working alongside Dr. Lewis to treat women and children. She's been doing that for the last three days. Although I admire her willingness to help, I hate that she's surrounded by germs all day long.

I pensively tap my fingers against the wooden counter under the window ledge. What if I go to her? How mad will she be? She already told me to stay away from the Medical Unit. She wasn't nice about it, either, but that's because she cares about me.

She scolded me when I came to see Emily the day Dr. Lewis released her. She'd slapped two hands around the middle area of her blue scrubs—clothing that must have once belonged to a thinner version of her. It wrapped her up like a piece of saran wrap around an apple fritter donut, making every roll and every bump visible.

"You listen here, and you listen good," she'd said with a finger in my face, reminding me of Mom. I went cross-eyed looking at the tip of her nail, and she kept jabbing it back and forth with every word. "This place isn't safe. It's crawling with bacteria. Now, I'm going to get your friend Emily, and you can take her back to her cell. Dr. Lewis says she's past the stage of being contagious. Keep an eye on her in her cell, but I don't want to see you around here again. Are we clear?"

I finally looked away from the tip of her index finger and found myself staring into her small, beady eyes squinting harder than I'd ever seen before. Distracted by the surgical mask hanging around her neck, I wanted to ask, "So why are you here?" but the longer I stared at the mask, the more I knew she'd use *that* to argue her case. She'd say something along the lines of "I used to do this for a living, Lucy. Dr. Lewis and I are taking every precaution not to contract the virus."

Nola's stubborn, too, so it's not like I could have argued any further. When she realized I wasn't moving, she told me she'd come to visit me at least once per day. That's when I threw my arms around her and hugged her tight, knowing all too well that there was a chance I'd lose her.

I swallow hard thinking of that hug. I can't lose Nola. Although she'll never replace my mom, she's become somewhat of a mother figure.

Turning away from the window, I reach for a head of garlic and start peeling off its mesh skin. But then, something strange happens—something... incredibly strange.

At first, it feels like an earthquake. The table vibrates, and all of Mavis's metal and wooden kitchen tools start dancing about beside her cauldron. Some of them even roll toward the cauldron, making a clanking noise against the metal and against each other.

I look up at Mavis, and then Perula, who both look like they've seen a ghost. What's weird about this is that the shaking doesn't stop. It's not inconsistent—it doesn't get worse and then better. Instead, it's long-lasting and doesn't change all that much.

So it can't be an earthquake, right?

What's going on?

I swing back around and stick my face against the window, the tip of my nose sliding over Mavis's grease smudge. Only minutes ago, the women around Eve were all on the ground, holding down Loretta.

But now, they're standing, and it doesn't look like they're wanting to fight. Instead, they all have hands over their eyes and heads tilted back as they point toward the sky. Eve, too, looks confused by what she's seeing. I hunch forward to try to see above the Herb Shack at whatever it is they're looking at, but the window's too small.

Oh God. Is it a comet? A missile? Are we all about

to die?

I rush past the Herb Shack's long table, my feet stomping on the wooden floor planks, and blast the door open. Mavis and Perula hurry behind me.

"W-would you calm yourself, you monkey-brained lunatic?" Mavis barks behind me.

She stomps so hard the Herb Shack shakes even more than it already has; obviously, she isn't accustomed to moving that fast.

I step out into the yellowing grass and gaze up toward the sky, blinking once, then twice, waiting for reality to set in. This can't be real. It's impossible.

"Holy mother of Athena..." Mavis shouts.

She has to shout, otherwise, no one would hear her. The plane is so loud, so powerful, that I can't look away. It's huge. Like, enormously huge. I've never seen anything like it. It looks like there are weapons, or huge missile guns attached underneath, which means it's a military plane. Its wings are as black as its metallic body, and they extend so far on either side of it that it almost looks bigger than all of Eden.

It's bigger than the Airbus Z900 that came out a few years before all this happened. I learned about it in school, and about how it was revolutionizing passenger aircraft by offering something like 600 seats and going twice as fast as the old models. Clearly, we were too young for them to go into detail about the specs.

What's so cool about this plane, though, is that it's floating in the air like a helicopter. It has drone functionalities mixed in, which isn't all that new, but it's shocking to see in something this big. There are over twenty giant propellers spinning around so fast and blowing air down on all of us.

My hair flies everywhere—in my face, around my neck, and even in Mavis's face who slaps a hand at it.

I watch Eve, not knowing who else to look at for comfort. Despite me thinking she's crazy, I also think she's the only one who can tell us what to do right now.

Is this thing going to kill us all? Are they from another country? Who's inside of that thing? Eve doesn't seem too sure, either—all she's doing is looking up like the rest of us with a scowl on her face, which is pretty worrisome.

And then, the wind slows down as the propellers shut off one by one.

The plane makes a left turn, hovering away from Eden, and slowly starts to descend.

Whatever that thing is, it isn't leaving—it's landing.

CHAPTER 10 – EVE

"Eve, what's going on?"

"What is that? Are we in danger?"

"Please, Eve, tell us what's going on!"

I can't speak. In fact, I can't even think. I march my way down the main hall, through the countless women bickering about my decision to isolate infected bodies. I don't care what they have to say—not anymore.

It's Freyda, isn't it? She's returned. It has to be. Who else would it be? When I reach the entrance hall, Nola comes running down from the Medical Unit's corridor. Her sneakers squeak and her breasts bounce up and down in her scrubs—something that looks like they've been taken off the corpse of a teenager. I don't understand why she hasn't had them resized.

She pulls her wiry hair out of her face, revealing a glistening forehead and sweaty cheeks, and ties a ponytail high on her head.

"D-did you hear that, Eve?" she asks, struggling to catch her breath. "The rumbling. Dr. Lewis heard it, too. I've lived through three earthquakes, and I can confirm that that was no earthquake."

Without saying a word, I jerk my head sideways as a way of saying, *Follow me.* Though I despise Nola for what she's done—for pulling Lucy away from me—I have more important matters to focus on right now.

She scurries behind me as I move, taking quick, uneven steps to keep up. I pass through the first set of doors leading to the main gates. The plane, or the ship—whatever it was—landed out there.

Swallowing hard, I open the penitentiary's front doors—two heavy bulletproof doors that swing with a swooshing noise—and make my way out into the cold autumn air. A gust of wind sweeps between the prison and the concrete barrier, sending dust into the air and into my mouth. Nola lets out a whimper and throws two hands over her eyes.

"A-are you opening those things?" she yells, pointing at the massive iron gates.

"Not yet," I shout back. "When I give you the signal, pull that latch over there." And I point at the same latch Freyda's pulled a dozen times over.

I climb my way up the concrete wall's tower, my palms numbing against the ladder's cold metal. My breath forms small white clouds every time I exhale, and I blow into my hands to warm them. The sound of the plane's engines can be heard from behind the wall, and without a doubt, across all of Eden.

My women must be panicking.

Little do they know that their entire world is about to change.

Once at the top, I peer down, seeing the plane in its entirety. It's the largest thing I've ever seen, with a wingspan of at least three hundred feet. It reminds me of large passenger planes my mother always promised to take me on, only bigger, sharp-edged, and black. Its nose is pointed, not round as I've seen on television, and its wings form sharp L shapes. There are massive propellers everywhere—on its wings, on its tail, and I'm sure, underneath its belly; these must be what allow the plane to hover the way it was doing moments ago.

The wind blows hard all around the plane, sending dust, debris, and even small stones flying into the air. The woman from earlier today—the one surrounded by men—is still standing outside of Eden's gates, yet now, she's standing far away with arms held over her face for protection.

Has she been waiting outside this whole time? Hoping I might change my mind and allow her inside of Eden? I would never allow men inside my paradise.

In an instant, the engines cut, and a high-pitched electrical sound lingers before a deafening silence takes over. An oversized door slowly opens, no doubt controlled by a hydraulic system, and continues to lower until it creates a platform capable of being descended on.

The moment I see her face, I almost drop to my knees.

Freyda is the first to exit. She pauses halfway down the platform, turns around, and encourages others to follow. Miller and Jada come out next, and then, Gabriel. I swing around, feeling a pleasant crack in my spine, and wave an anxious hand down at Nola.

"Open the gates!" I shout, wanting to jump up and down with joy.

Without looking at the plane again, I hurry down the ladder, careful not to slip and fall. The moment the gates crack open wide enough for me to fit through, I run through them and straight toward Freyda.

"Freyda!" I shout.

Her face lights up the moment she sees me. My heel stabs into the dirt and I nearly trip, so I kick them off and hurry to her.

"Oh, Freyda!" I say, throwing both arms around her.

She stiffens as if I spilled poison on her, and I realize I've never shown her any form of affection. I pull back, feeling embarrassed by my sudden show of emotion, and clear my throat. "I-I'm sorry," I say. "I was beginning to worry that I would never—"

"I'm okay," she says, a sweet smile embellishing that beautiful face of hers. She then turns toward the plane, and her smile stretches into a wide grin. "Can you believe this? I mean, it's crazy. I didn't think we'd actually pull it off."

All I can do is stare at her. She must think I'm insane. I don't care that they've returned with a plane, all I care about is that Freyda is safe and that she's standing in front of me at this very moment. God, I want to throw my arms around her again, but I'm afraid she'll pull away.

Instead, she takes a step forward and gives me a tight hug, surely sensing what I'm thinking.

"I'm okay," she repeats.

I let out a long breath, feeling whole—feeling as though I've been reunited with a severed limb. Freyda has always been my other half. If it weren't for her by my side, I'm not certain I'd have succeeded in caring for all the women of Eden all these years.

"Freyda," I say, remembering how I allowed things to end before her departure. "I'm sorry—"

She waves a hand and shrugs. "There's nothing to apologize for." She playfully punches me on the shoulder, and although months ago, this would have infuriated me, I can't help but smile. It's as if I've reverted to my teenage years. "I know you better than anyone here," she says, her perfectly shaped lips hypnotizing me as they move. "You were scared."

Scared? I, Eve Malum, was not scared.

"And unwilling to admit it," she adds.

I glance sideways to ensure no one heard her. She's right—I was scared. Terrified, even. It doesn't bother me that she knows this, so long as she keeps it to herself.

"I shouldn't have taken it out on you," I say.

She parts her lips to say something else, probably something along the lines of *That's how you are, and it's okay,* when voices coming from inside the plane capture my attention. They're deep—too deep to be female voices.

I look at Freyda and she retreats into herself, undoubtedly aware that I'm about to flip out.

"Eve, please—" she tries.

"Are there fucking men with you?" I growl.

Suddenly, Freyda's back to being my beta—not my friend, nor my confidante, but someone who is fully conscious that I'm in charge and she's nothing more than a tool kept nearby for the sole purpose of being given orders.

Men are forbidden from entering Eden.

Freyda knows that.

How could she do this? How could she bring men back to my paradise? I feel completely betrayed. She takes a step back, surely sensing the rage building in me.

"Eve, I had no control—"

"I should have never trusted you with this," I hiss, pointing a stiff finger at her face.

She pulls her face back and widens her eyes, looking into me as if I've mutated into a monster.

"Eve, you don't understand—"

I raise a tight fist and she takes another step back, but when I see the fear in her eyes, I stretch my fingers apart and clench my teeth.

What don't I understand? Are they prisoners? Was Freyda captured by these men? There's no way. If Freyda were a prisoner, she wouldn't have been the first one off the plane. Furthermore, her captors would be much closer to her to ensure she doesn't run off.

She's no prisoner.

She brought them here.

Fucking bitch.

Calm down, Eve.

Everyone's watching.

Both Jada and Miller keep their distances, observing with confusion and curiosity. Then, from behind them, the voices louden and a dozen men come marching out with advanced-looking guns held firmly in their hands.

I turn to Freyda, prepared to kill her with my bare hands.

How could she do this?

How the fuck could she bring soldiers into Eden?

I'm going to kill her.

I'm going to fucking kill her.

I turn around to see Nola standing by the front door, mouth wide open and hand hovering over the lever. I'm surprised she hasn't closed it already, but she must be waiting for my command.

The thought of running back inside of Eden crosses my mind, but there's no time. I'll never make it, and chances are, I'll be shot the moment I turn my back.

"Nola, close the gates!" I shout.

"Eve!" Freyda growls as the gates begin to slide across the dirt, making a loud rumbling noise.

I turn around and with a full swing of my arm, slap Freyda across the face. She falls into Jada, hand pressed against her reddening cheek. Jada helps her up, but in an instant, the soldiers around her point their guns at me, postures hunched and eyes aimed down their sights.

"I trusted you," I say, my voice breaking.

Freyda parts her lips to say something, but a familiar voice carries over all of us.

"At ease."

At once, the soldiers lower their guns and split halfway in the middle, forming a path for whoever gave them the order to back down. Then, she comes walking out of the plane.

I stand up tall and stare at her, wondering if

maybe I've been shot and sent to the afterlife. This isn't truly happening, is it?

Vrin, looking the very same as she did the last time I saw her, extends her arms on either side of her body, cocks her head to the side, and smirks at me. "What's wrong, Eve? You look like you've seen a ghost."

CHAPTER 11 – GABRIEL

Eve looks pissed.

Not the obvious kind of pissed, though. The kind that sits right below the surface, waiting to burst out. She forces a smile and welcomes Vrin as she approaches, but it doesn't take a genius to see she's disgusted by her long-lost friend. And why wouldn't she be? Without warning, here we are with a bunch of men. And I know exactly how Eve feels about men.

"We heard you were in trouble," Vrin says. "Are you okay?" She reaches for Eve's shoulder but Eve pulls away.

"I'm fine," Eve says. And then, it's like she realizes everyone's watching her. She clears her throat, forces a smile, and touches Vrin's shoulder. "Thank you for coming."

What's she going to do? Send us away? Eve asked me to locate Area 82. She wanted this. She wanted out of Eden. Is she seriously going to throw all that away because of her hatred for men? I wouldn't put it past her.

"Is it true?" Vrin asks, leaning into Eve.

Eve pulls away with her neck tucked as if Vrin's breath smells worse than four-month-old tuna.

"Is what true?"

Vrin playfully taps her on the shoulder and Eve's eyes roll toward where she's been touched. If she had a lighter, she'd likely try to burn off the spot where Vrin touched her.

"The all-female colony," Vrin says. "A lot of rumors have been floating around, Eve. The women of Elysium are dying to meet you. To be honest, I didn't think you'd made it. You were so young..." She stares at Eve like she's trying to see what's inside. "They call you the Queen, you know."

Vrin looks like she's about to laugh. Like she can't believe how ridiculous it all sounds coming out of her mouth.

"The Queen?" Eve says.

Her posture stiffens a bit. It's obvious she's intrigued. The anger, the resentment... It's all gone now. It's like all she cares about is recognition.

"Yeah," Vrin adds. "You have to realize, Eve, that people have been talking about you for five years. You've become a bit of a myth."

"This... Ela—" Eve tries.

"Elysium," Vrin corrects, planting two veiny hands on her waist.

"How many women are there?" Eve asks.

Vrin scratches her chin. "The last time we did a headcount, we were at two thousand and forty-three."

Eve's eyes look like they're about to pop out of her head. And with good reason. Aren't there something like 300 in Eden? Give or take? That's a huge difference.

"Women?" Eve asks. "And what about—" she glances at me, and then at the soldiers behind me, but it's like she's too disgusted to even say the word *men*.

"One hundred and twelve," Vrin says. "Thirteen, if we're counting Gabriel."

I swallow at the sound of my name. Does this mean I'm staying for good? Am I finally going to be somewhere I belong? Five years of surviving wastelands is about all I can take.

Everyone watches Eve now. It looks like she's doing mathematical equations in her head. Why's she so interested in knowing how many men and women there are?

"Who's in charge?" Eve asks.

Vrin gives her a crooked smile and raises her chin. "You're looking at her."

Eve's stare becomes hollow. It's like she isn't even in there, or she is and she's talking to a dozen voices at once. What's she thinking about?

Vrin clears her throat. "Look, Eve, I'm not here to step on anybody's toes. I'm here on a rescue mission. Now, if you don't mind opening up those gates, we'd like to start bringing women up onto the plane."

Everyone watches Eve, no doubt waiting for her to snap. Freyda, especially, looks worried. There's a silence so heavy that it reminds me of a twig being bent. It's quiet, up until the pressure is too much, and then there's a loud snap.

Why isn't she reacting? Is she going to freak out? She's protective of her little paradise, after all. She's made it damn clear that she's worked her ass off to get her women to where they are today... That she's the reason they survived. I can't imagine her handing all that over to Vrin, even if it's for the best.

But then, without breaking eye contact with Vrin, Eve shouts, "Nola, open the gates!"

"Oh, yes, yes, right away!" comes a mousy voice.

Up to the tower, where Eve was standing moments ago, stands a straggly-haired woman waving frantically. She quickly then disappears behind the concrete wall. She must have been watching this whole time.

"Avi, Darnell," Vrin orders, "go see the family over there, follow protocol, and bring them on board."

She's referring to the people who've been standing at a distance since we landed. It looks like they've been waiting to get inside of Eden for days. They look related, all of them, and malnourished and exhausted.

Looks like we got here on time. For their sake, anyways.

Vrin takes a step toward the open gates, but Eve stops her with a firm hand on her chest.

"Vrin, wait," she says. "The influenza virus is spreading. Let me go inside, and I'll retrieve only those who are healthy."

"No need." Vrin's loud voice carries through the open gates and she widens her stance. "We have advanced state-of-the-art medical equipment and several world-renowned doctors in Elysium. Let's get everyone out and we'll focus on healing them afterward."

She clicks her fingers over her head, and her male soldiers start descending the door ramp.

Eve, having no other choice but to let them enter her kingdom, extends a welcoming hand as they walk by. "Come on in..."

That smile scares me. It's wide and forceful. It's so wide that I can see her molars.

God.

Doesn't anyone else see through her like I do? I glance at Freyda, but she focuses her attention on her feet. We've been here for all of ten minutes, and already, Eve's got a hold of her. Freyda's like a beaten dog who's been dragged back to her master.

"Freyda," Eve orders, her fierce eyes shooting up toward us. "What're you waiting for? Let's go."

I reach for Freyda but she yanks her arm away from me. She's back to being Eve's puppet. Back to obeying every order without question. How does Eve do it? How does she manipulate such a good, strong-minded person into being a brainless soldier?

* * * * * *

"He thinks we're all a bunch of brainless soldiers," James says, eyeballing Commander Howieson.

All that runs through my mind is, *Aren't we?* Or, more specifically, *Aren't you?* Why's James so upset about Howieson telling us to arm up? He's only doing his job. We're about to land any minute.

I think James has a problem with authority. If anything, he wants to be the commander, and he's pissed off that Howieson got the position instead of him. It's scary to think that James is jealous of someone like Howieson. The man has no soul. Every time he talks, it's like listening to a machine.

"Gentlemen, shoot to kill," Howieson says,

marching back and forth at the front of the plane. "Mothers, grandmothers, daughters—I don't give a shit. These women have become enemies of the United States of America."

We're on our way to the White House, and all of a sudden, we have a kill order.

My stomach, or at least what's left of it, feels like it stayed behind some thirty thousand feet below. Shoot to kill? Jesus Christ. This can't be happening. Minutes ago, we were on our way to provide relief to the White House, not actually *kill* everyone protesting.

A few guys around me shift in their seats, probably realizing that this is about to happen. We aren't playing in virtual reality anymore. We're being asked to kill real human beings... Real women and children. It's obvious that the ones who still have an ounce of humanity left don't want to do this, but what choice do they have?

Soldiers obey, and we're all in too deep.

Besides, the last time someone disobeyed a direct order on a plane, he was thrown out.

"Do we have a kill order from the president, sir?" someone asks.

Howieson turns his huge bearded face to the side like he's insulted that someone would even ask. He cracks his neck, something that's big enough to be someone's torso, and searches us to find who spoke out.

But Howieson doesn't have time to say anything. The door behind him opens with a loud *swoosh*, and out comes a man wearing a suit that must have cost more than the plane, shoes so shiny they cast an aura around him, and a smirk so arrogant I want to knock his teeth out.

But at the same time, I'd be afraid to. This man, whoever he is, is powerful. I can see it in his eyes. He looks like he owns the damn plane. In fact, he looks like owns all of us.

Isn't that what we are? A bunch of pawns in this sick war?

"The president hasn't given a kill order yet," the man announces. "But he will very soon." Then, he lowers his head forward like he's looking over a pair of sunglasses and observes each of us. What's he trying to do? Wait for us to realize who he is or what he represents?

I have no fucking clue who this man is, or who he thinks he is, but when his eyes meet mine at last, I know one thing: I'm sitting only a few feet away from the most dangerous man alive.

He pulls his chin up and gazes down at us as if we're nothing more than specks of dust on his high-end Italian leather shoes. "President Price does as he's told."

* * * * * *

"W-what's going on?"

"Oh my God."

"Mommy!"

The shouts carry through the huge main hall in Eden when Vrin and her men walk in like they own the place. The women look terrified like they're about to be slaughtered at the hands of these soldiers. Women grab hold of their little girls, and some girls crawl underneath the dresses of their mothers, grandmothers, or even their older sisters.

"It's okay!" Eve shouts, but no one seems to want to listen to her.

She raises both hands in the air and smiles, but that smile doesn't even last two seconds. Soon, it turns upside down when she undoubtedly realizes she has no control over her women. Not now. Not while they're being infiltrated by soldiers.

On the bright side, the men aren't holding their guns. They have them fastened to their backs and they form a straight line against the wall, heads held high and gazes aimed at the back of the room. A few of them, however, can't help but look at the women.

One young man, no older than twenty years old, catches a glimpse of a young woman with rosy cheeks and sun-kissed blond hair braided to one side. He smirks at her, and she offers the same shy greeting. But it doesn't last long. The woman standing next to her, assumedly her mother, grabs her arm and pulls her as far away from the soldier as possible.

"Everyone!" Eve tries again.

"You promised us safety, Eve!"

"What is this? Why are there men inside of Eden?"

"Tell us what's going on!"

"Everyone, please—"

Then, a loud whistle bounces off the walls and makes me wince. In fact, it makes everyone grimace and reach for their ears, which I'm assuming was Vrin's intention.

"Enough!" she shouts.

Her voice is so authoritative. Not in a panicked

sort of way, like Eve, but in an *I'm in control and I'll take care of you as long as you listen to me* sort of way.

Surprisingly, everyone goes quiet. Eve doesn't seem too impressed by this. She searches her people with wide eyes and a wrinkled forehead. She must feel betrayed.

"My name is Vrin, and these are my people." She rests a hand on her padded military vest and then points at her men. "We're here today because Eve sent a search team to locate a safer living space for all of you."

The crowd's focus shifts from Vrin to Eve like they're trying to spot the truth in one of them. I don't blame them. Who can they trust? A woman who, despite her faults, has managed to keep most of them alive, or a complete stranger?

Eve has her problems, that's for sure. But I feel a bit bad for her. She seems devastated. It reminds me of when I was eight years old and a new kid joined our class. All of my friends thought he was the coolest thing because he could ride a skyboard. My talent was being able to ride a horse. Mama didn't have the money to buy me a skyboard. In fact, most parents didn't.

We were poor, but my friends loved me and always loved visiting my grandpa's farm, where I'd show off by standing on the horse while it was moving. But then little Eduardo came along with his fancy clothes and thirty-thousand-dollar skyboard and it was like I'd disappeared. He had the SB-9000, which was the best in its class. It flew up five hundred feet and even had protective crash-preventative mechanisms that brought the board down safely if the person riding it lost control. When kids asked him to ride it, he'd let them, even though he wasn't supposed to; a special license was needed.

I'd never understood how he got the license at eight years old. His family was rich, and they must have paid someone off.

Now, Eve reminds me of young me. She doesn't show it on the outside, but I can sense how terrified she is. Any moment now, she could lose total control over her paradise. If these women decide to follow Vrin, what's Eve supposed to do about it? The worst part is that in the eyes of Eve's women, it's her fault all of this is happening. She authorized the mission to Area 82.

That could either be a good thing or a bad thing.

"We hear there's a virus going around," Vrin continues.

Rapid nods fill the room, followed by coughs and sneezes.

"In Elysium," Vrin continues, "we have high-end medical equipment and incredible doctors and surgeons. Whatever's spreading here can be treated. I assure you that you will be very comfortable inside of Elysium. We have clean running water, electricity, heat, and even central air."

The women's nods turn into excited grins, and for a second, it's like everyone's cured of their illnesses. Like no one's sick, and they're perfectly healthy. I guess it would be like telling someone with a broken arm that they just won a million dollars. It's unlikely they'd still feel any pain for a while after hearing that.

Or at least, they wouldn't focus on it.

"We have aircraft, functioning vehicles, hydroponic farms, livestock, and a cutting-edge defense system to protect you from any exterior threat."

Okay, now, she's showing off.

The women already look sold on the idea.

"If you're willing to join us," Vrin continues, "I assure you that you'll be comfortable and well taken care of. Now, I can't force any of you to make that decision. It's up to you. The plane will be leaving in one hour." She pulls her sleeve back and glances down at her wristwatch. I haven't seen one of those things in ages. "If you're joining us, please grab your belongings and meet us at the front gates."

She glances at Eve, almost like she's asking for permission.

Eve nods, but when she doesn't say anything, Vrin claps two solid hands together.

"All right, people, let's move out."

CHAPTER 12 – LUCY

I feel like I've gone back in time to when I was six years old on Christmas Eve. Mom said something about last-minute Christmas shopping and how everything was too late to find me a sitter. So instead of staying home and playing on my H-Cap, I was plucked underneath my arms, brought into the car, and forced to follow her around while she plowed her way through the massive crowd in the mall.

I hated it. People kept bumping into us, and every time, Mom apologized, even though they were the ones at fault. My mom was being polite, but by the end of the day, it was obvious she was getting annoyed. She mumbled, *Sorry*, and then rolled her eyes and shook her head so hard her hair swept her shoulders.

Today, that's what it feels like. Women are scurrying around Eden as if it's caught fire. They're rushing in every direction, looking for their friends or family members, and scavenging through their small, iron-gated cells to pack whatever cherished items they plan on bringing.

My H-Cap is the only thing I care to bring. From what the military lady said, it sounds like I'll be able to power it back up again. That's what I'm most excited about right now—getting to use my H-Cap again.

I'll get to play games, read stories, and who knows, I may still have my old pictures and videos on there.

Pictures of my mom.

"Is it true?"

I swing my body around to find Emily leaning against my gate, shoulders slouched and a single duffel bag resting by her feet. A big hole decorates the side of it, and it's obvious that she tried to fix it on her own. Small beige threads criss-cross over one another and form a hectagon. It looks sloppy, and the color clashes with the bag's forest green exterior. She must have tried to fix it when we first arrived in Eden, assumedly to avoid asking Sahana, who was already in over her head with repair requests.

"Is what true? That we're leaving this place for good?" I try not to scoff—I'll come across as an entitled brat. The truth is, I couldn't be happier that we're leaving this place. Mom didn't come here with me, but for some reason, Eden reminds me of her. Maybe it's the heartache. Everything about Eden—the humid scent, the main hall's white tiles that get clay brown every autumn, the women gathering together in the cafeteria to reminisce about old times—reminds me of what I've lost.

A fresh start is exactly what I need. Admittedly, everything feels surreal. The thought of leaving Eden feels like a dream, but it's happening, and I need to hurry up if I want to make it on that plane.

"It's hard to believe," I say, "but it's really happening, and so much is going to change." I reach for my *Magic of Herbs* book and squeeze it into my backpack. Whether or not I'll even need this at the new place is beyond me, but the truth is, it's interesting. "Were you there when the lady explained everything?"

Emily moans and rubs her pink eyes. "What?"

"Did you just wake up or something?" I ask.

She nods and wipes a line of drool from her lip. "Y-yeah. Malory came running down the hallway squealing about boys or something." Poor Emily looks pissed off about the rude awakening. "What's going on? She said we're all leaving. Now even the kids are running around. I packed my stuff"—she points at her beaten and deflated duffel bag—"but I still don't get what's going on."

I crane my neck and gawk at her bag as if gifted with x-ray vision. "What're you bringing?"

She shrugs. "Two pairs of jeans, two shirts, and a picture of—" But she stops herself short.

It's obvious Emily is still afraid to talk about her dad. What she doesn't realize, though, is that this new place isn't only filled with women. There were about a dozen men standing in the main hall. Some had beards, which was weird to see when you're accustomed to being around only women, and others clean-shaven heads. They were so big, too. Two of them who stood nearest to Eve towered over her, their chests puffed out and their shoulders wide. I imagine she didn't like that very much.

"It's okay," I tell her. "I don't think you'll have to keep your dad a secret anymore."

Her big, swollen eyes stare into mine. Is she about to cry? Is she relieved, or is she sad? Without saying anything, she nods weakly and reaches for her bag. "Malory said something about medicine, too."

"Yeah," I say. "I'm telling you, Emily, this is a good thing. I get that it's scary right now, but do you honestly want to spend the rest of your life living in a prison cell?"

She shrugs.

Poor Emily. She seems so depressed.

"Puppy!" a little girl suddenly shouts.

She waddles from side to side, running across Division Three's opening and straight toward where everyone is standing.

Emily and I look at each other, but only for a moment. Within seconds we're running down the hall chasing after the little girl. She runs with her chubby arms swinging over her head, her thick pigtails swinging like horsetails and her red puffy dress bouncing up and down. Her mother follows closely behind, and together, they disappear into the dense crowd of women.

"Easy, easy," comes a man's voice.

Then, a whimper fills the air, and I look at Emily again. Could there actually be a puppy here? Where did it come from? The last time we saw a puppy was when Freyda brought Ruby, Eden's favorite and only golden retriever—into Eden for the first time. She'd said something about the dog having been saved from death and how she'd done everything she could to save its brothers and sisters.

So where does this new puppy come from? I hurry toward the crowd and elbow my way through the adults seeing as it seems to be what all the kids are doing. When I finally break through into the open, children of all ages surround a man at the front of the group, some on their hands and knees, others, on their butts. They're all squirming and wiggling in their spots, obviously wanting to get closer to this man.

I don't know who he is, but there's something soft about him. His brown eyes remind me of warm honey. He smiles at the children and regrips his hold around the puppy. He, or she, squishes its face into the hairs of the man's bushy beard.

"Let's all be really quiet for her, okay?" he says, eyeballing all the kids. He's a bit awkward, undoubtedly because he hasn't been around kids since America went to hell. But he's trying, and that's all that matters. "Her name's Justice," he continues, petting her soft-looking head.

She's a light gray color, almost blue from where I'm standing, and the tips of her paws are white. Or at least, they seem to be. She keeps kicking the air and tucking her feet inside his thick, dark-haired forearm. Her tail, too, is tucked. According to Freyda, this means she's scared. When Ruby first came to Eden, Freyda took it upon herself to give everyone a crash course on canine body language to avoid any problems. Fortunately, Ruby is about the most docile dog in the world. She can be poked, prodded, and even pulled at, and she doesn't seem to care. She loves kids, no matter how rough they are with her.

I wonder if Justice is the same.

"I'm gonna put her down right here," the man says, leaning forward. "Would one of you like to pet her?"

The main hall explodes with little voices—

screams, pleas, and bare feet clapping against the hard floor.

The man bites his bottom lip and glances up at the mothers, probably wondering if he made a mistake by offering.

"Shhh," a few women say.

"You have to be quiet. The puppy doesn't like loud noises."

"Leeanne, sit down, honey."

"Mushi—" And the woman points toward the ground—an obvious translation of *Sit down, or else.*

Quickly, the room returns to the way it was, and the man slowly kneels to release the puppy onto the floor. At first, she squirms and shoves her face further into his neck, but he pries her away and places her gently onto her four legs.

She seems uncertain; her tail wags but then disappears between her two small thighs. The man lets a few kids pet her head but then scoops her up.

It's too much for her to handle.

"All right, everyone," comes the army woman's voice. I say army woman because she's the only woman wearing a military outfit. And by the way she's talking, it's clear she's in charge. "Gather around over here, and let's make our way to the aircraft."

Whispers break out, some panicked, others excited. I catch a glimpse of ditsy Malory, who keeps flirtatiously pulling at her flowing hair and combing it over one shoulder. She keeps looking at the youngest soldier standing against the wall.

He looks back and smirks but doesn't maintain eye contact. He's either shy, or he was trained not to allow lust to get in the way of his work. Malory picks up a small purse, then shoves it into her tomboy friend's arms without looking away from the young soldier.

Malory will always be Malory, even in a world like this.

"You ready?" I ask Emily.

She nods, though it looks like she'd rather be sleeping.

"Are you feeling *any* better?" I ask. I don't mean to come across as rude—I want the old Emily back. Sick Emily is lethargic, depressed, and unenthused. It's not her fault, but I'd be lying if I said it wasn't a bit of a downer.

Still staring at the floor, she shrugs. "I think so."

"Well, like I said, they have advanced medicine at the new place. So they should be able to get you back to normal in no time."

She tries to smile, then picks up her bag and pulls it over one shoulder.

"Here," I say, pulling it out of her hands. "I'll take it."

"I'm sorry," she says.

I stare at her. What's she sorry about?

"For being like this," she adds.

"It's not your fault—"

"My mom got the Lazarus virus when I was little," she says.

I don't say anything—I know what she's talking about, and I can't even begin to imagine how hard that must have been. Millions of people died from the Lazarus virus and it got all the conspiracy theorists worked up. I remember Mom talking about how the government had released a virus to try to control the gender ratio. She explained to me that women were being way more affected than men—thousands were dying, while men spent a few days in bed with flu-like symptoms. How was it that a virus could target one sex over the other? Although it made absolutely no sense to me, it didn't change the fact that it was happening.

"I don't remember much of it," Emily continues, "but I remember seeing how my dad took care of everything. He cooked, cleaned, ran errands. He was always gone doing everything for us. He even worked double shifts to get us by." She looks up at me and swallows hard. "And despite all of that, he'd still tuck me in at night, read me a bedtime story, and lie down with me until I fell asleep."

She tugs at her fingers. How do I respond to something like that?

"She miraculously survived," she says, "but I saw what it did to my dad. I'd never want to make someone my caregiver."

I part my lips to say something, but she reaches for her bag around my shoulder and pulls it off. "I can take this, thank you, though."

As she walks away, I watch the back of her wild hair, the result of lying flat on a pillow for over a week, and wonder how often she thinks about her dad. I think about Mom every single day, and although I don't talk about it, it eats me up inside. I want her here with me. It's not fair that I'm alive and breathing while she's... gone.

Clearing my throat, I follow Emily. No way am I

allowing myself to get all emotional around so many people.

* * * * * *

"So you're an orphan too?" comes a mousey voice.

I turn sideways, my eyes most likely red and swollen. A luminous fluorescent light makes it hard to look at her and it's killing my head. I've been crying so long I think my head's going to explode.

And what's she talking about? An orphan? I'm not an orphan. I have Mom and I have Aunty Eve.

She looks the same age as me. Eight or nine. She looks sick, though. Kind of like she's been sitting in this basement, or warehouse, for months. Her skin is so pale it looks blue a bit. And those veins... They're popping out beside her eyes and on her forehead like they're going to rip through her skin any second. Maybe she's been crying for days, too.

"I'm not an orphan," I say.

She looks at me funny, and so do a few other girls and boys in the room. They're staring at me like I just told them I have superpowers. Like I'm not one of them.

"Everyone here's an orphan," the girl says. She looks around, and little heads nod up and down.

"What're you talking about?" I ask. "My mom's coming back for me."

I'm trying not to get mad, but it's hard not to. I'm scared. Mom will come back, right? There's no way she left me here forever. Why would she do that? Is this about all the fighting? Did Mom decide to go fight with Aunty Eve? She wouldn't. She has me. Aren't I the most important thing to her?

"Now, now, girls and boys," comes Clarissa's voice. She's the nicest adult I've ever met, aside from Mom and Aunty Eve. She keeps telling us we're *hiding out* until everything is safe, and then we'll get to come out of hiding. She's also the only adult in here, so we sort of have to listen to her. "We talked about that word."

That word.

She's talking about the word *orphan*. Bella, the oldest kid here, is the reason all of this started. She's the one who told all of us that the sole reason we're here is that our parents abandoned us. And kids whose parents abandon them are called orphans.

"But Miss Clarissa," says the girl beside me.

"Ming," Clarissa says, sounding more serious than usual.

Ming, I guess is her name, bows her head and pouts with her arms crossed like the little kids do when teachers get mad at them.

I turn away and drop myself down into my bed of old clothes and blankets. Then, the crying starts again. I hate this. I've never been the kind of kid who cries in front of other kids. But ever since Mom left me here, that's all I can do.

I wish I could push a button and make all of this stop.

* * * * * *

Why are they crying? Shouldn't they be happy? A handful of women are hugging each other, crying. It looks like they're saying goodbye. Are some of them staying behind?

"Come on," someone says, and I'm pushed forward.

Everyone's rushing to get to the aircraft. This is all happening so fast. I can't believe that in a few minutes, we're going to be up in the air, flying away from here.

When I step outside, it's hard to believe what I'm looking at. The plane is huge. I mean... huge. I've never been on a plane before, and now that I'm about to climb onto one, I'm sick to my stomach.

What if it crashes? Oh God.

"Are you okay?" Emily asks.

Without looking at her, I nod, still staring at the plane. Women are going up the ramp, dragging bags behind them. Some are excited, waving their arms over their heads and talking loudly, while others keep quiet and follow the lineup.

"You don't look so good," Emily says.

I turn to her. "I-I'm fine. I just... I've never been on a plane before."

She smiles at me for the first time in a long time. Does she find it funny that I'm scared? I'm never scared. At least, I don't show that I am. The last time I showed any kind of vulnerability, I was told I was an orphan. Some days, I wonder if all of my crying is the reason Mom died. If I somehow made it happen. It's completely irrational, but I need to put the blame somewhere.

That's why now, I don't let people know how I'm feeling.

"It's not that bad," she says. A bit of color returns to her cheeks. She's obviously excited to tell me about her experience on a plane. "At first, it's freaky, because, well... It's really loud. But then you get used to it, and it's kind of exciting. Especially once it's high up in the air."

I swallow hard. How high does this thing go?

"I've only been on a plane once," she admits, "but it was awesome. We took one to go visit my grandma when my dad said she didn't have much longer to live. Before we took off, my dad explained to me that flying is kind of like being on a boat. And I'd gone on a boat that summer when he took a day off from work to bring me on a local cruise. So when he compared the bumps in the air to waves, I understood. It was pretty bumpy, but after a while, it was like being on a ride at an amusement park. So... that's what it'll feel like."

I stare at her.

"Like waves," she repeats.

I stop walking, and someone bumps into me.

Emily clears her throat, drops her bag, and starts making gestures in front of her. She raises two hands pressed firmly together to replicate a plane.

"It'll be bumpy, like this," she says, moving her hands up and down.

Is this supposed to reassure me? It doesn't. If anything, it's stressing me out even more.

"You're telling me that huge thing"—I point at the plane—"is going to be moving up and down in the air?"

"It's called turbulence," comes an adult's voice, and I jump, startled by the way he's hovering over my shoulder.

I swing around. It's a man in a weird black suit and a gun strapped to his back. With two hands planted on his waist, he smiles down at us as. At first, I'm a bit intimidated by how tall he is and by the black beard on his face, but he seems nice. And surely, he knows much more about planes than we. I'm hoping he can explain to me what turbulence is... better than Emily, who's making my anxiety way worse.

"Turbulence only affects passenger aircraft," he says, his voice deep and grumbly. "This thing's way too fancy for turbulence."

When we don't say anything, he adds, "There are a lot of causes for turbulence... Wind, storms, hot air rising from the ground. Like your friend here says, it's like waves in the ocean. One moment things can be smooth, and the next, you're bouncing in your seat. It's nothing to be afraid of. It's perfectly normal. In fact, you should count yourselves lucky that you're about to board a Falcon—" He sticks a thick thumb out at the massive aircraft ahead of us. "This thing has hundreds of equilibrating functionalities that reduce the effects of turbulence. In other words, you don't feel it as much."

It's making a bit more sense to me.

"My dad told me that planes used to be a lot softer in the air," Emily says. "Is that true?"

"Your dad's right," the man says. "If you read up on the history of flying, you'll hear the year 2031 mentioned a lot. That's when climate change finally caused turbulence to become so severe that people didn't want to fly anymore and the air transportation industry lost billions of dollars. That's also when they started developing technology to reduce the impact of turbulence. I'm not a pilot or an aircraft engineer, so I can't explain it to you, but all I can tell you is that you'll be perfectly safe and it'll be so smooth, chances are you'll fall asleep."

When we don't say anything, he jerks his head sideways, his beard brushing against the collar of his shirt. "So, you coming, or what?"

CHAPTER 13 – EVE

I dig my fingernail into the chair's armrest, creating grooves in the gray leather. Women bicker around me, an annoying hum like insects buzzing around a camper in a humid forest.

They appear excited—full of vibrancy and enthusiasm. So much so, in fact, that I don't recognize half of these women. Their smiles stretch the skin of their faces, and their eyes light up with so much excitement that for a moment, I'm reminded of my Devil's tea.

Only now, these women are not high. They're not under any spell other than that of this new place. They speak of it as if it's paradise—as if it's the holy land they've spent the last five years waiting for.

That was supposed to be Eden. Why did they not feel this much excitement in Eden? I claw down again, this time, causing a small piece of leather to tear out and fall to the matching gray floor.

This was your idea, Eve.

You wanted new land.

I didn't want new territory ruled by someone else. We aren't traveling to new grounds to build a new society for ourselves—we're entering a preexisting society of people who have most likely spent the last five years living far more comfortably than us.

How will my women ever forgive me for this? They will blame me for their suffering. Who will I be if I don't have them? If I don't have Eden? Eden is who I am.

I am Eden.

And now, they speak of Elysium.

I grind my teeth and attempt to block out the voices around me. I want to shout and tell everyone to shut up, but I must remain calm. These women—the ones who will always see me as their savior—need me to be the strong leader they believe me to be.

"You okay?" comes Freyda's voice.

I swallow hard, refusing to look at her. How can I despise someone so much, yet want nothing more than to be near them? She betrayed me.

Air blows out from the padding of her seat as she sits down beside me. "I know apologizing will never be enough. I didn't mean for any of this, Eve."

She reaches for my hand that's gripped tightly around the armrest and I pull away.

"I should have turned back when we saw the plane fly overhead—"

Glowering at her, I lean in. "You knew the place was inhabited before getting to it?"

"I didn't know it was—" she lowers her voice. "I didn't know it was full of men, Eve. How was I supposed to know that? I thought maybe we'd found the Binaries. It was a plane, Eve. All I saw was technology. I thought maybe the Binaries were rebuilding civilization. And for all we know, they might be. They might be in there. Wouldn't you have done the same thing? Wouldn't you have wanted to know? Or would you have wanted to stay in the Dark Ages?"

I grind my teeth. Freyda has no right speaking to me about the Binaries. For the longest time, she ridiculed me for believing that one day, we'd find the them—women specializing in various trades... women capable of rebuilding civilization from the ground up. And now, what? Is Freyda going to sit beside me and preach to me about the possibility of the Binaries living inside Elysium?

It makes sense, I suppose. How else would someone like Vrin get technology up and running again? Vrin is a military woman—she's no expert in engineering or technology. She also mentioned advanced medical equipment. Surely, the Binaries are responsible for this.

"What?" Freyda asks, searching me. "What're you thinking about?"

If she knew what I was thinking about, she'd get up and move away from me. While I may hate Vrin for ruling over this new land, I should also be thanking her for building such a large society that apparently worships the idea of me.

All I have to do is convince these women that I'm a more capable leader than Vrin, and Elysium is mine.

CHAPTER 14 – GABRIEL

Poor kids.

They remind me of puppies at a shelter trying to get past the cage gate that's preventing them from reaching human visitors. They're excited and want to be close to me to see Justice on my lap, but their mothers keep telling them to sit down and to keep quiet. So they wiggle in their seats, readjust their seat belts, and stare at me as if I'm the one who's going to tell them it's okay if they come closer.

But I don't say that. It isn't my place. Besides, we're about to take off, so it's important that they sit still in their seats.

I rub my finger between Justice's eyes. She closes them, rests her snout on my shoulder and lets out a tired sigh through her dry little nose. I'm hoping they have a vet in Elysium. God knows how long she's been alone. She could be dehydrated, or malnourished. She could even have worms, for all I know.

"I don't want to see you anywhere near that thing," comes a mother's stern voice. She glowers at me, and then at Justice like she's the ugliest thing in this world.

Justice is far from ugly. She's beautiful, perfectly

structured, and has vivid blue eyes that are to die for. She'd probably win awards if she was in some sort of dog show. So what's this mother's problem? How could anyone look at a puppy like that?

"But mom—"

"Bee, don't make me repeat myself," the mother orders. "Do you want to lose an arm?"

"But she's a puppy—"

"She's a pit bull," the mother growls, and a few other mothers turn their heads as if they're only now realizing what kind of dog Justice is.

Didn't they already know? I thought it was obvious.

Now, I'm getting a bunch of nasty looks. Not from everyone, but from a handful of women all wearing similar dresses. They're looking at me like I'm carrying a live bomb. What's their problem?

Another mother pulls her child's face against her chest. "You keep that thing away from my kid," she hisses.

"It's not even muzzled!"

There's no point trying to argue with them. Mama told me that this has been an issue for years. Apparently, in 2027 (if I'm remembering that right), the government went on a mass killing spree, euthanizing a bunch of innocent pit bulls after it became illegal to own them anywhere in the United States. The fighting continued for years. People protested in the streets, crying out that owners were to blame, not the breed. And this went on for years and years. They lifted the ban in 2040, and everything was great for a while. But then President Price came into the picture, and everything went to shit again when the government became a dictatorship.

So, I get why these women are all riled up. They've been brainwashed into believing all the horrific campaigns operated under President Price's rulership. He even made announcements online about how pit bulls were Satan's creations, and how the world would be a better place without them. He made some pretty similar comments about Rottweilers and Dobermans, but pit bulls got the shittiest end of the stick.

"What's going on here?" comes Vrin's voice.

She stares at the women, then follows their hateful eyes to Justice.

"If you have any concerns, please direct them to me," she says, though I can hear the frustration in her voice. "Lockjaw's a myth, and so is aggression, so unless there's anything else you'd like to discuss, I'm going to assume this matter is resolved."

She reaches for Justice and scratches her behind the ear, and it flaps up and down.

"You're a good man, Gabriel," she says.

Not knowing how to respond to that, I nod and focus my attention on Justice.

"Seat belts on," Vrin shouts all of a sudden. "Takeoff is to commence in five minutes."

Resting my head against the chair's headrest, I suck in a long breath.

There's no reason to panic. There's no reason to panic. There's no reason to panic.

God, I hate being like this. I squeeze my eyes shut, then open them again. The flight here lasted all of fifteen minutes. I can handle another fifteen minutes again to get back to Area 82. It was shitty and stressful, but I survived. I'll survive this, too.

I'm about to close my eyes again when I see a young girl sitting a few aisles ahead of me. She's turned sideways, talking to someone I assume is a friend, so I can see her perfectly. Her hair, a mess of chestnut brown and frizzy waves, hangs over one shoulder, making her already pale skin look even paler.

Why does she look so familiar? I don't know this kid. But she looks like Castor. A lot. She has the same nose, only much smaller and more feminine-looking, the same thick brown eyebrows, the same soft round jaw.

I swallow hard at the thought of Castor.

* * * * * *

"Hands over your head!"

I'm already on my knees, but I do as told and slowly raise my hands above my head.

"State your name!"

"Rodriguez," I say. "Gabriel Rodriguez."

I look up at the guy holding the gun, who jerks it in the air the moment we make eye contact. He reminds me of those over-the-top soldiers, the ones who feel the need to yell every few minutes. His head is shaved, though not cleanly and which is no doubt due to the conditions out here. His eyes, two sparkling blue dots, sit in the middle of his acne-scarred skin which is now red from all the yelling. It's obvious he's the one leading the group, and it's also obvious he's the last person who should be leading the group.

"You armed, Gabriel?" he asks.

I nod. I'm not going to lie to the guy. Who isn't armed out here? If I say I'm not and he finds out later, he'll kill me. That's how it works in the wild. The part that pisses me off is that I've managed to keep under the radar for the last four or so years. Why was I found now? Did I get sloppy? I'm kneeling in a pile of debris alongside an abandoned school.

Guess I wasn't the only one who thought of looting this place.

He jerks his head sideways, which is obviously translation for *Search him*, and three of his guys start poking and prodding me. They pull my pistol out of my ankle holster, remove my knife from my belt, and even find the small knife I have tucked inside of my boot.

Goddamn bastards.

"I'm Adam, by the way," says the guy with the gun. "That right there's Masterson, McGaver, and Castor. The rest of my boys are waiting in the woods. You're with us, now. And if you try to run"—he swings his rifle from side to side—"you can expect a bullet in the back of your skull."

Great.

So now I'm basically a prisoner. I don't bother making eye contact with the men circling me. I don't give a shit who they are. But then, one of them taps me on the arm and whispers, "Sorry about this."

It's that Castor guy, and he's looking at me with slanted eyebrows and big doughy eyes. A dark messy beard masks most of his face, and when he opens his mouth again, a rotten smell comes out. "You'll adjust."

Was he taken against his will, too? He seems like a decent guy, but that doesn't change the fact that I don't like him.

Adam whips his gun over his shoulder, and with a deep, authoritative voice, says, "Let's go, boys!"

A nasty feeling sinks in my stomach.

I don't like any of these guys.

* * * * * *

I wish I'd known back then how good of a guy Castor was. Instead, I bunched him in with the rest of those pricks and only got to know the real Castor months later. He was a good guy. A great guy, even, and it's my fault he's dead. If I hadn't run out into the field to save that woman, to confront Adam and his goons head-on, maybe Castor would still be around.

I should've planned the attack better.

But then again, I didn't have the time. The woman was being raped. I couldn't stand around and let that happen.

I miss Castor. It's easier not to think about the people I miss, but he gave me hope. He reminded me of the good men—it was hard to remember they existed when I was around Adam every day.

Now, I'm staring at a spitting image of him.

I reach into the pocket of my cargo pants and pull out the keychain Castor used to carry around with him all the time. It's silver, oval-shaped, and has a capital E engraved at the very center. Although it took him awhile to finally open up about it, he'd told me it belonged to his daughter.

The plane's engines kick in all of a sudden, and I

lean back into my chair, fingers wrapped tightly around the armrests.

It'll be over soon. There's no reason to be scared. You're a goddamn marine. Toughen up.

"Prepare for takeoff," comes a voice over the plane's speakers, and within seconds, we start floating up into the air.

It's smooth and balanced, which makes me feel even dumber. This is one of the softest plane rides I've ever been on.

With my thumb, I wipe off the sweaty fingerprints I've left on the keychain. Am I imagining things? No way that girl is Castor's daughter. That's ridiculous. He even admitted to me there was a chance she wasn't alive.

I'm sure some kids look like me, too. That doesn't make them mine.

Closing my eyes, I draw in a deep breath. Now, all I can see is Castor's goofy face.

"Told you it wasn't bumpy," I hear.

I crack my eyes open again to find that same young girl smiling from ear to ear.

Jesus.

She looks even more like him when she smiles.

She pokes at the other girl beside her, which I'm assuming is her way of teasing her about the plane ride.

The other girl, the one with the long red hair, slaps her friend's hand away and says, "Stop it."

The Castor look-alike reaches down and tickles her friend's side.

The redhead laughs and squirms, then in a loud

choppy voice, says, "Emily, stop it!"

My stomach sinks.

CHAPTER 15 – LUCY

"Okay, okay," Emily says, raising two hands by her face. "I'll stop."

"Someone's feeling better," I say.

She's probably still feeling like crap, but I think all of the excitement—being on this plane, being around new faces, and heading toward new territory—is getting her all worked up. She's hyper, and I haven't seen Emily hyper in forever.

"You think they'll be like us?" Emily asks.

I'm not sure what she's referring to when she says *us*, so I cock an eyebrow and wait for clarification.

"You know, like us. What if they're all military kids? What if they've been trained to be like robots?" She leans in closer, and the smell of an empty stomach combined with sickness makes me pull away. "Will we get along with the kids our age? Well, if there *are* kids our age."

I shake my head. She's talking to me as if I have all the answers. I don't know any more than she does and I think she realizes this. She sits up in her seat and breathes out.

"I hope it's better than where we were before."

I'm about to say, *Me too*, but I immediately think

of Nola and twirl in my seat, frantically searching the plane.

Where is she? My heart picks up in pace.

Oh God. I was so preoccupied with the puppy, and with Emily, that I forgot to find Nola. She came on board, right? And then, as if having tuned into a specific radio wave frequency, I overhear a conversation behind me.

"It was her decision, Asha. You couldn't have done anything to make her follow."

The other woman whose face I can't see lets out a muffled whimper and sniffles.

"Shhh, it's okay."

Who are they talking about? I've never heard the name Asha before, so I'm certain they aren't talking about Nola. I'd have known if Nola had a friend named Asha.

"What's up with you?" Emily asks.

"D–Did some people stay... stay behind?" I ask.

She must think I've lost my mind with my wide eyes, agitated motions, and choppy speech. But I can't help myself. I'm downright freaking out. Why would she do this? Nola wouldn't do this. She wouldn't stay behind without at least telling me.

What if she *did* try telling me, but couldn't find me? My palms and the back of my neck get clammy.

"Um, yeah, I think so," Emily says. "I saw a few women hugging goodbye and crying like they were being separated forever. But that was their choice. No one forced them to stay there."

Oh my God.

"Oh, shut your flipper floppin' trap!" I hear. "That

ain't true. Never was, never will be!"

Mavis's familiar voice soothes me, but only for a second. She's swatting at the air a few rows down from me, glaring at a woman across from her and pointing a crooked finger in her face.

Beside her, Perula sits quietly, eyes rolling and head shaking. They resemble two witches in this crowd. Especially Perula, who's wearing a black beanie hat that's obviously far too big for her head. It's folded at the top and hangs halfway down her face.

Mavis, on the other hand, couldn't wear a hat if she wanted to. Her hair, a tangled mess, sits atop her head like dried tumbleweed.

If Mavis and Perula are here, where's Nola?

I can't do this without her.

* * * * * *

I lift my fist to knock on Aunty Eve's door, but I stop before I hit the wood.

She's crying.

Why's Aunt Eve crying? I was mad at her for telling me not to call her Aunty Eve, but it still makes me sad to know she's sad. All I wanted to do was come see her. Maybe she'll say sorry for the hurtful things she said to me when we first got here at this Eden place. She has to say sorry. I need her. I don't know if I'll be okay without her.

That Nola lady said she'd take care of me, but it's not the same. Aunty Eve is like family. Mom always says... said Aunty Eve is like a sister to her. That's why I call her Aunty Eve. She's my aunt. Kind of. Mom says... said that Aunty Eve is my godmother. I didn't know what that was at first, but now I understand.

Now that Mom isn't around, I understand what she meant when she said, "Honey, if anything ever happens to me, Aunty Eve will be the one to look after you, okay?"

She'd brushed her hand along the side of my face and I almost started crying. I was five or six at the time, and I didn't understand what Mom meant when she said, "If anything ever happens to me."

Or, maybe I didn't want to understand. But now, Mom's gone, and Aunty Eve needs to keep her promise. She needs to be my godmother and she needs to take care of me.

"Oh God, Ophelia," I hear through the door.

I feel like I'm going to throw up. Why's she saying my mom's name like that? It hurts me to hear my mom's name. I'm not ready to hear it. It makes me miss her even more, and I don't know how that's possible since I miss her so much already.

I take a step closer to the door and press my face on it so I can hear better. Aunty Eve sounds like she's going crazy. She keeps making weird hiccup noises and then talking to herself. I think she's crying really hard. It makes me feel like I have a frog in my throat. At least that's how Mom used to describe that feeling before you cry. It used to make me giggle... picturing a frog wiggling around in my throat. But now that I know the feeling, it isn't so funny.

It's not a nice feeling at all.

"I-I'm so sorry, Ophelia. Oh God, what have I done?"

What's she talking about? It isn't her fault Mom's gone. I guess it's like when Fuzzy died. Fuzzy was my cat. A big fat orange cat. Mom kept saying sorry to me while I cried, but I knew it wasn't her fault. Maybe that's what Aunty Eve's doing now. She doesn't seem to know what else to say, so she says sorry.

I feel bad spying on her now that I know she's crying, so I take a step back and start walking away from her room. Maybe in a few days, I'll come back. I'll try again and see if she can be my godmother, like Mom wanted.

* * * * * *

My hands begin to tremble as I claw at my seat belt.

I need to get up—I need to search this plane until I find Nola. The moment I unlatch the seat belt's clasp, the military woman's voice carries throughout the plane. "Listen up, everyone. Please make sure your seat belts are fastened. We'll be landing in approximately five minutes."

Turning my head slowly, I realize I'm not the only one who wants out of my seat. Kids are stirring, forcing their mothers and guardians to discipline them. At least the mothers aren't dealing with toddlers anymore. Eden's youngest children—the ones who arrived as babies—are all young kids now. I can't even imagine how hard it was on the mothers to migrate a bunch of babies and toddlers.

"Lucy!" Emily shouts as I get up.

"Excuse me!" comes that military woman's voice, but instead of turning around, I ignore her and march my way toward the back of the plane.

"Nola?" I ask, swaying my head in every direction. "Nola? Where are you?"

Instead of Nola's face, all I receive are slanted

eyebrows and wide glossy eyes. The women must know how much I'm panicking, and instead of doing anything about it, they sit there, feeling bad for me. It's as if they know something I don't—they know Nola stayed behind and they're too afraid to be the ones to break the news to me. Or, maybe that's me being paranoid again. Maybe they don't know anything at all, and they're simply feeling some empathy for me given my anxious state.

"Nola!"

This time, my voice carries all the way down the plane

"Honey... Sweetheart," says a sweet-looking woman. She looks old enough to be my grandma with her round glasses, large veiny nose, and curly white hair atop her head. The only difference between her and Grandma is that she has what looks like a snake tattoo running down her neck. It's withered and blue-looking, but at some point in her life, this woman must have looked pretty badass. "Are you talking about Nola the nurse?"

I'm scared to answer her. I'm afraid that if I tell her yes, she'll tell me Nola stayed behind. But even though my lips remain sealed, my head starts nodding on its own as if disconnected from my brain.

"Nola's on the second level, love. She's with Dr. Lewis, tending to those who are severely sick."

I follow her eyes to where a metallic gray ceiling sits overhead. Upstairs? What's she talking about? She must sense my confusion; she smiles, her pale lips looking like dead skin, and points at the far corner of the plane. "There's a door on your right. The stairwell leads to the second floor."

A second floor.

Of course.

Why didn't I think of this? I saw how big this plane was. I should have assumed. I should have—

But then a vibration tickles the underneath of my feet, and the women around me start telling me to sit down. The plane must be landing, but it isn't the kind of landing I'd have expected. It's smooth—so smooth, in fact, that I don't understand why we were asked to sit down and wear our seat belts.

I glance back toward the front of the plane to catch the military woman glaring at me. It isn't a mean glare, but it's enough to make me realize that my disobedience is being noticed. She crosses her arms over her chest and raises one eyebrow as if to say, *Do I really have to repeat myself?*

Although I want to rush upstairs to find Nola, this older woman's affirmation is enough to comfort me. Besides, first impressions only happen once, and I get the feeling this woman's some sort of boss at the new place.

The last thing I want to do is piss off the big boss.

So I spot the nearest empty seat and plop myself down into it like a stubborn child told to go on a timeout.

The moment I click my seat belt in, the girl sitting next to me nudges me in the ribs as if we're long-lost friends. I've seen her around, and we're around the same age, but I've never actually spoken to her. She grins from ear to ear, her heavily freckled face inches from mine and her narrow, button nose barely visible this close to my face.

I instinctively pull away, which seems to make her want to move closer.

"Did you hear?" she asks, her sour breath making me tighten my lips.

She's so animated that if I didn't know any better, I'd think someone told her that this new place has an indoor amusement park. I don't say anything. I get the feeling she's chatty—like, super chatty. If I open the floodgates, I'm done for.

"This new place," she blurts, flicking both her wrists in the air, "is called Elysium. Did you hear what's inside? Did anyone tell you? That's what everyone on the plane's been saying, by the way. Elysium."

I don't know why she's asking me if I've heard—it's not like she's even giving me the chance to get a word in. Now I understand why no one's sitting next to her.

"Isn't that a cool name? Elysium." She giggles. "Kind of sounds like asylum, if you think about it. Which is freaky, right? I mean, who in their right mind wants to go to an asylum? Someone said the name has something to do with Greek mythology. Something about gods. Does that, like, make us godly?" She laughs again and slaps my wrist with her cold, clammy fingers. "Oh my God, I'm rambling again. I'm so sorry. My name's Abigail Powder, but my friends call me Abi."

Her friends? I don't see anyone sitting here. I swallow hard, attempting to push these harsh thoughts away. Why am I judging her? I barely have any friends myself and there's nothing wrong with that.

She points a finger in my face, her speckled features hardening. "And don't even think about making stupid jokes about my name." She starts chuckling again, then stares at me with wide, expectant eyes. Her lips remain parted, revealing corn-yellow teeth.

"Oh, um... I'm Lucy," I say.

Without giving me the chance to offer her my hand, she grabs it and shakes it vigorously.

"Nice to meet you, Lucy."

Still shaking my hand, she asks me again, "So, did you hear?"

"Hear what?"

She releases her grip and plants a firm hand on my forearm. "Apparently, they have a huge cafeteria with dozens of chefs who serve breakfast, lunch, and supper!"

At once, I feel nauseated. Have we been lied to? Something's fishy. I'm beginning to think that all of this talk about a new paradise-like haven is too good to be true.

CHAPTER 16 – EVE

Vrin walks to the front of the plane as if she's God's gift to humanity—as if without her, Earth would shatter into a million jagged pieces. With shoulders drawn back in her military uniform, she exudes pure confidence and fearlessness, which makes me admire and detest her at the same time.

I should be the one standing in front of my women. Not Vrin—not some stranger to my people. The worst part in all of this is that they're looking at her as if starstruck, or worse, as if only she possesses the means of delivering a life of freedom, abundance, and prosperity.

Is this not what I gave them? Do they honestly forget how hard I've worked to ensure their survival?

I get up and make my way to Vrin's side. I won't allow her the satisfaction of taking my people from me.

These women are mine.

"Listen up, everyone," she says, and I cringe.

Why does she speak to them as if they're like her? As if they're friends? Is that how she expects to earn respect? Is she not supposed to be a leader?

"I want to go over a few things before we go inside

Elysium," she continues.

I look at the women sitting in the first aisle, and the moment their eyes meet mine, they look away from me and focus their attention on Vrin. Clenching my fists, I remind myself that I'm the reason millions of people didn't die on Inauguration Day.

Had I not gone against Bethany and warned the underground resistance of President Price's kill order, these women wouldn't even be alive.

How dare they turn their backs on me?

I cleanse my thoughts—if I allow myself to feel hatred, they will sense it. It's important that they continue to see me as their strong and capable leader, not as someone who's afraid to lose control.

The truth is, I am afraid. If I lose these women, what will I have left?

The plane's tires make contact with the ground—a subtle vibration in our seats.

"We've landed," Vrin says proudly, and all I want to do is tear that smile off her face. "Before we enter those doors," she says, "I want to make one thing very clear." She pauses, surely trying to dramatize the point she's about to make. "Inside of Elysium, we don't tolerate hatred, racism, sexism, or any form of discrimination." Her scrutinizing gaze lands on me and I turn away.

"I understand you've all been through a lot. I'm fully aware of the war that took place on American soil. I was there. We all were. But I want to assure you that Elysium is nothing like the America you once knew. I will not tolerate hatred between the sexes, nor will I tolerate alienation or animosity. In Elysium, everyone is equal. Do I make myself clear?"

I nearly scoff, but instead, bite the inside of my cheek until I taste blood.

What is she thinking? These women have been taught that men are the reason our world has fallen apart. Does she honestly believe they will follow her?

But to my surprise, everyone nods.

What are they doing? Why the hell are they agreeing to lower themselves to the same level as the male species? I clench my armrests so firmly two of my fingernails bend backward. How is this happening? Why aren't they standing up for what they believe in? I part my lips, prepared to berate Vrin for even suggesting that men are worthy of being considered equals, when I realize doing so would only tarnish my plan.

I cannot take over Elysium if I'm denied initial entry.

If I plan to be ruler of Elysium—Queen of the New World—I must be discreet in my approach.

CHAPTER 17 – GABRIEL

"Watch your step," says Vrin, helping women off the plane. She reaches for duffel bags, pillows, blankets. Anything she can grab to take some weight out of their hands.

I admire Vrin, I really do. Although she may walk around with a flexed back and arms dangling a bit too far from her body, it suits her. She's a military woman, and she exudes confidence, fortitude, and boldness.

She's nothing like Eve, which is exactly what these women need.

The moment that thought crosses my mind, Eve steps out into the cool autumn air with squinted, rapidly-moving eyes. She searches the premises, the people, and even Vrin. It's like she's calculating everything in that messed-up head of hers.

What's she planning? It's not like she has any power here. At least not yet. I hope to God she never does, but Vrin made it pretty clear that she's worshipped by a lot of women on the inside. She also made it clear that discrimination won't be tolerated, which means Eve needs to be cautious.

"Whoa, careful," Vrin says, catching a six-year-old girl by the arms. She pulls her back up onto her feet.

"Watch your step, sweetheart."

To my surprise, a boy appears out of the crowd like a piece of coal on a bed of snow. He's the only young male around and it looks like he's lost. Where did he come from? No way he's from Eden. Eve wouldn't have allowed...

"Zack, stay close!" hisses the woman beside him.

It's obvious she's Hispanic with her tanned complexion and long wavy hair. She reminds me of my mother but curvier and a bit taller. That kid, Zack, reminds me of myself when I was young. He's awkward and jittery and keeps glancing down at his mom for direction.

Eve turns his way when his hoarse, teenage voice carries over the crowd. "I *am* staying close, Mom."

Eve doesn't appear confused or disgusted by him. Obviously, he's here because she let him inside of Eden. How is that possible? I thought Eve hated men more than anything. Is it his age that saved him? Or is it his mother?

The Hispanic woman reaches for Eve's arm with a smile on her face. The second her fingers touch Eve's skin, though, Eve flinches away as if a spider landed on her.

She's on edge. That's clear.

The woman, still smiling, mumbles something to Eve, but I can't make it out. Maybe she's thanking her. It would make sense, after all. If Eve let her son inside of Eden, that's something worth celebrating.

"All right, everyone, my men here will lead the way inside. Follow them and they'll take you to your new living quarters."

The women start whispering excitedly, leaning into each other and wrapping their arms around one another.

"Did you hear that?" one of them says. "Living quarters!"

"Not a prison cell!"

"No more cells!"

I kind of feel bad for Eve. She's looking at them from her peripheral while walking down the plane's ramp, but she doesn't make eye contact. She must be pretty hurt about the whole thing. And while I don't think she's stable enough to lead hundreds of women, she still deserves to be happy.

Even people who've made horrible mistakes deserve some happiness.

Turning away from the plane, I make my way toward Area 82, or Elysium, as Vrin calls it. It looks the same as it did the day I started my training. The only difference is there aren't a dozen shuttle vans carrying hundreds of military personnel.

Another major component is missing: men in fancy black suits with pistols on their waists. Everything's so calm. From out here, it looks like the place is vacant. The main building, a giant concrete structure with glossy black windows and metal doors, is as clean as it's always been, which means it's being maintained.

The grass around it, though now a bit yellow, was recently cut, though it doesn't smell like fresh grass. Instead, it smells like engine fumes and crisp air. The kind of air that slides inside your lungs, making them feel clean.

Along the side of the building, carefully trimmed shrubs decorate the edges of the wall. Everything's so immaculate. It's like I've traveled back in time. Like America's still the America it used to be, with running water, a nationwide electrical grid, and working gas lines. I look at the ground, where Area 82's main runway extends another several hundred feet. Not a single leaf, grass trimming, or rock litters the asphalt.

Behind the Falcon, a few other planes sit in the grass, their blacked-out windows clean and their widespread wings dust free. We've landed pretty close to the building, but that's because the Falcon can land vertically. I'm sure the runway is used for the other planes. It must be if it's this clean.

Kids tug at their mothers' arms and point toward the other military vehicles: planes, helicopters, heavily equipped cars, and even a few tanks.

"Look, Mommy!"

"Can we go in that?"

"Can I go see it?"

One kid suddenly runs off, and two women chase after her in a panic.

It's hard to tell how the mothers feel about this place. They seem excited, but now that the whole military aspect is visible, it's like they're cautious. Most of them wrap their arms around their kids' shoulders and pull them closer. These kids don't know anything about war and I'd be willing to bet the mothers don't want them to, either.

Ignorance is bliss, right? Mama used to say that. Though when she did, it came out more annoyed than anything. It also didn't make as much sense as she thought it did, but I knew what she was trying to say. If somebody upset her by doing something thoughtless, she'd roll her eyes and say in a sharp whisper, "Ignoringness is bliss, isn't it? I wish I could be more blissy." The last word came out a bit hateful, but she had every reason to be annoyed. When she said this, I knew that whatever the other person did was *really* stupid.

Even though I'd correct her and tell her it's *ignorance* and *blissful*, she'd always react the same way: she'd flick her wrist at me and say, "Ah, my beautiful Gabriel. *Mi ángel.* I teach you to be such a smart boy."

She'd kiss my forehead, and several months would go by before she'd make the same comment with the exact same errors.

I smile at the thought of my mama. She was always so—

Out of nowhere, a loud explosion blasts behind me and my entire body jolts.

* * * * * *

"Get down!" shouts one of my comrades.

His mouth is wide open, blending in with the dark green of his shirt, his war paint, and even his dark eyes. Sweat drips from his forehead, leaving streaks of brown over his skin. His woolly beard, something that's been growing for the last two weeks, is even darker than usual with all the blood soaked in it.

I don't know how I'm noticing all of this, but I am. It's like time's stopped, giving me the opportunity to take in everything around me. Marcel's still standing there, shouting at me and pointing behind me. His voice barely carries over the sounds of gunfire and explosions. I don't understand what he's trying to tell me.

What's going on?

A few minutes ago, we were sitting in our tent playing cards. Now, Rashid and Carlo are lying by my feet and I'm covered in blood... There's blood everywhere. Carlo yells with squinted eyes, reaching for what used to be his leg. A pointed femur bone sticks out through broken skin, hanging muscle, and torn tendons.

My head spins. I grab my gun and dart toward the tent's opening when another explosion goes off and I find myself lying flat on my back, ears ringing, vision blacked out.

* * * * * *

"Get off!" several people shout.

A lot of people.

What's going on?

"Gabriel!"

"Gabriel!"

"Oh my God, he's gonna kill them!"

I come to and find myself lying atop five women, the weight of my body crushing them. One woman's face is so close to mine my cheeks are warmed by her radiating heat. Her face, a swollen red ball, looks like it's on the verge of popping.

Then, solid arms grip me around my torso, my shoulders, and my stomach.

"Grenades! Get down!" I shout.

What're are they doing? What the fuck is happening? I swing a fist at the nearest guy I can find, and a loud crack vibrates against my knuckles. He falls back with two hands over his bloody nose, his hateful eyes fixated on me.

Who is he? Who are they?

I'm about to take another swing when something hard hits me against the side of my head. Everything around me goes fuzzy, and all the noise, all the panicked shouting, disappears as I fall to the ground.

CHAPTER 18 – LUCY

I should be moving forward with the crowd, but instead, I'm holding on to my bag, staring at the man who was freaking out. Why was he freaking out? That's the guy who had the puppy. He seemed super nice

Now, he's lying facedown in the grass when seconds ago, he was screaming with a puffy red face and bulging eyes—so much so that his neck got all lumpy and veiny.

The last time I saw a man this worked up was the crazy guy on Seventh Avenue. Mom explained to me that he had mental problems and told me to ignore him as he did this daily. He'd stood there, shouting at the sky and pulling so hard at his own hair that I expected it to tear out of his skull. Now that I'm older, I realize he was most likely on drugs.

Thank God this man passed out. Well, I suppose God had nothing to do with it if there even is a God. It's the youngest soldier who knocked him out. And now Malory seems to be all over him, calling him a hero.

"Are you okay, sweetheart?" Nola asks in a panic. Nola.

Dropping my bag, I swing around and throw my arms around Nola's neck.

"Whoa," she says.

She isn't used to me being affectionate.

"Nola, I thought—"

Pressing a firm hand against the back of my head, she pulls me in again. "Hey, I'm right here."

"Who's this?" comes Abigail's voice.

Seriously? Can't she see I'm having a moment? Irritated, I pull myself out of Nola's arms.

"Abigail, this is Nola. Nola, Abigail."

"Lovely to meet you," Nola says, offering Abigail a hand.

"You can call me Abi," says Abigail, grinning the same way she did when she introduced herself to me. And now, she's following me as if we're best friends. Emily's my best friend, and nothing's going to change that.

Nola looks down at her, then at me. "Why don't you go on inside, sweetheart? I have to stick around." She twirls a finger toward the airplane, which I'm certain translates to *My nursing abilities are required.*

Even though I don't want to say goodbye, I nod, reminding myself that it's only temporary. When everyone's feeling better, I'll get to spend more time with her again.

"You'll find me, right?" I ask.

Her eyes narrow playfully, and she smirks as if to say, *Of course I'll find you.*

"Are you sure?" Abigail cuts in. "I mean, the place is huge. How're you going to find—"

"Come on," I say, tugging on Abigail's arm and

plowing through the crowd.

It's become so condensed that it's hard to see anything. The man who passed out is now out of sight, but I can hear people scurrying around him, most likely tying him up or maybe even helping him. I'm not sure which.

Right now, all I care about is finding Emily before we get inside.

"Emily!" I shout.

But I can't find her.

"Move along," someone says.

I'm pushed forward, all the way to the massive side doors of this Elysium place. Two men stand right outside holding big black guns. Maybe it's protocol, or maybe it's them being paranoid. I can't blame them. No one's forgotten about the war that happened years ago.

I'd be willing to bet that some women are going to have a hard time adjusting to this new place. Why wouldn't they? There are military men everywhere. The last time these women saw men in uniform, it was during the war.

No one says anything as we walk past the two soldiers. They don't make eye contact, either.

But the moment we enter those doors, I stop caring about the military men, about the plane, and about the guy who freaked out on the runway; I'm way too blown away by the inside of this place.

It's nothing like Eden. Everything is so bright and crisp—the result of fluorescent lighting overhead. It reminds me of a hospital but without the hospital smell and with a much higher ceiling. The floors, shiny white slabs of marble or something expensive, look like they were cleaned and waxed only minutes ago. Every few feet, little blue and red lights decorate the walls, and although I don't know what they're for, it's obvious by the way they're flashing that they're being used for something.

The massive room we're standing in reminds me a bit of the main hall. At the far end, straight ahead of me, a massive hallway continues into another opening, and right before this hallway are two glass elevators sitting on either side of the entryway.

A woman wearing cotton blue pants and a plain blue top approaches the one on the left. Her appearance makes this place feel even more like a hospital. She's so immaculately dressed and groomed, and her clothing reminds me of a nurse's outfit. Atop her head sits a brown bun so cleanly tucked it looks like a ball. She glances our way, curious dark eyes lingering for several seconds.

She reaches a hand beside her, where a young girl, no older than five years old, is standing. The two of them keep looking back at us without saying a word. It's likely they haven't seen anyone new for years. The woman, assumedly the mother, opens her mouth and says something, and the elevator's glass doors open with a soft *swoosh*. They enter, almost backward by the way their necks are craned, and stare at us from behind the safety of the glass.

"Mommy can I go?" asks a little girl near me.

She points at the elevator and hops up and down as if seeing a roller coaster for the first time in her life. Her mother plants a firm hand on the little girl's chest to keep her from running toward the elevator.

"Later," she says.

The room begins to fill as the crowd squeezes its way through Elysium's side doors.

"Where's your friend?" Abigail asks. "That Emily girl?"

She seems genuinely concerned, which makes me feel bad for finding her annoying. I'd once thought Emily to be annoying, too. Maybe I've spent so much time in isolation these last few years that I have a hard time connecting with anyone.

"I'm not sure," I tell her, "but we'll find her."

Her eyes scan the women around me, undoubtedly searching for Emily even though she has no idea what she looks like—at least, I don't think she does.

"Ladies." Vrin's voice carries across the hall as if being blasted out of a megaphone. "And gentlemen," she adds softly, which I assume is because she's now eyeing Zack, the only boy in Eden. She claps both hands together and smiles. "Welcome to Elysium. What you see here"—she expands her arms over her head and looks up at the ceiling—"is Elysium's West Wing. It's used mainly by flight operators and resource experts."

"Resource experts?" Abigail asks, leaning into me.

I'm doing my best to pay attention to Vrin, so I don't answer her.

"While you're welcome here any time, know that the door you've just entered will remain locked from here on out for your safety. We don't want children running about near the aircraft." She winks at two little girls in front of her and they giggle. "Next, I'll be bringing you all through Elysium's Hub. For those of you who aren't familiar with the term, all it means is the center. Think of it as—" she pauses and glances toward Eve.

"The main hall," Eve says dully. It's like she's bored and has no interest in being here. I wonder if she's already fallen into a dark depression again. I already know she's gone cuckoo as my mom would say. I caught her talking to herself in the mirror. But I've never seen her like this—not in front of us, anyways. She seems defeated; it's as if she's coming to terms with the fact that Vrin is now the new leader.

I expected her to be angry to the point of wanting revenge—not weak and vanquished. She hasn't even put up a fight. Something's up, and it isn't good. When I finally get the chance to talk to Nola in private, I'm going to tell her all about Eve and how she's lost her mind. An adult needs to be made aware of how dangerous she is.

"Like your main hall," Vrin repeats.

The women seem to like her. They're watching her every movement. A few of them keep looking at Eve for guidance, but since she isn't giving any, they return their attention to Vrin. Hopefully, Eve snaps out of whatever it is she's going through. A lot of women still follow her, and if she isn't a leader to them, they'll start following Vrin. It's like she thinks it's already happened and she's accepted it. Well, miserably.

"Ah, Nayma," Vrin says as a new face enters the room.

The woman seems to be around Vrin's age, which, if I were to guess, is in her late thirties or early forties. They're definitely older than Eve, which I think intimidates Eve a bit. This woman, Nayma, smiles a set of teeth so white you'd think she works in a dental office. Maybe there's a dentist here. I sure hope so because Eden didn't have one, and a lot of women complained about it. In fact, one woman died two years ago, and all everyone kept talking about was an "abscess," whatever that means.

I run my tongue along the back of teeth, feeling grime and what I assume is a lot of plaque buildup. Mom used to bring me to the dentist twice a year, even though we didn't have insurance. She said my teeth were more important than I thought they were, and that they deserved to be as healthy as me.

"Welcome," Nayma says.

Her skin, a lovely light brown color, makes her teeth look like little pieces of gum. I can't tell whether her eyes are brown or green, so maybe they're a bit of both. Hazel, my mom once explained to me. She's wearing a pair of brown khaki pants and a beige shirt that has a dozen or so buttons at the front. It's fancy, but not over the top. It was obviously custom-made here. From one of the pockets over her chest, she plucks out a pair of metallic blue-rimmed glasses and slides them over the bridge of her nose.

"I'll be registering all of you to Elysium," she says.

Someone in the back whispers, "Registering?"

Nayma clears her throat and taps something on the metal frame of her glasses. Nothing happens, at least not on our end, but she's now looking through her glasses rather than at us. She must be seeing something we aren't. She taps the glasses again as if adjusting a setting.

"Nayma's our systems expert," Vrin says. "She controls APHRODITE, Elysium's Intelligent Control System."

Why's she talking about a control system as if it were a person? And why'd they give it a name like that?

Vrin then points at the corners of the room, at the elevators, and at the doors. "Everything in here is controlled by APHRODITE. Think of her as... central intelligence," she says.

Everyone around me stares as if watching a magician perform a trick. Their eyes scan the areas she pointed at, and they break out into whispers.

Vrin smirks proudly, almost as if she's the one who built APHRODITE. "She controls the temperature, the security system, the lighting. You'll notice speakers built into the walls throughout all of Elysium. APHRODITE takes commands whenever spoken to." She playfully points a finger at the crowd. "Telling her to change the temperature when you're cold won't do anything, though."

A little girl giggles as if that's precisely what she was thinking.

"There are strict voice recognition settings in place," Vrin adds. "Only select people have access to make commands depending on your whereabouts in Elysium. You'll each be given access to make commands inside your room and only your room."

Abigail nudges me so hard in the ribs I'm certain

I'll bruise later. It's not easy to get mad at her, though; she's grinning so wide I can see her pink gums.

"If you could all form a line," Vrin says, "Nayma here will have you registered with APHRODITE."

"What do you mean, registered?" asks one of the women.

Nayma takes a step forward and pushes her glasses up the bridge of her nose. "Think of it as being included into APHRODITE's core. In order to have access to make commands, you'll need to be registered into her system. She'll need your name, your appearance, and a sample of your voice."

"Our appearance?" someone else asks, her voice quivering.

The crowd starts whispering again, obviously concerned about privacy. I don't blame them; when President Price was in power, he basically stripped everyone of their privacy. He made it legal for the government to record anyone anywhere at any time. He also made it legal to use evidence obtained this way against a person. So if someone said (inside the privacy of their own home) that they wanted to kill someone, the cops showed up within a few hours and arrested them.

That's why Mom was so scared of talking near electronics.

So it makes sense that these women are scared. They don't want to live like they used to—nervous of constantly being watched.

Nayma smiles, and it's comforting. She doesn't seem like the kind of person who would deceive someone. There's something very genuine about her, and every time she speaks, I want to listen to her.

"I can assure you," Nayma says, "that APHRODITE has only your best interests at heart. Well, in her M85 TU Operating System." She almost starts laughing but instead tightens her lips when no one reacts. "APHRODITE is a tool. That's it. There's no secret organization running in the background of Elysium. APHRODITE's physical appearance registration is both a safety feature and a facial recognition feature."

The women nod, including Abigail, who looks like she's hypnotized.

"Last month, we lost Thomas Avehnos, a little four-year-old boy," Nayma continues. "Elysium is incredibly large. Larger than any building you've likely entered, I'm sure. It was only because of APHRODITE's facial recognition system that we found him within a matter of minutes."

Now, most of the women seem convinced. Several of them pull their little girls closer. Who wouldn't want a safety feature like that?

Nayma pulls her arms behind her back, elevates her chin, and smiles crookedly. "So, who wants to go first?"

CHAPTER 19 – EVE

"Eve Malum," I say, staring into Nayma's unusual-looking eyes. It's almost as if she's wearing green contact lenses over a set of brown eyes or isn't from this planet at all. Then, following the oral script we've been given, I continue. "Lock the door. Unlock the door. Turn off the lights. Turn on the lights."

It appears APHRODITE's functionalities extend far beyond simple commands, such as unlocking doors or turning off lights. But Nayma explained to us that a basic voice sample is all APHRODITE requires in order to associate our voice with our name.

Nayma gives me a brief nod, which must translate to *Thank you. You've been registered*, and I step out of the line. Then, without even looking at me, she reaches into her pocket and extracts a bead no larger than a fisheye and tosses it into the air. It lights up an aqua blue and hovers midair, unmoving.

I still can't wrap my head around this form of technology, but Nayma assured us that these beads, or marbles—something she called a Luminus Sphere—are incredibly advanced and that we should not be fearful of them. They're programmed to lead us to our quarters—each and every one of us. I'm not certain how she does it, but upon registration, she assigns a room to an individual and connects a Luminus to that individual. In other words, this little flying ball knows where I'm intended to sleep and its sole purpose is to lead me there.

Several other women in front of me are following their Luminus Spheres.

"Clarissa McAdams," says the next woman in line. She goes on to continue the script, but I walk away, not wanting to waste my time listening to every woman's registration.

I observe the light blue glow being emitted from a small line splitting my Luminus in half. It's approximately half the size of a golf ball and floats in the air as if surrounded by magic. Its exterior is a glossy metallic white, and at the center of its upper half, right above the split line, is a small lens.

Nayma explained that it had something to do with its technology being able to alter the vibrations around its proximity. In other words, its technology is so advanced that it can literally manipulate nearby atoms. I don't pretend to understand it, though I must admit that I'm rather intrigued by it.

I take a step forward and it moves away from me, but not too far.

Is it looking at me?

I wave a hand in front of the lens and it releases a small beeping sound as if responding to me. I smile, amused by this new gadget. I take another step forward, and it hovers backward, still watching me.

"Well," I finally say, "take me to my room."

Another beep comes out of the ball and it floats

away from me as if being carried through the current of a river. I follow it, my steps rapid and my head held high. Several other women around me giggle as they wave their hands in front of their new toys.

I wonder how long Nayma's been working on these pieces of technology. Is she one of the Binaries? Vrin knew about the Binaries—she's the one who told me to keep my eyes open for them. Surely, she found them before I had the chance to. It's the only explanation.

The Luminus leads me through the West Wing's main entrance, which assumedly leads into the Hub. Or, as Vrin explained, the main hall. It will take some time for me to adjust to this new living space. Though I was hesitant at first, I can't help but see an opportunity here.

I crane my neck the moment I walk into the Hub. The ceiling, which is barely visible, surely reaches several hundred feet in height. In fact, there is no ceiling. Like Eden, it appears to be made of glass, allowing natural light to flood the entire hall.

Reaching up to this glass ceiling are levels upon levels of floors, and on each one, several men and women can be seen roaming the halls through glass walls. Most of them wear the same clothing—blue pants and blue button-up shirts that cover their necks.

I'd thought Eden to be clean—to be free of debris and germs—but as I stand here, I realize Eden was filthy. This place is immaculate. At the center of the Hub is a stone statue of a naked woman with wings wrapped around her body. Her left hand sticks out, palm facing up, and from it pours a clear stream of water. It lands in a pool around her feet, where two little girls, no older than three years old, are found giggling and slapping their hands in the water.

Around this fountain are several Egyptian blue benches—so blue that I have a hard time looking away. I wonder what compelled them to select such a vibrant color. Perhaps it has something to do with the psychological effects of colors.

On either side of these benches are gorgeous trees planted in gray stone pots. I can't tell what they are, but their trunks appear to be made of several trunks intertwined around each other like braids. Their leaves, although mostly vivid green, have purple veins running through them. Are these some sort of hybrid plants? Are they experimenting with botany?

I instantly catch a woman's gaze. Her eyes, two brown dots on her youthful face, are fixated on me as if I'm a different species. Do I have something on my face? Does she recognize me from somewhere? How could she possibly recognize me? I've remained in Eden for the last six years.

She leans into her friend, another woman who appears to be the same age as her, and whispers something into her ear. Now, the two of them are gazing at me in awe. I take a step forward, hesitating as my Luminus hovers several feet away from me, waiting to guide me to my new living quarters.

Should I say something? Ask them what they're staring at? I find it rather rude. Tempted to tell them to look elsewhere, I turn away and continue following my little guide. The last thing I need right now is to make a scene and to convince my women that I'm no longer fit to lead... if they don't already believe that.

The whispering continues as I turn my back to them, and it's only when I reach one of the eight elevators in the Hub that a voice captures my attention.

"Eve?"

I pause.

Maybe they're speaking to another Eve. Surely, there's more than one in all of Elysium.

"Eve Malum?"

* * * * * *

"Eve Malum?"

I glance back to find several filthy faces gazing toward me. Some are covered in ash, others, blood. It's like nothing I've ever seen before, and it makes me sick to my stomach. My name is being repeated over and over again, but not in an attempt to call out to me—rather, they're repeating it as if it holds some magical power.

"She knew about the attack," someone says.

"Yes, she did," Vrin finally shouts.

She's standing by my side, which is something I need right now. All I can think of is Ophelia. I can't believe what I've done. Everything feels so surreal... like a dream. And now, these women speak of me as if I'm some hero. As if I'm something more than an eighteen-year-old girl who murdered the president and her best friend.

What am I?

A monster?

"She's the reason you aren't all dead," Vrin

continues. She climbs atop the hood of a police cruiser and sticks two firm hands over her belt. "Eve Malum went against orders and scheduled an attack to prevent a genocide."

I look up at her, ashamed. Why is she talking about me like that? Why's she defending me? She saw what I did, and she's acting like it never happened.

"The world you know is over," Vrin continues. "Shit's about to get even worse. I'm not saying this to scare you. I'm trying to make you realize that it isn't going to get better. You need to be prepared. You need to survive."

Panicked voices carry throughout the crowd of grieving women. I've never seen so much hurt in my life. Now that the electrical grid's been fried, all I hear are voices—nothing more. Wailing, shouting, and even pleading. Everyone is hurting one way or another, whether physically or emotionally. Everyone's lost someone they care about, and everyone's terrified of what's to come next.

"My women will be doing everything they can to help out over the next few days, but for those of you who are ready to leave, I suggest you pack your things and follow Eve."

Follow me? My heart skips a beat. I knew this was coming, but I'm not prepared for it. I can't possibly guide hundreds of women outside of the city without knowing where I'm going or how I'm going to survive.

Vrin continues to talk about the after-effects of the EMP, but my ears are ringing too loudly for me to hear any of it.

What have I done?

In an instant, I'm drawn back to reality by Vrin's breath against my face.

"You can do this," she whispers. "These women need you. They need a leader, and right now, you're the best we have."

* * * * * *

"Eve Malum?" I hear again.

I swing my body around to find the two women standing side by side, fidgeting with their fingers. They appear intimidated—starstruck. They avert their eyes toward the ground as I stare at them until finally, the first women I caught staring at me clears her throat.

"Is it really you?"

I've never seen this woman in my life. How am I supposed to respond to her? I elevate my chin, cautious. Is this some sort of trap? Some sort of mind game? Vrin told me that several women knew *of* me. How does this woman *recognize* me?

When I don't respond, she continues. "I-I was there that day. W-when you... When you came out of the White House."

I clench my fists. What does she know?

"I couldn't leave my husband and son behind, but I... I wanted to come with you. You saved us. You saved us all."

Finally, she looks up at me, her eyes soft and frightened, and I unclench my fists. Was she one of the women who stayed behind with Vrin in Washington DC? It only makes sense.

Then, without warning, she drops to one knee and bows her head. I'm too taken aback to know what to do with myself. Her friend, too, replicates her movement. Why are these women bowing before me? For a moment, I feel like my eighteen-year-old self—unworthy of being treated like royalty. I haven't earned it. But then, I remember who I am, who I've become, and I relish in it.

I deserve this.

I'm Eve—Eve Malum of Eden.

These women should worship you, Eve. It's what you've always wanted. It's what you've worked so hard for.

Unexpectedly, all the fear and uncertainty that's been crippling me washes away. Several other women in the Hub notice what's happening and begin whispering among each other.

"Is that her?"

"I think so. It looks like her."

"Oh my God, is that Eve Malum?"

"How do you know what she looks like?"

"I thought she was a myth."

"Shut up!"

A dozen more women gather, observing me like visitors crossing through an exotic zoo. It's as if they believe that if they stare long enough, I'll satisfy their curiosity by making an exaggerated movement or by saying something of immeasurable value.

Is that what they're waiting for? For me to speak to them?

I place my hand alongside my face, and at once, the room fills with a heavy silence. Eyes remain fixated on me, and pink lips part in awe.

"Hi," I say, smiling, and everyone breaks into

discussion again. Raising my voice louder this time, I add, "Yes, it's me—Eve Malum."

It looks as though they're on the verge of talking again, but my stare keeps them quiet. They want more—they need more.

"I realize it may come as a shock for some of you to see me here after all these years. I'm certain you've all heard the rumors... some good, some bad."

It's important that I approach this carefully; many women expressed hatred when we left Washington DC because I was unwilling to allow males to follow.

"I truly hope that most of you found safety with your families."

In my peripheral, the Hub is filling with my women who are exiting the West Wing with their Luminus Spheres. Along with them comes Vrin, and then, Lucy.

Everyone's watching you, Eve.

Don't fuck this up.

This is it. This is the first impression I have to make here in Elysium, and it's the only chance I have to redeem myself with my women even though most of them resent me for the way I handled the quarantine in Eden. The women who are sick have already been taken by Vrin and transferred to another wing—a wing she says is dedicated solely for medical care and scientific advancements. Without her, and without Elysium, those women would have died. I must remind everyone that the only reason we're here in Elysium is because of me—I'm the one who ordered Freyda and Gabriel to seek this place out.

"I want to start by apologizing to all of you," I say, and some of the scowls in the room soften. I can't recall the last time I apologized to anyone, so I'm certain my apology is coming as somewhat of a surprise to most. And although I don't want to apologize—although I don't believe I've done anything wrong—it's important these women view me in a certain way.

"First, to my women," I say. "I'm so sorry for what happened in Eden—" I turn away, feigning remorse. "I should have approached the situation differently. You deserve better than what was given to you, and I truly hope that my desire to relocate Eden—my drive to find Elysium and to seek out advanced technology—will remind you that you are…" I make a point to look at as many women as possible, one at a time. "Each and every one of you… are so incredibly important to me. I view you as… as family." I cover my mouth and turn away. Then, through broken speech and warm tears filling the corners of my eyes, I add, "I would do anything for you, and I can't express how sorry I am for letting you down."

Part of me is frightened by my own approach. I risk making myself out to be weak—vulnerable. But at the same time, I truly believe that this is precisely what these women want to see. No one wants to be led by some cold-hearted bitch. They need to see that I'm human and that not only do I make mistakes, but that I'm entirely willing to own up to my mistakes and to seek out a remedy.

Clearing my throat, I turn my attention to the women who don't yet know me.

"To meet all of you is an honor," I say. "I wish I could have taken everyone with me, but at the time, given all the hatred spreading across America, allowing both genders to cohabitate would have been too risky. All I wanted was to build a haven for the women... for all of you... who experienced trauma and heartache at the hands of men. I hope you can understand that."

Even those who, minutes ago, seemed to loathe me entirely are now nodding their heads. It's as if they're upset with me on a personal level, but on a different level, they understand why I did what I did and why I rejected the male gender.

They were all there—they saw what men in power did to our country.

The silence grows heavy, and at once, I'm sick to my stomach. Have I ruined it all? Have I destroyed my chance of ever holding a position of power again? I need this. I need to rule over followers. It's all I know, and right now, it's the only thing pushing me forward.

I part my lips to speak, but nothing comes out. I've run out of words. I'm prepared to walk away when a voice erupts from the crowd.

"E-Eve!"

The woman who spoke pushes her way out of the crowd, elbows nudging from side to side. She's incredibly short—no taller than five feet—and comes at me like an excited bulldog. Her face, a square shape, rounds off when she smiles from ear to ear. She's wearing the same blue cotton outfit as the women of Elysium, which means she isn't one of mine. It covers most of her neck, which is thick like a tree trunk and muscular.

"I want you to have... I want you to have my room,"

she says, and whispers break out again, reminding me of insects on a hot summer night.

I cock an eyebrow at her. What is she talking about? Why on Earth would I take her room when I have my own?

"Mary-Anne!" someone says.

Mary-Anne, the small woman, flicks her wrist and tells her friend to *shush*. She then looks up at me, her orange-brown eyes narrowing into happy lines. "I won the Monarch Suite in last year's Synergy Tournament, but I want you to have it."

Everyone around her is exchanging big-eyed glances, obviously taken aback by Mary-Anne's generosity.

"Monarch Suite?" I ask.

She nods rapidly, the skin of her tight face barely moving. "Think of it as a luxury suite in Elysium. There are only a few of them, and the one I have is the only one that was given to one of us common folks."

Her friend slaps her as if to say, *Don't call us common folk.*

"It's four times the size of any regular room, has three washrooms, a kitchen, a jacuzzi tub, a private bar, a fountain, a huge bay window..." She counts on her fingers and stares upward. "I-I can't think of it all right now, but it's fit for royalty."

Again, she grins at me, and although I hate physical contact, I suck it up, bend forward, and wrap my arms around her shoulders, squeezing her tight.

"You are an absolute gem, Mary-Anne."

CHAPTER 20 – GABRIEL

"Give him some space."

I clench and unclench my fists, letting my fingers hang at the end of the chair's armrests.

Vrin bends forward, penetrating eyes fixated on me so intently it looks like she's trying to read my mind. If there was a light bulb dangling over her head, and if we were in a dark room, I'd think I was in a torture chamber. It's so quiet I can hear myself breathing.

"What's going on?" I ask.

Rubbing the back of my head, I look around. The room isn't much larger than an average master bedroom, and it reminds me of a hospital, like Area 82 always did. It's so damn clean, and everything is white. Lights flicker every now and then across the walls, which means this place has power up and running no problem.

Behind Vrin is a twin-size bed. It doesn't look like much... Doesn't look comfy at all. But I've slept on beds in Area 82, and they're as comfortable as clouds even though they look like cardboard boxes. Sky blue sheets sit on top of the mattress so tightly you'd think they were glued to it. Beside the bed is a door, and I only know that because I used to live in Area 82. It's hard to tell it's a door. It's a rectangle in the wall that opens when commanded to do so. Kind of like a peekaboo door but way more advanced and without needing manual touch. I'm sure it leads to a bathroom.

"You're in Elysium," Vrin says, matter-of-factly.

"Area 82," I correct her.

She smirks, probably amused that I already know this place.

"Same thing," she says.

"What happened?" I ask.

She glances sideways at a slender woman standing next to her. I don't recognize her, though it isn't hard to tell she's a therapist of some kind. A tight-knit bun sits right at the top of her head like it's been sprayed with polyurethane and left to dry for months. Her glasses, big square things with metal-blue rims, mask half her face. I never understood the big glasses fad, but apparently, it's *in*. Well, was.

On her face, though, they must serve a purpose. I have no doubt those ugly things contain more than corrective lenses. She looks at me through them, analyzing every movement I make. First, she stares at my feet and all I want to do is slip them under my chair to avoid any kind of judgment. Then, her eyes roll up to my knees, my waist, my shoulders, and then my face.

Is she analyzing me, or is she *analyzing* me? Technically, I mean. Are those things scanning me?

"State your name," the woman says.

Clearing my throat, I look at Vrin. She gives me a brief nod, which I'm sure is translation for *Go ahead.*

"G-Gabriel. Gabriel Rodriguez."

I wait for her to say more, but all she does is stare straight ahead without looking at me. I take in her blue skirt, her button-up shirt, and the white pearl necklace that sits around her neck, wondering if she wears the same thing every day. If I were to guess, I'd say she has seven of the same outfits and seven of the same necklaces.

"Repeat after me," she says. "Open door. Close door. Turn off the lights. Turn on the lights."

Now I get what's going on. She's setting up my profile here, which means mine's been erased. I do as told, wanting to get this over with as soon as possible so I can lie in what I assume is now my new bed.

"You suffer from post-traumatic stress disorder," she says.

I cock an eyebrow at Vrin. I don't think the woman's crazy, but something's off. Why's she talking like a robot? Oh God... Is she a robot? Is that how advanced things have gotten around here? She looks pretty damn real to me.

"You'll have to excuse Valeria," Vrin says. "She's very... goal-oriented and doesn't like to beat around the bush."

Without even looking at Vrin, Valeria taps her glasses and with her left hand, makes a swiping motion in front of her like she's sorting through folders. She taps the air, then touches her glasses.

I'm getting impatient sitting here. I don't even know how I got here. Where's Freyda? Eve? Everyone else? Where's Justice? My heart starts beating a bit faster than normal.

"Could someone please tell me what's going on?" I ask.

"I have a two-week therapeutic program designed to resolve your condition," Valeria says, pinching the air in front of her. "It has a ninety-five percent success rate."

It's like she's reading it off whatever's in front of her. Is this woman for real?

"What the fuck's going on?" I ultimately snap.

Without removing her fingers from the corner of her glasses, Valeria stares at me until at last, Vrin steps in.

"You jumped on top of several women," Vrin says.

Shocked, I lean forward to get out of my chair only to realize a cable's wrapped around my waist.

I'm tied up. Great.

"W-what do you mean?" I ask. "Did I hurt them? Fuck. I'd never—"

"No," Vrin says. "They're more shocked than anything, but you could have done some real damage."

"I don't remember—"

"That's why Valeria's here," Vrin says. "She's one of America's most reputable therapists in advanced techno-psychology."

I nearly scoff, but I hold it in. Advanced techno-psychology? It sounds like a load of shit.

Vrin must realize I'm not buying into it. She crosses her arms over her chest and parts her legs, a stance she likes to use, and one that tells me she isn't messing around.

"I'm not going to get into details with you, Gabriel.

But let me be very clear. I don't allow loose cannons inside of Elysium. You can either follow Valeria's program, or you can leave."

Although skeptical, I'd be lying if I said I wasn't interested in fixing what's wrong with me.

"Ninety-five percent?" I ask.

Without saying a word, Valeria nods.

"You'll remain confined to this living space until Valeria confirms your recovery and clears you for collaborative living," Vrin says.

And with that, she turns around and heads for the main door.

"Wait!" I say and she turns around.

It doesn't look like she's in the mood to have any further discussion.

"What about Justice? She's only a puppy. Where is she?"

Vrin sighs. "She's fine. Just focus on your program."

CHAPTER 21 – LUCY

It's still weird to think that some robot lady has all of my information stored in an invisible system. While it might freak me out because of how bad things got in the past (the government trying to control everyone), I'd be lying if I said I wasn't intrigued.

Being able to open a door with my voice? That's pretty cool. The most I ever did with my voice was make commands on my H-Cap. I didn't do it often, though. Mom was often on the phone or talking with Eve in the living room when I got home from school. Well, before I stopped going to school because of the war.

So this little floating ball is apparently what's going to bring me to my brand new room. I can almost sense Abigail's wide-eyed stare before I even turn to look at her. She's so ecstatic her gums make up half her smile.

"This is so freakin' cool," she says, pointing at her own Luminus. "I... I think mine's trying to take me this way." She takes a step in the opposite direction of me and her Luminus glides through the air and toward a set of elevators at the back of the main hall—well, the Hub, as Vrin called it.

Although I want to take everything in—the fountain, the gleaming white walls, the bizarre green and purple plants that droop as if weights are fastened at their tips—all I can focus on is Eve. She's standing next to a woman who appears to be half her height and twice her size in muscle mass.

But what surprises me is the look on Eve's face. She's smiling—so much so that her eyes are squinting. What's she so happy about? Minutes ago, she looked so pissed off that even Abigail pointed it out. Is this another one of her mood swings? Or is this something else? Eve's little sister, Mila, had a similar mental illness, but she didn't act like this. She wasn't so extreme. Then again, Mila was also taking medication.

God. Why do things have to be so complicated? I should be wary of Eve right now. After what I saw—after catching her basically yelling at herself in a mirror—I should be warning everyone about how unpredictable she is, but I can't bring myself to do it.

She's still my Aunty Eve, as much as I hate to admit it. I don't trust her and I want to stop her from whatever it is she has planned, but I love her, and I can't bring myself to turn on her.

Maybe she's not evil. Maybe she's just... unstable. A lot of people are unstable and they don't hurt anyone, right?

Eve suddenly lets out a loud laugh and women gravitate toward her like mindless sheep around a shepherd. It's easy to understand how she draws people in as if powered by a magnet—she does it to me. There's something intrinsically captivating about Eve and there always has been.

It's hard to explain.

She isn't loud or obnoxious, but she has a strong personality. Well, at least she does now. It's like a calm strong, if that makes sense. Way before all of this happened, she wasn't like this. Then again, she was also much younger. But over the last few years, a fearlessness has come out. She isn't afraid of anyone, and she walks around like a goddess, although she's likely waging a war within herself.

Right now, all I want to do is walk up to her and say hi, which is ridiculous. I think deep down, even though I want to stop her from harming others, I also want to save her; I want to help her battle whatever illness she's suffering from.

It sounds so pathetic and I'm embarrassed for even thinking it. If Mom were around, she'd likely tell me she's proud of me for wanting to help rather than destroy.

The short stocky woman standing by Eve waves her arm over her head and says, "Come on, I'll show you."

In one quick motion, Eve snatches the Luminus floating beside her head and tucks it into her pocket. Obviously, she isn't going to her room; she's following this woman, whoever she is and wherever she's taking her.

I take a step forward as if prepared to follow her, even though it's none of my business, when Emily's voice slips into my ear.

"Hey, stranger."

"Emily!"

Beaming, she wraps her arms around my

shoulders and gives me a tight squeeze. "You okay? Did you find Nola?"

I nod. "She's taking care of people. Apparently, there's some advanced medical facility somewhere in here. I'm assuming that's where she went. I don't know how I'm gonna find her when she gets out... This place is huge."

Craning my neck, I gaze up upward at the glass ceiling that appears to be a mile away. There must be at least ten levels in here, and I can only imagine how big each one of them is.

"Everyone's saying to go get settled and that we're going to be given a tour afterward," Emily says. She then points at her Luminus. "How cool is this thing?"

I smirk. "Pretty cool. You feeling okay?"

She doesn't look as bad as she did earlier, likely the result of her excitement. Emily's still recovering from her pneumonia, but all in all, it looks like the worst of it has passed.

"I'm fine," she says. "Come on, let's follow these little things and see where they take us."

She takes a step toward hers and it hovers away so smoothly it looks like it's on an invisible track. Emily starts jogging toward it, and with every step she takes, her Luminus moves farther away.

"This way!"

We aren't the only ones chasing after our Luminus Spheres. A bunch of young girls keep hopping up and down to catch the little ball like cats swatting at butterflies while their guardians try to hold them back.

"Rashi, that's enough!" one mother says, tugging

at her daughter's wrist. Rashi, her little girl, slaps both hands over her eyes and starts crying, though it sounds more like a tired whine.

"It's going to the elevator," Emily says.

"So is mine," I say. "You think we're close to each other?"

Emily shrugs. "Maybe."

There are a dozen elevators lined up against the back wall. They look like glass tubes—slender, cylindrical shapes with a medium-sized platform large enough to fit a small crowd of people.

Emily stands in front of the elevator farthest right, waiting for it to do something. When nothing happens, she bends forward, her back round, and starts jabbing her thumb all over the metallic frame. "How does it work? There's gotta be a button somewhere."

I plant my feet in front of the elevator next to hers and stare at it. There's a reason they asked us to repeat scripts, isn't there? Maybe these only work through voice recognition.

"Open door," I say, and with a soft swoosh, the glass door slides open. Grinning, I turn to Emily. "It works!"

"Open door!" she shouts, her voice carrying across the Hub but then quickly slaps a hand over her mouth when several heads turn our way. Then, before stepping inside, she turns to me and says, "If I don't see you up there, I'll catch you later."

We both step inside our elevators at the same time and the doors close behind us with a swoosh. Through the glass, I watch as women and children gather in Elysium's Hub, arms waving and lips flapping. There's so much liveliness—so much emotion. Above their heads, hundreds of Luminus Spheres float quietly, waiting to take each one of them up to their rooms. Surely, once they've finished meeting new faces, they'll follow their spheres like we're doing and settle into their new living spaces.

I turn to my left and spot Emily smudging her hands all over the elevator's glass from the inside. What the heck is she doing? Is she seriously looking for a button again? When she catches me staring, she flattens her palms on either side of her face as if to say, *What do I do?*

The doors opened through voice command, therefore, it would make sense that the elevator also functions through voice command. So, without knowing for certain, I point at my lips and Emily lights up. Though I can't hear her, her lips move, and at once, her platform disappears up into the air.

"Take me to my room," I say.

At the very center of the elevator's glass door, a blue screen appears with my name written on it: Lucinda Cain. Under it, it says, Fifth floor, room 591.

And with a sound so soft I barely hear it, the elevator levitates, making everyone in the Hub look smaller and smaller. It blows my mind. The last time I was on an elevator, I could hear the cables dragging it up. This thing, from what I saw before stepping in, doesn't even have cables. I have no clue how it works, but it feels like I'm being brought up on a cloud.

And room 591? How many rooms are there in this place? I don't have the time to put too much thought into it; the moment the elevator's glass doors swoosh open, Emily's face appears. Had she been standing any closer, she'd have fallen into the elevator with me.

"Emily!" I shout with excitement.

Several eyes turn toward us, but she doesn't seem to mind.

"Looks like we're on the same floor," she says, smirking the way she does when she's up to no good.

"What?" I ask. "Why're you looking at me like that?"

"Because you should thank me. I asked to be next to you."

I'm a bit surprised to hear this—not that Emily would make such a request, but that Vrin or that Nayma lady would actually do it. That was incredibly nice of them. They didn't have to do that, and they did it anyway.

I get the feeling this place is going to be great.

"You realize we could have taken the same elevator—" I say.

She dismisses me with a flick of the wrist. "That would have ruined the surprise."

Swinging my bag over my shoulder, I smile at her. "So what's your room number?"

"It's 592," she says, and she's still smirking like she orchestrated the whole thing—which, I guess, she did.

"Thanks for doing that," I say. The last thing I wanted was to end up beside someone I don't know, or to end up all alone. I glance behind Emily, where dozens of kids and adults sit around tables that appear to be made of resin—they're shiny, light gray, and reflect the pod's fluorescent lights overhead. The ceilings are uncharacteristically high, and combined with the lighting, they make the tables even shinier.

On either side of us are corridors with glass walls, which I assume must wrap around the entire building. You can see the Hub perfectly through the glass. It's filled with scores of women, and from up here, they look like dots across a white canvas. I may only be five flights up, but it feels like ten because every floor is so tall.

The same green and purple plants that decorated the Hub are lined up throughout the corridor, slouching slightly away from the walls. The distance between each one seems almost too perfectly measured, and underneath them, small shadows spread across white floors that are so glossy they look like glass.

At the far back of the room is an entryway without a door—instead, a large metallic border frames the opening. People come out through it carrying plates with food and making their way to the large tables which are also meticulously positioned across the room.

Then, the smell hits me and I nearly fall flat on my butt. It smells of warm salted roast beef—the kind of roast beef only a grandmother can make—and of buttery potatoes. I can practically taste the butter sliding across my tongue, and my mouth fills with saliva.

Emily's jaw drops and she looks at me with big bug eyes.

She doesn't have to say anything, and neither do I. Snatching my Luminus the way Eve did it, I stick it into my pocket and march toward the crowd of food-carrying people.

I don't care about finding my room, or even about finding Nola right now. All I care about is this food. And meat. God... I haven't tasted meat in forever. For the last four years, I've basically led a vegetarian, almost vegan, lifestyle. I can't complain about it, though. Eve did a good job at making sure we were getting proper nutrients, but the smell of that beef...

A string of drool slips out of my mouth and I quickly wipe it away. Several eyes turn on us as we walk forward and it isn't until we reach the actual source of the food that I realize how quiet everyone's gotten. No one's eating anymore; they're staring at me and Emily. Some of them are even midbite, mouths partially open with stringy beef hanging out.

"What're they all looking at?" Emily asks, lips close together. If she were a cartoon character, she'd have spoken out of a hole at the corner of her mouth.

I gawk around the room, and then it hits me. They're all wearing sky blue outfits with buttons up to their necks—they're nice, much nicer than Eden's hemp clothing, but they all look alike... like clones.

Emily gives me an up-and-down look no doubt reading my mind. Her jeans are as worn out as mine are, and we're both wearing ratty old sneakers. Today, I managed to slide on an old pink hoodie that I've had since I got to Eden. When it got too tight, I stretched it out until I heard the seams snap. Its sleeves are too short for me now, so I roll them up to my elbows.

Emily's shirt, an old T-shirt that looks like it may have belonged to her dad, hangs down to her waist.

Compared to what everyone else is wearing, it looks like a rag you'd find in a mechanic's toolbox.

"Is that them?" someone whispers.

The person sitting next to the young boy who spoke, a spikey-haired blond woman with glasses and a bird nose, shakes her head, which I assume is translation for "I don't know."

Weren't they expecting us? Surely, Vrin announced to everyone that newcomers were on their way. Maybe I should have waited for the adults to take the lead instead of running ahead of everyone. Emily bites her lip and tugs at the bottom of her torn T-shirt.

I bet she's thinking the exact same thing.

"Lucy Cain and Emily Wilmer," comes a man's authoritative voice.

My first instinct is to look at the walls, and then at the ceilings. I don't see anyone, so I can only assume it's coming from that robot thing APHRODITE. Then again, APHRODITE is a female voice, so I don't know who's voice this is.

Whoever is speaking clears his throat and I feel stupid. The man is standing near the entrance to the kitchen wearing a strange outfit—a long yellow cotton jacket that sits over a plain white T-shirt and hangs over the top of loose fitting pants.

Who is this guy? And why's he dressed differently from everyone else?

He smiles at us, revealing perfectly white teeth. Though I can't see his face in its entirety because of his bushy brown beard and shoulder-length wavy hair, he does seem like a nice guy. Thick flat eyebrows sit over his eyes like fuzzy caterpillars. Although exceptionally big, they suit his face. He's older than my mom was and definitely older than Eve. His sideburns, long hairy things that attach to his beard, have a hint of silver in them. They don't make him look old, though; they kind of make him look mature and responsible if that makes sense.

He's about to repeat our names again with that same smile on his face when I nod and say, "Y-yes. That's us."

How did he know it was us?

That's when I see an odd handheld device in his hand. I only notice it because he taps on the screen, inputting information. Then, when he catches us staring, he lets out a grumbly laugh and says, "I don't wear glasses, so you won't see me wearing anything fancy like Nayma."

The glasses, I remember. They must have been advanced versions of his device. What did he do? Scan us? Is that how he knew who we were?

Instead of waiting for us to walk to him, he makes his way to us. At the same time, he waves a hand in the air and says, "Resume," and everyone goes back to chatting, eating, and scraping their utensils against their plates.

When he reaches us, I have to crane my neck back to look at him.

Holy crap is he ever tall. He's taller than that guy with the gray dog, and that guy was pretty tall.

"My name's Adimmer," he says. He rests a hand over his belly and bends forward, reminding me of how Mom used to describe *gentlemen*—polite, kind, and caring.

"I'm one of Elysium's Facilitators," Adimmer says. "Think of me as the male version of Nayma, only... with less power." He taps the tip of his handheld device and slides it into his overcoat's pocket. "I'm responsible for the fifth floor, while Nayma oversees all of Elysium."

"How many of you are there?" Emily asks.

Without blinking, he says, "Eleven, including Nayma. There are ten floors in all of Elysium, and they're all similar. Well, at least in the main building."

The *main building*? In my peripheral, Emily's jaw drops. Though I don't react the same way as her, I'm equally as stunned. It's hard to get over how big this place is.

"I'm responsible for showing you the ropes around here," he says, planting two hands on his waist. "But there'll be plenty of time to give you a tour. You must be hungry. Come on, I'll get you both a plate."

Nearly stumbling over my own shoes, I follow close behind, grinning at Emily from ear to ear.

CHAPTER 22 – EVE

Monarch Suite, I think, drawing my shoulders back.

"Ain't she a beaut?" says Mary-Anne.

She reminds me of a child who gives their parent a Christmas gift for the first time in their life. It's obvious she wants to be thanked and told what a wonderful, generous woman she is for giving me her Monarch Suite.

"I got our Facilitator to transfer your profile over," she says, and although I have no idea what she's talking about, I'm assuming it has something to do with my access to this room.

Something tickles my thigh, and out comes my Luminus.

Mary-Anne lets out a chortle as it makes its way to a flat platform at the center of a glass coffee table. The moment the Luminus lands on the platform, its light flickers, which leads me to believe it's made its way to a charging station.

"Thing's pretty smart, isn't it?" she asks.

I nod, but I'm far too mesmerized by my new space to pay any attention to her. The room itself is five, six times the size of my room in Eden. A kitchen built of high-end glass appliances, marble countertops, and metallic cupboards sits at the right of the room. The counter curves around the kitchen, and two bowls of fresh fruit sit on top of it. Between these is a dazzling jug of water with lemon halves floating inside.

Slowly, I turn to a massive bay window that takes up the entire back wall of the room.

"If you prefer darkness," Mary-Anne says, "all you have to do is ask."

I'm not quite certain what she means by this.

She raises two playful eyebrows and directs her gaze to the ceiling, no doubt referring to APHRODITE.

"Just ask?" I say, and she nods with so much passion that her entire body shakes.

"Close the blinds," I say. I'm about to ask Mary-Anne if *blinds* was the right term to use when the glass of the window darkens. And then, as if by magic, its pigmentation changes to match the color of walls around it.

Mary-Anne must be staring at my big-eyed face; she lets out a laugh so loud and abrupt that I flinch. "It takes awhile to get used to, but that's only the beginning of it. Come here."

As I follow her, pot lights overhead increase in brightness to make up for the darkness in the room.

"You can turn those off, too, but I wouldn't recommend doing that until it's bedtime."

She's still laughing as if everything she says is intended to be a joke. I'm not quite certain how to respond, so I simply smile at her.

"Oh, by the way," she says, stopping midtrack and causing me to bump into her, "That fridge isn't any ordinary fridge, either. It's a Chepire model, if you've ever heard of it."

I stare at the fridge, wondering if Mary-Anne is pulling a prank on me. I can't possibly be standing in the same room as a Chepire fridge.

* * * * * *

"Money doesn't grow on trees!" my mom shouts.

She isn't usually *this* upset about money, but today, she's having a bad day. And she isn't usually mean to me or Mila, either—especially not *Mila*, her baby girl, as Mom calls her.

"Mom, that's not what—" Mila tries.

"I don't want to hear it!" my mom says. I can tell she's really pissed off when the veins on her temples pop out, looking like little electrical wires. Her hair almost seems like it's been in contact with those electrical wires; it's frizzy and damaged and appears bleached white underneath our kitchen's fluorescent light.

Mom only gets this upset for two reasons: men and money.

Ever since all this crap started—ever since men started freaking out about women outnumbering them—Mom's been on edge all the time. All she does is rant about how *dumb* men are and how they all belong in hell.

Every day, that's what she talks about; every day, that's what I hear and what I'm starting to believe.

And as for money, well, Mom's never had much of it, and now she's responsible for the two of us. I hate it when she takes it out on Mila. All she did was ask for a new school bag. Any other day, Mom would have sighed and walked away, too overwhelmed to think about another expense. But today, I guess she's had her fill.

"I'm so sick of you kids taking everything from me! It's never enough, is it?" She digs her fingernails into the kitchen counter, the skin of her face as tight as stretched elastic.

I glance around, observing our twenty-year-old microwave, our empty cupboards with missing doors, and our fridge that works when it wants to. She's trying her best. But some days, her best doesn't feel like enough.

I'd never admit this to her, but the thought pops up every now and then.

Out of nowhere, my mom slaps a can of beans off the counter, smashing it into the kitchen sink cupboard. It leaves a small dent in the wood before rolling by Mila's feet. She then lets out an annoyed sigh and storms out of the kitchen, mumbling to herself.

Mila looks like she's about to cry. "My backpack broke…"

I wrap an arm around her shoulder and squeeze her tight. "Don't worry about it, Mila. Mom's being Mom. I'll get you a backpack."

What I'm honestly thinking is: I'll get you a new life. A life away from here. I'll make sure you never have to suffer the way Mom lets us suffer.

* * * * * *

"You have to wave your hand in front of it for it to work."

"Eve?"

"Hello?"

I blink twice and follow the voice.

Mary-Anne is standing next to me with two hands planted on her waist. Her eyes dart between me and the Chepire fridge.

"You okay?" she asks.

I look at the fridge again, and Mila's face is no longer in its reflection.

Mary-Anne waves a hand in front of me, though what I think she's actually doing is activating the fridge.

The glass of the fridge darkens to a deep ocean blue and small letters float in front of my face. They appear to be listing all kinds of food, assumedly meals to be created by the fridge. Mary-Anne flicks her finger on the glass, her fingernail making a soft ticking noise. Then, a long list of options appears on the screen in front of me: peanut butter sandwich, peanuts, nachos, cheese sticks, veggie platter... The list goes on.

If only Mila were here with me. If only she were still alive to see all of this... All I can think about is how every time Mom snapped at her, I promised her that one day, I'd be so rich I'd buy her a house with a Chepire fridge.

My throat swells and I turn away.

"Wait!" Mary-Anne says. "Don't you want to see it in action?"

"I'm not all that hungry, but I'm excited to try it later."

She seems satisfied enough to step away from the fridge.

Although I want to explore the rest of the Monarch Suite, Mila is all I can think about now. I make my way to the white leather sofa—it sits directly atop a zebra skin rug, something I assume cost thousands of dollars when money still existed.

The leather feels cool against my palms as I lean back and close my eyes.

"Are you all right?" asks Mary-Anne.

I crack one eye open and roll my head sideways to look at her. Slouching, her hands fidgeting in front of her, she reminds me of a queen's servant—someone prepared to jump off a cliff if ordered to do so. Is that what she wants? For me to lead her?

Sighing, I say, "A lot has happened, that's all. I wish I could draw a map of my brain and—"

Unexpectedly, the coffee table in front of me—with a sleek glass tabletop supported by silver cylinders—vibrates and lights up a bright aqua blue. The transparency is gone, and the zebra skin rug can no longer be seen underneath it.

Instead, a digitized design appears flat on the table where the glass used to be. It looks like a map or a blueprint.

Leaning forward with elbows on my knees, I slide my fingers across the table's hard surface. "What is this?"

Mary-Anne looks as confused as me. She plops herself down beside me and I inch away from her. She bends so far forward it's as if she's trying to kiss the glass, then bends even farther, peering underneath.

"It must be hardwired right into the ground," she says. In an instant, a childish grin stretches across her face. "I've been here six months now and I had no idea about this!"

Gliding my finger across the glass, I touch numerous rooms outlined on the map. Each one is numbered, and some of them even have names, such as Storage, or Electrical Room.

"Is this Elysium?" I ask.

She drops to her knees on the rug and hovers over the map. "Sure looks like it. Look at that—" She points at the center. "Looks like the elevators to our floor. And check this out—"

But as she motions her hand across the table, the screen changes, and at the top left-hand corner is bold text that reads: Second Floor.

"Do that again," I say.

She doesn't seem to know what she did, so she swings her entire arm in the same direction again and the screen changes to Third Floor.

"I think it's a map to all of Elysium," she says, looking as dumbfounded as I am. "Like, every single part of it."

"Does everyone have a map in their room?" I ask.

Mary-Anne scoffs, and then, as if realizing she should be careful with how she speaks to me, shakes her head. "Vrin is pretty secretive when it comes to Elysium. We're allowed in certain areas, but there's a lot of technological advancements that are being done behind closed doors. So, no, I highly doubt this is a common thing."

Though I remain tight-lipped, I'm beaming inside.

"Do you think anyone knows about this?" I ask.

She shakes her head.

"Good," I say, resting a gentle hand over hers. She seems to like this; she smiles shyly and turns away. "Let's keep this between you and me, okay beautiful?"

CHAPTER 23 – GABRIEL

The wall feels like ice against the back of my skull.

It's like a prison cell in here, only, some messed-up version of it. It's a bit luxurious if you ask me. It sucks being confined to one room, but at the same time, I get it. It's for my own good, and for the safety of others.

Vrin has every right to integrate only stable people into Elysium. I threw myself on top of women, for fuck's sake.

"How would you rate your nightmares on a scale of one to ten?" Valeria asks.

She crosses her skirted legs and leans back into the white plastic chair. I can't help but feel like I'm being judged, though I know I'm not. Valeria's done a lot for me these last few days. I don't like her approach, but it seems to be working.

And how am I supposed to measure something like that? How does someone rate their nightmares? "Five, I guess."

"Are they less frequent?" she asks.

I don't have much to go on, here. It's been four or five nights, but I guess they have been better, yeah. Meaning, I haven't had as many nightmares, and the ones I did have weren't as violent as usual.

Even though I haven't yet said anything, the way she's looking at me makes me feel like she already knows what I'm about to say. So I keep it short. "Yes."

She nods slowly and taps her fingers in front of her face, taking note of what I'm saying through those weird glasses of hers. Then, she taps the side of the frame, which I've come to realize is her way of *turning off* the screen, or the projection, whatever you want to call it.

"Today," she says, "I'd like to advance to level three." She pauses, no doubt waiting to see how I react.

I'm not excited about having to jump up a level. It hurts. But, at the same time, it's the only way forward. Valeria explained to me that the program has a total of five levels. I've been on level two for the last few days, so it makes sense that I move up.

I give her a brief nod.

Without saying a word, she extends her hand toward the Nepalt 4000 chair. Apparently, that stands for Neuro Pathway Alteration, or something like that. Honestly, I don't care what it's called. All I know is that it works even though the process is shitty. The damn thing looks like a spaceship. It's made of metal for the most part, but a thick layer of padded leather sits on the surface. At the headpiece, a bunch of wires wrap around the base and lead to small pointed tips. I don't stare at it too long; otherwise, it'll freak me out.

Some days, I wonder if it's frying my brain. Valeria wasn't scared to admit that the machine used to be used for brainwashing during the war. So, yeah, it has the ability to fry a brain. But she's assured me time and time again that they've rewired the thing to become a *medical miracle*. Supposedly, it can cure all kinds of psychological disorders.

She also said they're working on making it look less scary and less painful.

I get up off my bed and make my way to the Nepalt, turn around, and plop down into it.

Valeria gets up and moves forward, her hips swaying like a cat on the verge of pouncing on a mouse. She locks the metal clasps around my ankles and then around my wrists.

It's cold against my skin, and so is the chair's leather, but it doesn't bother me. Right now, I have to focus on Freyda and Justice. The sooner I finish this program, the sooner Vrin will let me out of here and back into society.

I'm curious to know how it's going out there. Are men and women living together? Are they getting along? Are there any rules, like having men stay on one floor, and women on another? I'm pulled back into reality when Valeria grabs my face and tightens a strap around my jaw. Then, she pulls down small arms around the headrest and carefully places each one around my forehead. She's so focused it's as though she were performing surgery.

Every time she puts them around my head, it needs to land at a precise point. That must mean there's a technique to it.

Then, like every other day this week, she reaches into her black briefcase and extracts a mouthguard.

"It may be more uncomfortable than our last

sessions," she says, forcing it inside my open mouth.

I already know it's going to hurt like hell, so I nod quickly. That's my way of saying, *Look, can we get this over with?*

"Close your eyes," she orders.

I do as told with my fingers wrapped around the edges of the armrests.

The sound of machinery warming up fills the room. It's a low hum, followed by a high-pitched tone that makes me wince. Then, blinding lights flash over my eyelids and a sharp pain fills my head. At first, it feels like a headache, then a migraine. But as it progresses, it gets so bad that I feel like my eyes are literally going to fall out of my skull.

I bite down on my mouthguard and the plastic cracks.

"You're doing great," her voice resonates in the distance.

It sounds like I'm underwater. Or somewhere. I can't even think anymore.

Jesus Christ, I'm going to die. Fuck. Fuck. Fuck. Make this stop.

Freyda, and Justice, I remind myself.

Freyda and Justice.

Freyda and...

Freyda.

CHAPTER 24 – LUCY

"What is that?" Emily asks.

Turning to face her, I wonder if maybe she didn't have much growing up. Most kids know what an H-Cap is. Mom compared it to a tablet from Grandma's time—a portable electronic device that could be used for a bunch of stuff.

"You've never heard of an H-Cap?" I ask. "A Holographic Capsule?"

She moves toward me and plops herself down on my bed. "Well, yeah, I've heard of it, but I've never seen one."

I gently place it in her hand to let her have a look at it, and I think she knows how much it means to me; she grabs it so delicately you'd think she was grabbing a flower.

"How do you turn it on?" she asks, twirling it around in her palms.

"Well it needs to be charged," I say.

She looks at me like I'm missing too many brain cells for my age. She points at my night table, where a small white pad sits perfectly at its center. "All of our rooms come with charging stations."

Adimmer told us about it—that's the only reason

we know it's a charging station. He taught us everything there is to know about our rooms, like how we can make a fake window appear to make us feel like we're looking outside. It's some sort of screen that looks like the wall until it's activated. We can even choose any scenery we want, like a neighborhood to feel a bit less alone.

Sighing, I pluck the H-Cap out of her hands. "I'm just scared."

"Of what?" she asks.

"Of seeing my mom, I guess."

Without saying anything, she pulls the H-Cap out of my hands. I'm about to yell at her for being so aggressive about it when she places it down on the charging station.

"What are you—" I try.

With eyebrows close together and lips forming a flat line the width of a wool thread, she points a finger at me. "You have memories to look at. You have something left from your mom. Do you know what I'd do to have something of my dad's? I'd do anything—" Her voice cracks and she turns her head away.

"Emily—"

It's no use. How can I explain to her that all I want is a minute to compose myself before breaking down? Or, maybe subconsciously, I don't want Emily around for this.

Now, she's standing at the door of my room.

"Open your door," she says choppily.

"Emily, please."

"Open it!"

"Open door," I say plainly, and the wall opens up

with a soft sound. The moment she's gone, I drop myself into my bed, a large breath blasting out of my lungs. "Close door."

I turn to my side and punch my pillow for better head support, all the while staring at my H-Cap and wondering what life would be like if Mom were still with me.

* * * * * *

"Mom!" I shout, laughing so hard my stomach's starting to hurt.

"What?" she exclaims in a panic. She jabs the air in front of my H-Cap and her whole hand goes through the holographic screen, causing little pixels to break apart.

"You have to control how hard you hit it." I try to show her how to do it, but she's so caught up in her game that she doesn't want me interfering.

"Get over here, you son of a—" She bites down on her lip and jabs hard again.

Then, the screen disappears, and large letters come floating up: Game Over.

"No!" she shouts, and even though she seems pretty upset about losing, I'm having so much fun that all I can do is laugh.

* * * * * *

I stare at my H-Cap.

Why isn't it lighting up? The little blue light is supposed to light up when it's charging. I yank it off the charging station, analyze the station, and place it back down.

Nothing.

My palms get clammy and my throat tightens. I'm not sure whether to scream, throw something, or cry into my pillow. This is all I have left from my mom. I need it to work. I need to see my mom again. Even if it's only a picture of her at Christmas or a video of her making supper and dancing by herself in the kitchen.

I squeeze my fingers around my pillow and clench my teeth.

This is bullshit.

I'm about to angrily pull my H-Cap off the charging pad again when someone screams down the hall.

I lunge to my feet and say, "Open door" while walking straight for the wall. The door opens in time for me to not smash my face into it. Down the hall to my left, there's a big commotion. It sounds like it's coming from the eating lounge.

What's going on?

I rush toward the sound as it amplifies. Women are shouting, followed by rumbly, authoritative male voices.

"Back away!" one man shouts, his voice carrying over everyone else's.

Then, a woman shouts, "You fucking pig! Fucking pig!"

By the time I make it into the eating lounge, two men are holding a woman back by her arms. One of them seems to be having a hard time keeping her still; she kicks and claws the air in front of her. I can't tell what she's trying to get at until I move a bit closer, shoving my way through the crowd.

"Come on, let's get him to Medical."

Who said that? Is someone injured?

"Move!" someone shouts and the crowd starts to split.

Then, out from the crowd come two women wearing all white with red cross pins fastened over their chest pockets. Between them, a tall stretcher sits on two wheels and rolls toward the elevators.

"Move!" shouts one of the doctors or nurses. I'm not certain what their status is, but I do recall Adimmer saying that each floor has medical staff present at all times in case of emergencies. I never imagined an emergency to be a fight—not in a place like this.

The man atop the stretcher doesn't make a sound, but his large hand is clasped around something metallic that seems to be coming out of his neck. At first, it looks like a metal rod, but as the stretcher rolls closer toward me, I realize it's a fork.

Holy shit.

I avert my attention to the woman who's now pinned to the ground with both hands behind her back. Blood covers her knuckles and smudges against the tile floor as she squirms.

Did she stab him?

"Fucking pedophile piece of shit!" she continues.

The two men holding her down—who I assume are trained guards given their dark gray uniforms and large combat boots—scoop her back up onto her feet with her arms fastened behind her back. Without a word, they drag her down the hall at the very far right corner of the eating lounge. I have yet to see someone with basic blue clothes enter those doors, so I assume it's a staff-only area.

Then, as if this sort of thing happens every day, a young man moves toward the bloodstains on the floor with a mop and a bucket. He shakes his head, pulls out the wet mop, and begins cleaning up the mess.

"What happened?" I ask aloud, though I'm not even sure where I'm directing my question.

A young guy who looks my age turns around with both arms crossed over his chest. He's about a foot taller than me and somewhat lanky, though also defined with round, muscular biceps. Dark brown scruff runs along his strong jaw and chin, resembling a shadow. His eyebrows are thick and full, as are his lips, making it difficult to look away from him.

He smirks, revealing a sharp white tooth at the corner of his lips. "Justice happened," he says.

I'm not sure what he means by this, and I'm about to ask him when he shakes his head and adds, "Turns out Pat Walsh wasn't the guy we thought he was." He rubs his scruff and averts his honey-brown eyes.

For a second, he almost looks hurt by what happened. Did he know this guy, Pat?

"That lady they took away says he touched her daughter," he says.

I stare toward where they dragged the woman away. "Is it true?"

He shrugs. "I don't know the woman. She just got here. But a mother wouldn't lie about something like that. And she sure as hell wouldn't attack a man for it."

I'm not sure what to say, so I don't say anything.

"It's a shame," he says. "Vrin's been fighting so hard to make sure Elysium only has good people, you know? Both men and women. Then once in a while, we find out some creep or psychopath's made their way in."

"So this *has* happened before?" I ask.

"Only twice," he says. "One time a woman started trying to fight every man she saw. Kept accusing Vrin of allowing *demons* into this place. Another time it was a guy with anger problems."

"What did Vrin do with them?" I ask.

"Banishment," he says as if answering a simple mathematical equation.

I stare at him, taking in his high cheekbones and smooth plush lips.

"I'm Lucas, by the way," he says, extending a hand.

The moment we touch, it's as though my blood's turned to warm maple syrup. His hand is strong, though not in an intimidating way, and it makes me feel safe.

"L-Lucy," I stammer.

He smiles again, this time, revealing perfectly aligned teeth.

"Lucy," he says, and my name sounds like magic slipping off his tongue. "Wanna see something cool?"

Without thinking, I nod rapidly. Anything *cool* sounds like fun right now. I've been living in a garden for over five years—I'd say I'm ready to see something new.

"Come with me," he says, turning around and heading for the elevators.

The only time I've used those elevators, aside from when I first got here, was to visit the courtyard when Abigail made her way to the fifth floor and asked us to join her. She said it was nice out there and that fresh air would do us some good. Within five minutes, I got bored and wanted back inside. I'm not sure if I've offended Abigail. She hasn't come back to see us, and I don't even know what floor she's on.

As we arrive at the elevator on the farthest right, the one beside it opens up and a woman walks out, bumping into me.

"Oh, shit... Sorry," she mumbles."

"Freyda?" I say.

She's sweating—her whole face is glistening as are her shoulders. She chugs a gulp of water from a stainless steel water bottle, swallows hard, then nods with a smile.

"H-hey, Lucy!" She swallows again, obviously trying to catch her breath. "How're you doing?"

"I'm good," I say. "Are you okay?"

She takes another gulp of her water. "I'm good. Just training." Then, her scrutinizing eyes roll toward Lucas. "Who's this?"

How am I supposed to introduce him? As a friend? I barely know the guy.

"Lucas," I say.

"And where's Lucas taking you?" she asks me, though she's looking at him.

"Just showing her around," Lucas says.

He doesn't seem intimidated at all. He smiles at her sweetly and extends a hand. But instead of taking it, she takes another gulp of water and rolls her eyes. "Lucy, if you ever want to learn how to protect yourself"—her eyes roll toward Lucas again as if he's someone I should know how to protect myself against—"feel free to join us outside."

I don't say anything, so she adds, "And both of you, stay out of trouble."

The moment we step into the elevator, Lucas grins at me. "She seems nice."

"She usually is," I say, scratching the back of my neck.

What's gotten into her? She's bolder than usual. The Freyda I know used to follow Eve around without making a sound. She was so rigid all the time. This Freyda, however, seems carefree.

And where's Eve, anyway? It isn't like her to keep a low profile. Should I be worried? Oh God, what's she planning?

"You okay?" Lucas asks.

I swing around when I realize the elevator's sinking lower than the main floor. Was this a mistake? Is this what Eve warned me about? Is Lucas luring me somewhere to hurt me? Somewhere no one can find me?

"Where are we going?" I ask, my voice breaking.

He offers a crooked smirk. "Relax. You're safe. I'm taking you to Elysium's Core."

"Core?" I ask. "What Core?"

Without losing his smile, he shakes his head. "Be patient. I'm trying to surprise you."

Swallowing hard, I fight the urge to think violent thoughts. It's as if all the time I've spent with Eve over the years has influenced my thinking. She taught me to fear all men and to view them as nothing more than empty shells—weapons to be used solely for the purpose of gaining power through destruction and violence.

The walls around the elevator are so dark they appear black. But that lasts for a few seconds at most. Now that we've sunken deeper into the ground, soft blue pot lights fill the space with a somber atmosphere, worsening my anxiety.

"Only a few people have access to this place," he says.

My heart's beating out of my chest now.

What have I done? If he tries to hurt me, no one will be around to hear it. Are there even cameras down here? The elevator doors open without barely making a sound and Lucas steps out. He looks back at me, likely confused that I'm not getting out of the elevator.

"You okay?" he asks. "You don't look so good."

He's toying with me—making me feel like he's nothing but a sweet guy.

Maybe Eve was right all along... I can't trust men, or boys, for that matter.

"Lucy," he says, taking a step toward me.

I instinctively step back and regret doing so the moment I do; he looks devastated.

"A-are you scared of me?" he asks.

I don't know what to say. He's tall, way taller than me. And although he isn't a man yet, he's almost there. His muscles are visible through his shirt, veins pop out on his large hands, and he's already started to grow a beard. It isn't long—a small shadow—and if I weren't terrified right now, I'd be focusing on how good it looks on him.

His eyebrows slant and he looks at the ground.

"Listen, I don't know what you've gone through... I have no idea. Maybe you've been hurt before. Or, maybe the rumors about Eve Malum are true and you've been living in a world where men aren't even allowed inside."

Although I've never been hurt by a man before, I saw firsthand how terrified my mom was of Jason. And now, apparently, that psychotic bastard is my dad. To worsen that, all I keep hearing in my head are the stories women used to share in Eden—stories about both physical and sexual abuse. I wasn't supposed to be listening, but sometimes, it's hard not to overhear when someone's whispering, especially when you've trained yourself to hear every little whisper. The women would go into every detail about how violent some men got, almost as if having transformed into monsters, and how helpless the women felt. There were good stories, too, but no one was supposed to talk about those.

"Look," he says. "You don't know me, and I respect that. If you want to go back upstairs, we'll go. No hard feelings." He offers a sweet smile. "The room I wanted to show you is the second door on the right." He points down the hall. "Right there. See it?"

I nod.

"I don't know what you've heard about guys," he says, "but I promise you that Elysium isn't like that. Vrin makes every effort to only let good people inside. She isn't shy about banishing or locking up bad people, both men and women. Do you honestly think I'd want to get locked up or thrown out of Elysium and left to rot in the wild?" This time, he laughs and shakes his head. "It isn't even about not wanting consequences, Lucy. I'd never hurt you. I'd never lay my hands on any girl."

He seems honest, and I almost take a step forward.

But then I think if he did hurt me, how would anyone find out? Maybe that's why he's brought me down into this basement.

"Tell you what," he says, still smiling. "How about I bring the cool to you?"

"What do you mean?" I ask.

He beams and sticks out an open palm. "Wait here!"

He rushes into the room he pointed at and the sound of shuffling and metal clanging fills the hallway. Finally, he comes stumbling out with a small square-shaped and shiny gadget in his hands.

"What's that?" I ask.

"Something I'm working on." He sits on the floor and places the small box in front of him. Its sides are glossy black and a small, almost unnoticeable antenna sits at the top.

"Kind of looks like one of those ancient TVs," I say, laughing. "But way smaller."

He looks up at me, the blue lights overhead making his eyes look almost white. Any other time, I'd have found this to be freaky, but his smile is so attractive that it's hard to remain afraid of him.

"That's the point," he says. "I'm going retro."

Without thinking, I step out of the elevator and walk toward his small creation.

"So what is it?" I ask.

He points at the empty space in front of him, which assumedly means, *Have a seat.*

"So it's not perfect yet," he says. "I'm planning on catching every signal out there. But right now, all I'm getting is France."

He presses a button and in an instant, a large blue holographic screen appears between the two of us. The image is a bit choppy, and every time it breaks, I see his face on the other side, so I'm assuming we're both seeing the same thing.

"*Aides-moi à chercher, mon ami!*" comes a brittle voice.

A giraffe walks in a large grass field, searching for something. Beside the giraffe is a baby hippo that keeps hopping up and down.

I start laughing even though this is one of the dumbest things I've ever seen; it's also the only digital thing I've seen in years. So I keep watching, mesmerized by the colors, the sounds, movements. I'm not sure how long we sit there in the dark together, but it must be awhile. Pressed against the hard floor, my body starts to ache, and the show's turned into something else—some adventure with pandas and koala bears.

He turns off his small box and picks it up between his thumb and index finger as if holding the last diamond on earth.

"Pretty neat, huh?" he says.

I grin, happier than I've been in a long time. "That was awesome."

"It's a kid's channel, but I'm hoping to catch news channels soon."

"In France?" I ask. "What for?"

"Not only in France," he says. "Everywhere in the world." He rubs his thumb against his creation's glossy metal. "We need to know what's going on out there." He leans forward, shadows darkening his cheekbones. "Think of Canada, for example. If they weren't affected by this war, all I'll have to do is find a way to communicate with them. And then, maybe, who knows… We could go back to living a normal life."

I find it hard to believe that Canada is fine, given the fact that five years have passed. But he's so excited about it I can't help but feel hopeful.

CHAPTER 25 – EVE

Over the last few days, the whispering has gone down dramatically. The women don't point at me while leaning into their friends' shoulders. Instead, they glance at one another, at me, and then at each other again.

Some of them even fidget in their seats, assumedly contemplating whether or not it's appropriate to approach me. It reminds me of our old world, when a celebrity was spotted eating supper at a local restaurant—Do I, *or don't I ask for an autograph?*

Mary-Anne seems to be the only one who isn't afraid of upsetting me, and I enjoy her presence in an unusual way.

She's easy to control. Every few minutes, I sense her eyes roll my way, though I don't give her the satisfaction of returning the gaze. If there's one person I wish would look at me in such a way, it's Freyda.

Still, she hasn't forgiven me for what happened in Eden—for slapping her and accusing her of being a traitor. I don't blame her for holding on to resentment, but I truly thought that she would have moved past it by now.

Freyda has always been my other half. And where is she now? Making new friends and building a life without me. Perhaps this only further proves her betrayal. If she truly cared about me, she would forgive me for my outburst.

When I've earned my rightful place as leader of Elysium, she'll regret having abandoned me.

"You sure you don't want to go outside?" Mary-Anne asks.

She's been asking me every day to visit Elysium's courtyard—a common space for all to share. I think what I fear most is coming face-to-face with Freyda, or worse, seeing her smile without my being the cause of it.

But today, I'm ready to put this behind me. I elevate my chin and look down at Mary-Anne; she practically dances on the spot the moment my stare meets her gleaming eyes.

"Is... Is that a yes? Are you finally ready to visit the courtyard? The women have been dying to talk to you, Eve."

Why haven't they?

"They haven't wanted to bother you while you eat or while you spend time in your room," she says as if reading my mind. "But the courtyard... You'll see. It's where everyone socializes. The fact that you're stepping out there means you're one of us, you know?"

I'll never be one of you. I swallow back the bile rising in my throat.

But then I remember something: that's precisely

who I need to be. I need to be one of *them*. That's how I'll win them over.

I force a smile and squeeze the back of Mary-Anne's neck. "I would love nothing more than to finally sit down and chat with everyone."

She's so excited now that her gums are showing under her nose and saliva sticks to the corners of her mouth.

"Oh! Oh! Let's go!" she says, hopping in front of me.

She leads me out of the Hub and down a wide passageway illuminated by pod lights. Women turn as I pass them, and some of them even retrace their steps to follow me outside. The doors to the courtyard, two thin slabs of metal, automatically open and disappear into the walls on either side as four women leave the courtyard.

I catch a glimpse of the outside before the doors close again, and I'm completely taken aback. Mary-Anne's spent the last several days attempting to lure me to the courtyard by describing its unprecedented beauty—by gloating about how much the outdoor space resembled pure paradise.

While I should be ecstatic at the prospect of a new garden, it is precisely the reason I haven't wanted to visit the courtyard. Eden was meant to be our paradise; we were supposed to live in a bountiful space full of vibrant colors, vivid greens, fresh water, an abundance of savory food, and an atmosphere so pleasant that everyone envisioned growing old and dying inside of its walls.

Instead, resources became scarce, sickness

spread like wildfire, and exterior threats became all too prevalent.

This place... This Elysium... is the true Eden, and I simply have to make peace with that.

The door suddenly flies open again and sunlight fills the hallway, casting a radiant white light across the floor and along the side walls. Ahead of me, hundreds of women wander about—some aimlessly, others chasing children, and some reuniting with old friends with grand gestures and loud voices.

I take one step outside, my lungs filling with crisp autumn air. The sun, although not very bright, warms my face and shoulders as I step farther away from Elysium's doors.

The grass is yellow and dull and somehow reminds me of my childhood. In an instant, I'm taken back to the summer I spent at my aunt's cottage.

* * * * * *

"Eve, get your sister and you girls come inside!" shouts Aunt Peligrina.

This is translation for, *Supper's ready.* I can't even see Mila—last I saw her, she dived headfirst off the pier and into the deep blue lake water. I've never been a fan of lake water myself, but Mila loves it, so I watch her.

Besides, she's six years old. It's not like I can leave her alone. At least not the way Mom does. All Mom seems to want to do lately is leave us alone. Dad left us a few months ago, and ever since, it's like she's gone off the wagon. I don't think that's the saying.

Who leaves a six-year-old and a ten-year-old with their aunt over the summer? I mean, I guess it happens enough, but this wasn't something nice she did for us. It was more of a *Here, you take them Peligrina. I don't know if I'm coming back.*

She didn't give any of us a return date. For all I know, she's dead.

I get that Dad wasn't always around, but he was good to us when he was. Ever since he left, all Mom does is accuse him of all sorts of things. She's been talking about it so much that I'm starting to forget what Dad was like. It's almost like staring at a famous painting and then having someone throw a bunch of oil on it.

She's ruining my memory of him and making me hate him.

And every time I say something along the lines of "I miss Dad," my mom glares at me and shouts, "He left us!"

So now, I'm standing outside in a pair of old jeans and one of my dad's T-shirts without either one of my parents. Instead, I'm left with the responsibility of taking care of my six-year-old sister and hoping she doesn't drown. The last thing I want to do is jump in that water.

"Mila, come on," I shout, and her head resurfaces from the water. The sun reflects off of it, making it look like a never-ending sheet of blue glass, and Mila squints her big wet eyes.

Any other time, she'd have given me a hard time, giggled, and dunked her head back into the water. But ever since Mom dropped us off here, it's like she knows how much it's hurting me and doesn't want to add to the hurt.

She comes out of the water and I wrap one of Aunt Peligrina's towels around her. She shivers, her blue lips resembling pieces of candy.

"You're freezing," I say.

"I-I'm okay."

She runs up the pier, her bare feet slapping against the wood, and disappears into Aunt Peligrina's wooden cottage. I jog behind her and go inside, greeted by the smell of freshwater fish and steamed green beans.

Aunt Peligrina places two floral plates of steamy food on the table and smiles at us. She looks nothing like my mom; she's dark featured, taller, and healthier-looking overall. Her skin, a creamy beige, would look brown beside Mom's. I'd never admit that to Mom, but the truth is, Mom looks sick half the time. She also takes a bunch of meds, so I'm sure that's not helping.

I sit down at the wooden table. It looks like something Aunt Peligrina built herself, but in a good way. It's so nice and surprisingly comfy.

Taking a bite of my food, I thank Aunt Peligrina for supper and a piece of fish flies back out into my plate.

Mila bursts out laughing, and food flies out of her mouth, too.

Aunt Peligrina smiles but quickly clears her throat. "Mind your manners, ladies."

Manners? What does that even mean?

Mila giggles again and says, "Manners. Manners what? Mom says mans are all evil."

* * * * * *

Men *are* evil, I think, gazing around Elysium's

courtyard.

I feel sick to my stomach; for every six or seven women, a man is present. It's apparent that the female sex still outnumbers males, but what I don't understand is why Vrin's allowed them to coexist.

Elysium is large enough—why not separate the sexes?

Why put us in harm's way like this?

Most of the men are located at the far west side of the courtyard, which is surrounded by tall iron gates. I'm not sure whether the gates are to keep us inside or to keep predators out—perhaps a combination of both.

In this location, at the far west side is an area filled with obstacle courses, painted markings in the grass, shooting targets, bales of hay, and bags that appear to be used for either target practice or punching bags.

Two short men tackle each other to the ground, releasing muffled grunts. I clench my fists at the sight of the aggression, but when no one reacts, I realize they are either playing or training.

Fucking dogs.

That's when I catch a glimpse of Freyda—what I was most afraid of. She's staring at me, though the moment I make eye contact with her she turns away and fires an arrow at a target. The arrow lands at the very center of her target—a small red dot—and I can't help but wonder if she's visualizing my face.

How is she, anyway? She'll have to forgive me at some point. As I stare at her, I wonder where her horse Pearl is. I saw them bring her onto the plane. What about Ruby? The children love that golden retriever.

"Have a seat, Eve," comes someone's voice.

A crowd has formed around me. I was so busy observing Freyda that I hadn't noticed. She must be happy now; she's receiving precisely what she wanted—combat training and an army of women to train. Around her, dozens of women appear to be following her command. Men, too, are carefully analyzing her techniques.

"You ready?" comes a familiar voice.

I turn around in time to see Yael marching out of Elysium, head held high and intense green eyes gazing out into the courtyard. Her hair, long and dark, sits still all the way down her back until she scoops it up and ties it back.

This isn't the Yael I remember—the Yael I remember was timid and soft-spoken. Who is this woman? She's walking forward with drawn shoulders and a man at her side. They share similar features, which leads me to wonder if they're related.

She slaps two hands together—both of which are wrapped in elastic bands—and turns to the man beside her.

"I'm gonna kick your ass, *akhi.*"

Akhi? Is that his name? The way it came out of her mouth, it sounded like another language. It sounds Hebrew. What's happened to my women? Why is everyone so happy here? They're supposed to realize what a mistake this was—they're supposed to come crawling back to me, begging for me to help them.

"I don't think so, sister," says the man, rubbing his short bristly beard with the back of his hand.

His biceps form small balls at the ends of his T-shirt, and a rage rises inside of me. What is he going to do? Force her into submission? Teach her that men are superior because of their muscular strength? This is precisely how it begins—slowly, men feel superior to women until they choose, by force, to be in control.

I'm not certain what's caused Vrin to be so delusional. It's as if she believes that she's tamed the men enough for them to coexist within a female society. The truth is, no matter how tame they may be now, it is not their nature; sooner or later, they will want to rise and take her place.

As she passes me, Yael catches my eyes and smiles at me. "Oh, hey, Eve."

I'm too stunned to talk back. Not once has she ever called me by my first name or spoken to me as if we were friends.

Her brother shoves her and she playfully punches him in the shoulder, though by the sound of the impact, I have no doubt it will leave a bruise.

"Eve?" comes that voice again.

I turn sideways where a woman is standing next to an oak chair. I'm about to thank her and sit down when something hard hits me against the head. My vision blurs and I stumble forward, before falling to my knees.

What's happening?

"You fucking bitch!"

This time, the blow reaches my ribs. Although my attacker appears fuzzy, I know precisely who it is: it's Loretta, Ireela's mother—the same woman who tried to attack me in Eden, accusing me of being responsible for Ireela's death.

She raises her leg, prepared to drop her boot into my face when four women jump on top of her and pull her to the ground.

"Break it up!" comes a man's voice.

Women are piled on the ground, refusing to move. They're not Eden's women, either. I don't recognize them, and yet they still came to my defense without hesitation.

"Enough!" comes that same aggressive voice.

I sit up and rub the side of my face when the man storms toward the dog pile and with one hand, pulls one of my protectors away from the fight. They're so different in size that she dangles in the air as if she's made of paper, arm twisted backward and face contorted in pain.

"Let me go!" she shouts.

Then, without thinking, I lunge to my feet and charge straight for the man.

"Get your fucking hands off her, you fucking male piece of shit!"

Swinging both arms, I punch him in the chest and in the face. I'm not certain whether I caught him off guard, or whether I'm stronger than I give myself credit for, but he retreats covering his twisted face with his arms for protection, and I don't stop swinging.

A droplet of blood splatters onto my lip and I lick it up. Voices grow louder around me, but the only thing I can think about is killing this man. It's as if I've lost all control of my own body—as if it's no longer my own, but rather, controlled by some unseen force.

Adrenaline surges through me as footsteps approach.

I'm not certain who is near, or who is involved, but the next thing I know, I'm being pulled back by two firm arms. I kick the air and throw my head backward, attempting to break the person's nose.

"It's okay," comes the voice behind me.

It enrages me even more when I realize it's another man.

"It's okay," he repeats, his voice smooth and monotone. "I'm not going to hurt you. I need you to calm down."

I'm not sure how long it takes me to finally calm down, but once it happens, the pain in my face sets in and my eye begins to swell. I watch as Loretta is pulled away by two women in combat clothing. What are they going to do with her? Lock her up? What about the man who hurt that small woman? Are they going to do anything to him?

My heart is beating so hard I'm afraid I resemble a frog croaking with how hard my throat must be pulsating.

The man I attacked is on the ground with a face so bloody he's beyond recognition.

Did I do that? Why can't I remember? I remember attacking him, but I don't recall injuring him so badly.

Vrin storms through the crowd. She must have been contacted by one of her soldiers the moment the fight broke out. "What the hell happened here?"

"A woman attacked Eve," someone says.

"And he hurt Daisy," says another woman, pointing at the bloody-faced man. "So Eve protected her."

Vrin glowers at me. "You call that protection? You could have disfigured him."

She stares at me, nostrils flared, then at the man lying motionless in the grass. I can imagine what she must be thinking: she wants to punish me for my act of violence but is afraid of retaliation from her women.

If I were in her position, that's what I would be thinking.

She's powerless.

"I don't tolerate violence," Vrin growls.

Her stare is so hateful I wonder if she regrets bringing me along.

"She was protecting us!" comes another voice, and several supporting "Yeahs" spread through the crowd.

Vrin's jaw muscles pop out. Surely, her brain is firing so fast she doesn't know how to respond. So instead of punishing me, she threatens me.

"If this happens again, Eve, I'm locking you up."

I smile, and although it may come across as an apologetic smile, it's the farthest thing from it. The truth is, Vrin has given me power; she's unknowingly put me in an advantageous position.

I've proven myself capable of protecting these women, and now I'm being unfairly treated by the leader of Elysium. I, the one person who's responsible for saving all of these women's lives, am being threatened.

The moment Vrin turns away with clenched, bony fists, the women rush to my aid.

I reach for my bloody eyebrow and wince.

"Are you okay, Eve?"

"Oh my God, is she all right?"

I raise a hand, and when I try to stand, two women help me to my feet. "I'm all right thanks to you. All of you." I glance toward the beaten man, who is now being transported toward the Medical Unit on a gurney. "I'm sorry for how I reacted," I say, even though I owe no one an apology. "I didn't mean to become so violent. But the way he touched you—" I press the back of my hand against my mouth and turn away as if on the verge of crying.

"You did the right thing, Eve!" says a woman with chaotic hair and torn clothing. I'm assuming she's one of the women who grabbed Loretta. "We can't let men think they can get away with that!"

Everyone around me nods furiously.

I smirk. "No, we can't."

CHAPTER 26 – GABRIEL

It reminds me of my old room.

Overall, it's pretty plain. The walls are as white as they were when this place was called Area 82. The bed at the corner is perfectly made, almost like the sheets are made of plastic. Not a single ripple or crease is visible.

I drop my bag down and sigh.

Two weeks of therapy to end up where everything started. At least I'm not having violent flashbacks. I guess the therapy does work after all. It's sad to think that people in the past suffered from PTSD for years and years, or that a bunch of them committed suicide because of it.

Now, here I am, healed after a few lousy weeks. It makes me feel guilty, in a way, even though I shouldn't feel that way. That's how technology works. One day, some new piece of equipment is released, and it saves hours and hours of work in manual labor or it saves someone who would have otherwise died.

"How are you feeling?" Valeria asks.

She stands at my doorway with a small black booklet held firmly against her chest. I'm not sure why she's carrying around a booklet when all she does is take notes with her glasses.

"I'm fine," I say.

She lowers her head, and without saying anything stares at me over the rim of her glasses. I'm guessing that's translation for, *Are you sure?* Either that, or she's trying to figure out whether or not I'm lying about how I feel.

When I don't say anything, she straightens her head and says, "You may be tired in the coming days. This is a residual effect of the Nepalt 4000. I am, however, clearing you for release into the general population."

General population? What the fuck is this? Prison? I don't voice it. I'm scared she'll write me up as being aggressive or something. Then I'll really be in prison. Or, I'll be spending another two weeks with wires attached to my brain and a mouthguard in my mouth.

No thanks.

Again, I don't say anything, so she forces a smile that looks like a painful twitch.

"It was a pleasure working with you, Gabriel. If you begin to experience any side effects," she pauses like she's expecting me to ask her what she's talking about, "come and see me."

I won't lie. I want to question her on it. She didn't say anything to me about side effects before the program started. So what kind of side effects is she talking about? But I keep my mouth shut. All I want to do right now is sleep.

She spins on her heels and walks away. Without turning around, she says, "Close door 521," and my door slides shut. I'm guessing she has the authority to control pretty much anything around here.

The moment I throw myself onto my bed and close my eyes, I disappear like I drank an entire keg of beer.

* * * * * *

"Rodriguez!"

Where's that voice coming from? Why can't I see anything? A gunshot goes off, but the moment it does, I forget what the sound was. Fireworks? An instrument?

A flash of light makes the blackness around me go away, and for a split second, I see a lineup of men wearing military uniforms and firing guns at each other. But every time a bullet comes out, it melts to the ground and instead, confetti comes pouring out of the gun barrels.

What the fuck is going on?

"Oh, my sweet Gabriel."

I turn around to find my mom standing next to me. With rosy cheeks, she carries a tray of freshly baked muffins. A small line of steam comes out of them and the chocolate chips on top look soft and tender.

"Are you hungry, my sweet Gabriel?"

* * * * * *

A soft beeping sound echoes nearby.

I crack my eyes open. Where am I? I turn onto my elbow in my bed, realizing where I am. How long have I been out? And why's my back drenched in cold sweat?

The beep goes off again. What the hell is that?

"Gabriel?"

That voice. It's Freyda.

"Open door," I say.

The second the door opens, Freyda steps into my room with Justice by her side. I'm happy to see Justice, but I can't stop looking at Freyda. She smiles at me, her long dark hair pulled over one shoulder.

"How're you?" she asks.

I sit up, clear my throat, and rub my hand through my hair to try to make it look presentable. I'm sure it looks like shit. I haven't had a haircut in months and there's a good chance it's flat at the back from the pillow.

"I'm all right. Close door."

Then, almost as if Justice only now realizes I'm in the room, she freaks out and runs toward me. Well, she tries to, but the first ten seconds is spent running in the same spot, her nails scratching the hard, tiled floor.

She jumps onto the bed and lunges straight for my face. At first, it's warm and it tickles, but then it gets slimy.

"Okay, okay," I say, pulling her off. "I missed you, too."

She wags her tail as I pat her on the head. I make my way behind her ears and she closes her eyes.

"Someone missed you," Freyda says.

I look up at her. Maybe deep down, she's referring to herself. Probably not. But a guy can dream.

"Have a seat," I say, pointing at the white metal chair by my dresser.

Instead of sitting, she smiles and removes a bag from her shoulder. Justice hops off the bed and stands on her hind legs to sniff it. That's when I notice her pink collar and leash. It's pretty cute and it suits her gray coat. Her little tail wags from side to side and she tries to shove her whole head in the bag.

"So apparently," Freyda says, "pets aren't supposed to live in these quarters. Ruby and Pearl are both in the East wing."

I'm assuming she's talking about her horse and maybe another pet.

"But I spoke with Vrin," she continues, "and convinced her that Justice is going to be a therapy dog."

She pulls from her bag two stainless steel bowls and a container of dry food. It looks like kibble, only broken up in a weird way. It isn't the kind of dog food you'd find in a grocery store, so I'm assuming it's made right here in Elysium.

"When you run out," she says, "go see Hani Rahn in room 103 of the East Wing."

I cock an eyebrow at her. How the hell does she expect me to remember that? She must know what I'm thinking; she gives me a crooked smile, places the bowls down, and sits beside me on the bed.

My palms get clammy the second she sits. I look down at her thigh, now a few inches from mine. It's firm and small and makes me want to move closer to her.

Jesus Christ. How does she make me this nervous?

"Don't worry," she says, patting my thigh, "I'll remind you where it is when you need it."

I look at her, and for the first time, she doesn't look away or tell me off. Why? Before all of this, she was pretty harsh with me. So what's changed? Was it me being gone for so long?

She must have some sort of sixth sense. She forces a smile and looks away from me.

"I don't know you well yet, Gabriel, but I can tell you're a good guy. I'm sorry for being such a bitch before. You just..." She looks up at me, but only for a second before staring at her fingers again. "You feel familiar, and I guess that scares me. I've lost everything familiar to me. You know?"

I do know.

"When that engine backfired and you reacted the way you did," she continues, "I thought you were a goner. I was sure they'd either lock you up or throw you out of Elysium for being unstable."

I open my mouth to say something along the lines of *I'm still here*, but she lets out a soft sigh so I keep my mouth shut.

"I'm glad you're okay."

She looks up at me, and this time doesn't look away. Her eyes move from mine to my lips, and I can't help but do the same.

All I want to do is kiss those perfectly plush lips of hers. They're a light shade of red, and she licks them gently, making them look warm and inviting.

I can't even remember the last time I kissed a woman. I can't remember... I can't remember anything. I can't even think. Why am I trying to think?

Just do it, I tell myself, and without thinking, I move in, pressing my lips against hers. At first, it's soft and sweet, but then she digs her fingers into my thigh and lets out a hard breath through her nostrils. She slips her tongue into my mouth and makes swaying motions with her head, a steady rhythm that gets me excited.

Instantly, I go hard, feeling like a virgin teenage boy.

"Fr-Freyda—" I try. The last thing I want is for her to do something she'll regret. This feels like it's coming out of nowhere.

"Shut up," she says, pushing me flat on my back.

Her breath is fast and strong and her kisses are turning into teasing bites.

Holy shit. Is this happening?

She pulls up my shirt, slides her hand into my pants, and grabs my penis.

Everything around me starts swirling.

She's about to start teasing me some more, but I don't know how much more I can handle. I flip her onto her back and climb on top. She lets out a playful, excited laugh.

She wants this.

She wants me.

I want this.

I want her.

For a second, we make eye contact, and she stares at me like she's trying to read my mind. There's a strong connection between us, something I've never felt before. It's like our bodies are emitting some form of energy and the energy is merging and growing more powerful.

I smile at her before sliding her pants off with my

index finger, tracing her soft skin. She welcomes me by spreading her legs apart, her way of saying, *Take me.*

And that's exactly what I do.

CHAPTER 27 – LUCY

"What's up with you?" Emily asks.

I must be coming across as PMSing, which might be confusing for her if she hasn't yet gotten her first period. That's something I wish Mom had been around to explain to me. But Nola did a good job explaining everything. Plus, living in an all-female society helps with that. In Eden, everyone had access to clean cotton rags for the time of the month.

I haven't said a word for the last thirty minutes, so finally, before entering the Library, I let out a defeated sigh and raise my H-Cap into the air. "It's my stupid H-Cap."

"What about it?" she asks.

She seems genuinely concerned, which I'm guessing means she's over the little spat we had.

"It won't charge," I say, playing with it in my hands.

We turn the corner of the hall and enter the Library's massive archway. It's constructed of cherry wood and is as shiny as wet metal. The only thing that looks old in this entire place is the Library—not ugly old, but basic old. There isn't much technology inside the place, and although I love technology, it's nice to get away from it all.

It's the third time I've come here, and every time I do, I'm amazed at how huge this place is. Natural light fills the room through the windows overhead, and hundreds upon hundreds of finely polished wooden shelves decorate every wall in sight. They're all lined up evenly, and on them sit thousands of multicolored paperback books.

An entire section is devoted to fiction, but for the most part, the books in this Library are works of nonfiction on history, medicine, physics, psychology, politics, and so much more. I keep finding myself in the medical area. Once, I caught Mavis and Perula scanning the shelves. They made their way over to the botanical section, but it was obvious that they were also interested in regular medicine, too.

Today, I'm not studying medicine. What I need is an answer to fix my H-Cap. Surely, there are several books on electrotechnology. Maybe I'll even find something specific to H-Cap; it isn't far-fetched to hope for this. I've seen all kinds of instructional booklets and user manuals on the shelves. The other day, an S-MAID Robot user manual was left in the middle of the Library on the carpet floor. Someone must have dropped it, and I assume they're having trouble with a few of the cleaning robots around here.

"So, what do you need?" Emily asks, poking her head around and pulling books out with her index finger to see the covers.

"Anything on electrical devices or a user's manual for H-Caps."

She nods without looking at me and keeps scanning the shelves.

"Hey, look!" Emily shouts, and a loud *Shhhh,* echoes around us.

She tucks her head into her shoulders and slaps a hand over her mouth.

"What is it?" I whisper, moving toward her in a rush.

Did she find a manual? If so, that was fast. But when I reach her side, she giggles and points at the cover in her hands. The title reads, *Robots are Taking Over the World,* and I roll my eyes.

"Oh please," I say. "Apparently, they've been saying that for a century and it hasn't happened. Robots are tools, nothing else."

With flat lips, she pushes the book back into its place. "It was only a joke."

"Well, the book isn't," I say. "Whoever wrote it meant what they said."

"How do you know?" she asks. "Maybe it's satire."

Not quite certain how to respond, I stare at her. Being bitchy with her isn't my intention. I'm scared I won't be able to fix my H-Cap, and if I can't fix it, I'll never see my mom again.

She must sense what I'm thinking and pats my shoulder. "We'll find the right book, Lucy. Let's keep looking, okay? I'll stop messing around."

We scan the shelves for what feels like hours, pulling and plucking at all kinds of different books. Why can't I find anything? There has got to be something. When I reach the end of one of the massive bookcases, I swing around it to start walking down the next aisle, but I don't make it very far.

I'm stopped midtrack when I bump into someone

and they drop three books on the floor.

"Oh my God," I say. "I'm so sorry."

He picks up his books and stands up tall with that familiar sweet smile on his face.

"All good," Lucas says.

"Oh," I say. "H-hey. What're you doing here?"

This time, he grins. It's like he's addicted to smiling. "I come here every day," he says. "I grab a few books, sit by the window, and read through them."

I scoff. "In a single day? No one can read that fast."

He stares at me, looking confused. "What are you talking about? Of course they can. It's called speed-reading."

I'm at a loss for words. It sounds like a joke. Speed-reading? I've never heard of that in my life.

"I'm not joking, Lucy. How do you think I know everything that I know? I'm seventeen. It's not like I've gone to college or university. I didn't even finish sch—" but he cuts himself short and clears his throat like he's already said too much, or like the memory's too painful to revisit. "I can show you sometime if you'd like."

I brush my hair behind my right ear and smile up at him. "Um, y-yeah. I'd like that—"

"Who's this?" comes Emily's voice.

Lucas's piercing blue eyes roll toward Emily and he waits in silence.

Without looking away from Lucas, I say, "Emily, Lucas. Lucas, Emily."

They shake hands and both say, "Nice to meet you," but then an awkward silence weighs us down. Emily clears her throat and keeps walking down the book aisle. She looks back at me behind Lucas and with big bulging eyes, gives me two thumbs-up.

Fighting the urge to laugh, I look down and smirk at my own feet.

"That's not a book," Lucas says, pointing at my H-Cap.

I take it out from underneath my armpit and rub my thumbs against its exterior shell. "No, it isn't."

"Do you mind?" he asks, reaching for it.

I don't have time to react, so he slips it out from my fingers and examines it.

"Looks like second generation." He gently rotates it, inspecting every inch of it.

I'm not sure what he's talking about, so I don't say anything. Then, when he presses the power button and nothing happens, he cocks an eyebrow at me.

"Let me guess," he says, "it won't charge."

I nod, though what I want to do is cry.

"Mind if I borrow it?" he asks.

I'm about to argue that it's mine and I'd never let anyone borrow it when he adds, "I can fix this for you no problem."

My jaw drops and he laughs at what I'm assuming is the face I'm making.

"It's pretty common," he says. "I've fixed hundreds of little electronic devices around Elysium. There are certain components inside that were fried by the EMP, and all I have to do is replace the part."

I'm about to ask him how many spare parts he has when, as if reading my mind, he says, "And it's pretty easy to replace parts when you're the one who makes them."

"You *make* the parts?" I ask.

He shrugs modestly. "Yeah. It's not that hard. I mean, Vrin's given me access to all her labs, equipment, and tools."

I don't know what to say. How does a seventeen-year-old know so much? I'm going to be seventeen next year, and now, I feel like an idiot. The most skill I have is my ability to mix a few potions and tell someone to drink ginger tea if their stomach is upset.

This guy knows everything... What am I doing with my life?

"Sorry," he says. "I'm not trying to brag at all. That's the last thing I want to do. I love this stuff. I like to be kept busy and I like to work."

"You're smart," I say, and it sounds stupid coming out of my mouth.

He shrugs with one shoulder. "It's not about being smart," he says. "I'm resourceful. And in a world like this, you have to be resourceful and you have to be the very best version of yourself if you want to survive. The way I see it... if I'm really good at something, I become indispensable."

I arch an eyebrow wondering if he thinks I'm *dispensable*.

He quickly raises both hands and says, "I don't mean it to be offensive. Look, I-I'm gonna stop talking now since I keep putting my foot in my mouth. Can I please fix this for you? It would make me happy."

"Sure," I say. "I mean... I'd appreciate it."

He sighs and presses the H-Cap against his chest. Behind him, Emily is waving at me to come join her, so I step away from Lucas as a way of saying, *I have to go.*

"Thanks, Lucas... for doing this for me. It means the world."

"It's my pleasure, honestly," he says. "I'm sorry if I was offensive in any way. I think you're incredible. I'd never want you to think that I believe otherwise."

Incredible?

I smile. "I'm not offended."

He lets out a long breath and bows his head. "Okay, good. And I meant what I said. If you ever want to learn how to speed-read, I'm happy to show you. I've seen you in here with medical books. I could show you how to finish them within a few hours."

I'm too stunned to say anything. The thought of being able to devour a book in a few hours blows my mind.

"Just think about it," he says.

"N-n-no, yeah. I mean, yeah," I say. "I'd love to."

The corner of his lip reveals his sharp canine tooth and I can't help but stare.

"Lucy!" Emily hisses.

"I'll, um, catch you later," I say.

"See you later, Lucy."

My name sounds so good coming out of his mouth. He has a deep voice, though not too deep, and every time he talks, I feel calm. I step away before I make some cheesy comment or make a fool of myself. I've never felt this way around anyone before, and it's freaking me out.

"Check it out," Emily says, pointing at one of the Library's oversized windows.

I stare through the glass and into the courtyard.

At the very far back, Freyda is swinging a stick over her head, around her shoulders, and straight into the faces of men trying to take her down. It's obvious by all of the weaponry and wooden targets around her that she's training—not fighting.

"Holy shit," I breathe.

The best version of yourself, I think.

I turn to Emily, our noses nearly touching. "How would you feel about learning how to fight?"

CHAPTER 28 – EVE

I stare at the coffee table in silence, analyzing every inch of Elysium's blueprints.

Though I enjoy having someone nearby to obey any command, I miss being alone. For the last few weeks, Mary-Anne has followed me throughout all of Elysium. Today, however, she is attending a friend's wedding celebration.

It makes me sick to my stomach to think that a woman from Elysium would be willing to marry a man... After everything they've done.

That's unimportant—soon, I will be the one who dictates whether weddings are to be held at all. And if I'm to eventually become leader of Elysium, it's important that I know every corner. Returning my focus to the coffee table, I can't help but wonder: how did they miss this? How did they not know that this coffee table—a secret map of Elysium—existed? Perhaps back before the war, it was intended to be secretive.

Gazing around the bright-lit room, I wonder who used to reside in this Monarch Suite, before Elysium. A *man*. It had to be. Disgusted, I wipe my palms against the pants of my legs. It's irrational—no way have germs survived over six years—but I can't resist the movement. It soothes me.

So many details cover the screen: elevator counts, room dimensions, doorway entries, room numbers. For fun, I tap my finger against one of the bedroom numbers and a screen is projected into the air:

Felice Ramsay

Room 703

Above this text is a picture of the woman with dark skin and light gray eyes; I don't recognize her, which means she's one of Elysium's women. Does this mean I have access to locate anyone? Frantically, I start selecting various rooms one at a time and different names and images pop up as fast as lightning.

Where's Freyda? Lucy?

Does this table also possess voice recognition technology? All of a sudden, I feel watched. Are there cameras in my room? No, there can't be. Nayma specified that Elysium's cameras are limited to common living spaces and that privacy is always respected.

No one knows what you're doing, Eve.

Returning my attention to the blueprints, I whisper, "Find me Lucy Cain," and to my surprise, the table listens. A soft beeping sound is emitted before Lucy's picture flashes up in front of me.

She looks exactly like her mother, with long red hair, fiery green eyes, and an awkward expression that sits somewhere in between a smile and a frown.

Lucinda Cain

Room 591

She's growing up so quickly.

I stare at her for a moment until all I see is Ophelia. Then, angrily, I say, "Find me Freyda Mills."

Her image flashes before me, along with her room information.

Freyda Mills.

Room 570

It appears that most of my women have ended up on the fifth floor. I suppose it makes sense to keep the majority of them together.

I reach for Freyda's face and my finger distorts her beauty, making one eye break apart. Why has she not yet forgiven me? She's always been my rock. I need Freyda… I need her more than anyone.

You don't need that bitch, Eve.

Swallowing hard, I slap the air across her face and the image vanishes.

You have hundreds of women lined up to follow you.

Out of curiosity and out of a need to distract myself from emotion, I locate my room. It's amusing to see it from an aerial view. Everything is drawn out: the common space, the kitchen, my bedroom, the bathrooms, and even my bedroom closet. What surprises me, however, is the additional room I know nothing about. It's drawn beside my bedroom, directly behind my closet. Is it additional storage space? Or is this a mistake in the blueprints?

I slap the air at the corner of the table to turn off the display. The last thing I need is to accidentally leave it open for someone to see should they enter my room. Memorizing what I can of the map, I enter my bedroom and open its closet doors—two solid wooden slabs leading into one of the largest walk-in closets I've ever seen.

My white outfits hang at the far right and underneath these, my red heels, stilettoes, and boots. I have no intention of wearing Elysium's common blue attire.

The rest of the closet is bare, which is precisely how I like it. I stare at the side walls, the corners, the ceiling, and then the very back wall. According to the map, an entryway should be somewhere at the back.

I walk through the closet, brushing my fingers along the walls.

Is there a button? Or, is this also controlled by voice recognition?

"Open door," I say loudly, but nothing happens. Frustrated, I start prodding and pulling at anything I can find. "Come on. Open up."

Still, nothing happens.

Perhaps the map was wrong and is unreliable. It may have been drawn out but never built. I lean my back against the wall and, out of frustration, allow my head to hit the drywall several times.

Without warning, the wall behind me trembles and splits right down the middle revealing a large opening. It's dark—so dark, in fact, that I can't see anything.

"Turn on the lights," I say, and nothing happens.

It's apparent that this room isn't controlled by APHRODITE.

I reach a hand inside and cringe when cobwebs touch my fingers. But then, I feel a cold metal light switch and I turn it on. Bulbs flicker overhead, and within seconds, the entire room lights up.

Although dusty, it's in good shape. A dozen hanging lights are evenly spread out across the ceiling, though one of them is burned out. Their cool white light reflects off the round metal table sitting at the center of the room, and around this table are four chairs large enough to sit two people. Papers, books, and pens lie atop the table in a disorderly fashion. Some of these are news clippings from during the war with headlines such as:

WOMEN ARE OUT OF CONTROL

MEN, GET READY TO SAVE AMERICA

THIS STOPS NOW

It angers me to read the headlines, so I'm careful not to look at the articles. I move closer to the table and search through the hundreds of papers, trying to make sense of this place. Then, images of advanced weaponry jump out at me like ants on a white picnic table.

They're like nothing I've ever seen before—guns, launchers, and even military vehicles that look like something taken from the future. The guns are barely guns at all; they're small rods with simple handles, and underneath the images are descriptive details regarding their use, power, and purpose.

My heart begins to pound hard at the thought of men sitting around this table, discussing machinery capable of wiping out thousands of women. What happened? Did they not have enough time to build their precious weapons? Did the war happen too soon for their liking?

I'm about to start shuffling through the vehicle

prototypes when someone calls out my name.

"Eve?"

It grows louder and louder, and that's when I realize someone's inside my living quarters.

"Fuck," I mutter, rushing out of the secret room.

As I exit through my closet, Nola appears in front of me with her wild hair tied into a bun. She isn't wearing her tight nurse scrubs anymore—instead, she's changed into Elysium's standard blue cotton. I instinctively reach for my hanging clothes and pull them to the center of the closet, hoping to hide the opening.

"A-are you all right?" Nola asks, craning her neck to see behind me.

"I'm fine," I hiss. "How did you get in here?"

"Your door was open," she says, still trying to see behind me.

I move toward her so quickly that she backs out, and the moment we're both out of the closet, I slam its doors shut.

"What do you mean, *it was open?*"

"That nice lady Mary-Anne told me I could find you here. When I got here, your door was open. I thought maybe you were hurt."

I glare at her.

Is she lying?

But then, I realize something—I shouted "Open door" when attempting to enter the secret room. Perhaps APHRODITE misinterpreted my command and opened my main door.

Oh God. How much did Nola see? Did she see inside? Does she know there's a room hidden inside my closet?

"Are you all right?" Nola asks.

I force a smile—the last thing I need is to display fear or anxiety. All that will do is make Nola suspicious and she'll question why I'm being so paranoid.

"I'm doing well, Nola. I'm so sorry... I must have forgotten to close it. You know me"—I playfully flick my wrist in the air—"always so much on my mind." I force a laugh and it comes out sounding more genuine than I expected. "If my head weren't attached to my shoulders, Nola, I'm sure I'd lose it."

She lets out a soft laugh and shakes her head. "I'm glad you're okay. They're serving lunch. Someone told me that the alarm system for the twelfth floor isn't working right now. Something to do with upgrading APHRODITE. I thought I'd pop in to let you know."

"Oh, Nola," I say, tickling the back of her neck even though all I want to do is strangle her.

She's a traitor.

A fucking traitor who's making Lucy doubt you.

"You are so thoughtful," I say. "I'll be right there."

She smiles at me, uncertain. Does she know what I'm thinking, or did she see the room? I stare back, waiting for her to leave.

"Okay," she says at last. "I'll, um... I'll see you later, Eve."

She leaves my Monarch Suite, and I wait a few minutes. Once I'm certain she's far enough, I make my way to the eating lounge.

The moment I get there, a young woman wearing rimless glasses and a necklace resembling something made by a three-year-old child grins and points at the empty seat beside her. There are numerous other chairs across the eating lounge, but they all appear to be taken. It's obvious this woman jumped up from her seat to give me her spot.

I smile at her and sit, feeling dozens upon dozens of eyes on me.

How many days have they been waiting for me to join them? I've been spending most of my time in my Monarch Suite, eating foods produced by the Chepire fridge to avoid socialization.

Now, I feel pressured to say something.

"Thank you," I say.

With her grin now taking up half her face, the woman slouches down to whisper something to her friends. It's like watching high school girls giggle over a crush.

Then, one by one, chairs start to screech across the tiled floor. Slowly, women circle me as if surrounding Jesus himself. Not all of them—some remain at a distance, observing like curious gazelles in the wild. There must be at least forty women around me right now. It's become even more apparent that I've drawn a crowd now that half the eating lounge is looking emptier and emptier at the corners. Even children are getting up from their miniature tables and colorful play blocks to join their mothers.

"I suppose you're all waiting for me to say something," I say, forcing a silly laugh.

The women join in on the laughter, glazed eyes never leaving mine.

Who needs Devil's Tea when I have women like

this?

Then, the woman who gave me her seat gets down on one knee and looks up at me.

"You don't have to say anything," she says. "We—" she glances at the other women, almost as if waiting for their permission to say whatever it is she's about to say. Several of them nod at her, while others simply stare. "We have something to ask you."

I smile, the genuine reaction causing the muscles of my face to feel foreign to me. How can I not smile? These women are gathered around me as if I were some ancient Greek goddess.

"Anything," I say.

"C-can you talk to Vrin?" she asks.

This catches me off guard. I was expecting to be asked about Eden and how I saved hundreds of women following the war. Why on Earth are they talking to me about Vrin? What does she have to do with me?

Another woman steps forward, her freckled arms crossed over her belly. With shoulders slouched and brows so slanted they look out of place on her forehead, she reminds me of an abuse victim.

"Things have changed around here... gradually." She, too, looks at the women for either encouragement or guidance. She must have received what she wanted; she continues, her voice trembling. "When we first came here, Vrin separated the men and women. Within the first year, she reintegrated us. It was hard at first—"

"Hard? It was a nightmare!"

"It wasn't that bad."

"Maybe for those who have husbands or children."

"Guys, shut up. You know we can't talk about this."

"I'm not saying it wasn't a good thing," says the shy woman. "It was, for the most part. There are a lot of good men here. We're not saying they're bad."

I fight off the urge to glower at her for her ignorance.

"The problem now is that Vrin's using the men for combat. She uses women, too, but it's mostly men she has as soldiers."

I stare at her. I understand why she feels uneasy about the situation, but I want to allow her to voice it aloud. She parts her lips when another woman cuts in.

"We all remember how fast men turned on us back in the day. Sure, the good ones didn't agree with it. But what did they do? Nothing. They didn't do anything. So who's to say that one rotten apple won't spoil the bunch? It's only a matter of time before some new guy becomes a soldier and decides that men should be in charge of Elysium. They have the guns, the training... It wouldn't be hard for them. All it takes is one bullet to take Vrin out and force us into submission. We don't like it, Eve. We don't like it at all. We've dealt with male soldiers in the past... We haven't come this far to deal with it again."

I elevate my chin and smile down at her.

She needs you, Eve.

They all need you.

"Don't you worry, my magnificent ladies," I say, and the tension dissipates almost instantly. "I'll take care of this."

CHAPTER 29 – GABRIEL

"Room 700," Nayma says, pointing up at the ceiling like that's supposed to help me.

She's preoccupied. All I want to know is where to find Vrin's office, and she's trying to brush me off.

"You okay?" I ask. I barely know the woman, but it's clear something's bothering her. She waves a hand dismissively and stares at the wall, though what she's truly staring at is a projection in her glasses.

"I'm trying to fix something, Gabriel. Could we please talk later? I don't want to be rude with you."

Whatever she's fixing, it must be pretty damn important. So I nod, even though she isn't looking at me. "Of course. Good luck with the repair."

She doesn't say anything. Instead, her frown hardens, and she starts prodding at the air in front of her.

Poor Nayma. She looks stressed out. It's probably related to APHRODITE since she's the one in charge of all that.

I make my way to the elevators and up to the seventh floor. It's weird being out in public like this. Every now and then, a woman gives me a nasty look. It doesn't make me angry. It hurts. I didn't mean to jump on those women like that. And now, some of them look at me like I'm a ticking time bomb.

I can't focus on them, though. There are plenty of others who are welcoming me into Elysium's society and asking how I'm feeling and if I'm doing better.

Room 700, I repeat to myself, scanning the room numbers down the corridor. Every door looks the same until I actually reach Room 700. A double door stands tall with two big silver handles, something I'm not used to seeing anymore. Everything's so advanced around here, even more advanced than when it was Area 82, so it's rare to see a regular door handle.

I haven't seen Vrin since she first admitted me into Valeria's care, but I need to see her now. I have to tell her how thankful I am for everything she's done. Without her, I'd no doubt be back in Eden's basement, imprisoned by Eve.

Raising a fist into the air, I knock on the door.

"Come in," comes Vrin's voice.

I reach for the handle, twist it, and gently push the door open. At first, she seems surprised to see me. She's sitting behind a big black desk, leaning over it with both elbows resting on its surface. She stares at me from above reading glasses that hang off her nose. I've never seen her with glasses. It makes her look a bit older. She drops the pen she's holding, sits up, and takes off her glasses.

"Gabriel," she says. "This is a surprise."

When I don't say anything, she points at the chair in front of her desk. "Have a seat."

I do as I'm told and sit down, feeling a bit awkward. The last time I was in an office with Vrin, it was in the

Oval Office. The memory makes this office look like a broom closet. It's nice, sleek, and extremely modern, but it doesn't compare to the Oval Office.

I think back, remembering how she was yelling at Eve to leave while Eve held onto the woman she'd killed. She had no idea I was there, and she still doesn't know.

We stare at each other for a few seconds, and even though I'm looking right at her, all I see in front of me are vivid memories. I can't stop thinking about telling her that I *know*.

I keep my mouth shut.

Vrin seems nice, but I don't know her. At least not well enough to tell her I was there that day. What if she locks me up?

She leans back in her chair and it makes a creaking noise. "Are you all right?"

Clearing my throat, I straighten my back and force a smile. "Yeah, I'm good. Actually, that's why I'm here. I wanted to... I wanted to thank you." I stare at the boot marks on the floor. It's the first time I see a dirty floor in all of Elysium. Obviously, Vrin isn't as particular as Eve when it comes to cleanliness. I'm sure that's a good thing. "I, um, I can't thank you enough, Vrin. The nightmares have stopped. It's all gone. All the horrible memories. I mean, they're there, but they aren't *there* if you know what I mean."

She smirks and nods slowly. "I do know, Gabriel. You've disassociated from your memories."

She says it like she's been through it before. Maybe she has. She was in the military, after all. So no doubt she suffered from PTSD, too.

"So, thank you," I repeat.

She's still smiling with narrow eyes. The kind of eyes that express love and happiness. I'm assuming that's her way of saying, *You're welcome.*

I don't get it. She's nothing like Eve. So why'd she associate with her during the war? What's bothering me even more is… Why did she and Eve go separate ways? Why didn't they stick together? Maybe Eve wouldn't have turned out the way she did if Vrin had been in charge.

Did she disapprove of what Eve had done?

"Is there anything else, Gabriel?"

I shift in my chair. "Actually, I was wondering if I could talk to you about—"

But then, something fucked up happens. The lights flicker and a soft hum fills the room before everything goes quiet. It's so quiet that I hear myself take a breath.

I feel like I'm back in the Oval Office hiding in the dark cabinet.

"What's going on?" I ask.

Vrin growls. "God damn it. Nayma told me this wouldn't happen."

"What wouldn't happen?" I ask.

"APHRODITE's shut down," she says. "It's part of an APHRODITE update. We have a few backup systems, but everything locks down when this happens."

"So all the doors are locked?" I ask.

She waves a hand and huffs and I get the sense she wants me out of here.

"Is there anything I can do to help?" I ask.

"There isn't much anyone can do to help," she says. "Cameras are all out, so let's hope no one gets lost. Elevators won't move, so anyone with physical disabilities is stuck if they can't use the stairs. Unless Nayma gets APHRODITE back up and running soon, we're fucked."

CHAPTER 30 – LUCY

"Stay focused," Freyda says.

It's hard to stay focused with a dog that cute a few feet away from me. She barks, though it comes out as more of a high-pitched cry, and I melt.

"She only wants off her leash to play," I say.

"Gabriel asked me to keep an eye on her," Freyda says, "and I can't do that if she's running around the entire courtyard."

She swings a fist at me and I bring up a block pad like she taught me. She has a strong punch, but she's going easy on me. I don't even want to know how hard she can hit when she's not holding back.

"Right here." She pats her stomach and I throw a kick at it. "No, not like that. You need to stabilize your core when you kick. And keep your hands up to protect your face."

"Who's gonna hit me in the face when I'm kicking my whole leg out?"

I do it again and out of nowhere, Emily slaps me across the face.

I stumble backward and reach for my cheek. "Emily! What the hell?"

Freyda bursts out laughing harder than I've ever

heard her laugh before.

"Gotta have eyes all around your head," Emily says, repeating word for word what Freyda told us a few minutes ago.

Rubbing my cheek, I glare at Emily. "You didn't have to hit so hard."

"Come on," Freyda says, "try it again."

I do as she says, and my kick comes out much better this time. I've kicked at her over a hundred times now, and every time I do, she finds a way to correct me more and more. But this last kick, she doesn't say anything other than, "Awesome."

I must be getting a bit better.

Emily continues practicing with one of Freyda's friends. It's a young guy in his twenties who seems to be as good as Freyda. He knows what he's doing, and although Emily's having a hard time keeping up, she's learning slowly, like me.

Fighting to catch my breath, I raise a hand and say, "Time out."

My back's drenched in sweat and my throat is so dry I can barely swallow.

Freyda hands me a metallic water bottle and I chug the whole thing.

"I'm glad you came out here today," Freyda says. "I have a lot I want to show you."

I point at a dozen targets lined up against a wooden wall at the far corner. A handful of men and women are doing target practice with bows, crossbows, and pellet guns. "Like that?"

Freyda smirks at me. "Not yet. But we'll get there. Basics come first."

I wipe my mouth. "Where'd you learn all of this?"

She shrugs. "I grew up in martial arts. My dad was obsessed with them. He even taught me Krav Maga. Then when I grew up, I became a cop and learned how to handle weapons."

"Krav Maka?" I say.

Freyda chuckles. "Maga. It's Israeli. One of the deadliest martial arts out there." She turns her attention to a man and woman fighting each other. They look alike, both with dark features, and are fighting in a way I've never seen before. The man pulls out a knife, and within seconds, the woman has him on the ground and the knife's in the grass. "Yael and her brother are both heavily trained in Krav Maga. I'll teach you the basics, but if you want to learn from the best, that's who you want to talk to."

I recognize that woman, Yael, but I don't know her very well. I had no idea she knew how to fight. She's always seemed so quiet and reserved.

Freyda looks out across the courtyard toward Elysium. "Where the hell is he?" she breathes.

She's referring to Gabriel—the man who jumped on those women when we first got to Elysium. Apparently, he's all better now, and he and Freyda are friends. I wonder if Nola had anything to do with helping him get better. I barely see her these days. She's been so busy working in the Medical Unit that I've seen her maybe a handful of times. And every time I run into her, she says she's too busy to talk and is only out to get supplies.

I hope the virus will stabilize soon so I can spend time with Nola again. The last time we spoke, it was rushed and in the middle of a hallway. She said they had most of it under control and that so far, there were no casualties. I bet Eve isn't taking that too well—had she stayed in power and had we stayed in Eden, dozens of women would have died.

She must feel pretty stupid.

"He should be here—" but she stops talking and instead, glares with a hand over her eyes to block out the sun. "What's going on over there?"

I turn toward where she's looking. More and more people are coming out of Elysium and into the courtyard. Something's up; I've never seen the courtyard this full of people before. Why are they leaving Elysium to come outside? And why aren't the doors closing? Two men stand on either side like they've manually pried them apart.

"Miller," Freyda shouts.

A tall woman with shaggy brown hair over her eyebrows and a scrawny build turns around.

"What's going on?" Freyda asks.

The woman, Miller, shrugs and says, "Something about a system outage. A bunch of people are locked in their rooms, and us, well, we can't go anywhere."

Scoffing, Freyda picks up a bag of sand and repositions it in the grass. "Looks like we're gonna be out here awhile. Come on, let's keep going."

CHAPTER 31 – EVE

What the hell is he doing here? And why is it so quiet in the hallway?

I clench my fists as I watch Gabriel leave Vrin's office. He makes his way down the vacant hall, looking pressed for time. I know this is Vrin's office because of the blueprints I have access to. I made a promise to the women of Elysium; I promised them that I would discuss their concerns with Vrin.

And now Gabriel is in Vrin's office? What on Earth could he possibly have to talk about with her? I despise that man. He's always getting in the way of everything. I've seen the way he and Freyda have been looking at each other. Last week, I overheard Freyda asking the women of Elysium if they knew where Gabriel's room was located.

Why would she want to know where his room is?

I bite down and my jaw pops. The idea of Freyda and Gabriel together makes me sick to my stomach. Freyda is mine—she should be by my side, not with some *man*.

Stay focused, Eve.

I inhale a deep breath and slowly let it out, feeling my lungs deflate.

With my initial goal in mind, I approach Vrin's door and knock against the wood.

"Not now," she says, her voice stern.

I part my lips, taken aback by her rude response. No one's ever spoken to me this way—not since I became ruler of Eden.

You aren't ruler anymore, Eve.

Vrin's in charge.

You're nothing.

Shut the fuck up.

I knock again, this time, fist blasting on the door.

"What?" she snaps.

Without saying a word, I open the door and step inside. The moment she sees me, she sighs, rubs her forehead, and starts pacing back and forth in front of her oversized desk.

"Eve, this isn't the time. APHRODITE's down."

Does she not care about her women? Does she not care why I'm here? A true leader would care about their people the way I do.

You're the true leader of Elysium, Eve.

"I don't mean to walk in on you," I say. "I realize something's going on... The hallways are empty, and no one is taking the elevators."

"Yes, Eve, something's going on and I'm trying to deal with it."

"Well, there's something I need to discuss with you," I say.

She slaps two hands on her desks and leans forward. "What is it?"

"It's the women of Elysium," I say.

Before I have the time to say anything else, she

scoffs and throws her head back. "Don't you dare talk to me about the women of Elysium."

"Excuse me?" I ask.

I understand she's stressed out, but she's being a complete bitch.

"*Eve, ruler of Eden*," she says mockingly. "That's all you are. A ruler. You want power. I see it in your eyes. So don't you fucking come in here and tell me what's best for my people."

"*Your* people?" I say slowly. "*Your* people wouldn't even be alive if it weren't for me."

She jabs a finger in the air so aggressively I expect it to make a sound. "We wouldn't be in this entire mess if it weren't for you! The whole EMP bullshit! What the fuck were you thinking going through with that?"

I stare at her in awe. "What was I thinking? The EMP wasn't my idea. Zoey's the one who built it. Hundreds of women are the ones who pushed for it."

"No, you pushed for it!"

"And you were part of it," I say calmly. If I allow myself to get as worked up as she is, I'm afraid of what I might do.

She scoffs again and slaps her forehead as if I were some dumb kid. At once, I feel like I've traveled back in time during one of my mother's angry outbursts. "I didn't think it would actually work. At least not nation fucking wide!"

"You know damn well that a single EMP didn't cause this. Women were angry, Vrin. Women all over America. I didn't do this. You can't put this all on me. You can't even put it on Zoey. Thousands of women were involved."

"Maybe," she growls. "But you'd just killed the President of the United States."

Where is all of this anger coming from? I had every right to do what I did. That piece of shit didn't deserve to live.

I saved them.

All of them.

Who the fuck does she think she is putting me down like this?

I inhale a breath so deep it hurts my lungs.

Calm down, Eve.

"I'm not here to fight with you, Vrin. I'm here to ask you to stop arming men. The women aren't comfortable—"

"Don't you fucking tell me what to do!" she yells and saliva splashes out of her mouth. She points that same finger in my face. "Get the hell out of my office. If I ever see your face again, I'll have you banished. You hear me? Stay in your room and stop trying to brainwash my women."

An indescribable rage overwhelms me. How dare she speak to me that way? Threaten me that way? I'm the reason she's alive and yet she treats me like an animal. Had I not killed the president... Had I not pushed for women to attack when they did, we'd all be dead.

"I'm not going anywhere," I say, my voice trembling.

The next thing I know, I'm lying flat on my back atop her office table and her hot breath slips into my nostrils. She grips and regrips my white coat's collar, and if she weren't so angry, I'd think she was trying to kiss me. "Let me make myself perfectly clear," she breathes, and I stare back at her, my heart beating against her forearm. "I'm in charge here. Not you. You're a fucking poison, Eve. You intoxicate the minds of women with your hatred. You were never supposed to survive. Why do you think I went my own way? You're unstable—"

I gasp, realizing something.

"You have the Binaries..." I breathe. "That's why this place is so goddamn advanced. You never wanted me to survive. You sent me on a wild goose chase."

For a moment, it looks like she's about to start laughing. She doesn't—instead, she lowers her head and her brow bones appear to double in size. "You seriously think I'd have let you have power over the greatest minds? You killed your best friend, Eve. You're fucking sick in the head."

"That was an accident!" I snap. I suck in a long breath. I need to calm down. "Why convince me to lead surviving women? *You* did that, not me. You encouraged hundreds of women to follow me!"

She regrips her hold around my collar, her hot breath now slipping into my mouth.

"I had no choice. Countless women would have died if I didn't give them someone to follow. They weren't willing to come with me because of the men. I had to give them someone as angry as you to get them out of the city."

She breathes out again, her warm body pressing hard against mine. "The difference between you and me, Eve, is that I'm a good person with a solid head on my shoulders. I still let you all inside of Elysium because I wanted to save your women. They aren't at fault in this. They're sheep, and all they need is a good shepherd. Not you. They deserve long, happy lives. You're not fit to lead—"

I can't take it anymore. I'm shaking so hard my teeth are clattering.

In one rough movement, I shove her off me and she stumbles backward. I slap my hand on her desk, searching for something I can use to defend myself, and papers fly up into the air. Eventually, something cool touches my fingertips and I snatch it. It feels like a letter opener, but I don't waste any time trying to figure out what it is.

The moment Vrin comes charging back toward me, I swing my arm as hard as I can, aiming the object at her neck, under her jawline.

The first attempt felt like trying to push a pin through a thick piece of rubber—nothing penetrated, but Vrin is so confused by the blow that she reaches for her neck while stumbling backward. She pulls her fingers away from her neck, no doubt expecting to find blood.

With clean fingers, she glowers at me and clenches her jaw.

I can't give her the opportunity to strike. This time, I run toward her with the object held in both of my hands in front of me. She swings a fist but misses and I thrust my two-handed fist up underneath her jaw as hard as I can.

We both grunt at the same time, though Vrin's sound is followed by choking and gargling. Blood splatters across my face—it's warm, silky, even. A few droplets enter my mouth but I don't mind; in fact, something about it satisfies me.

Only moments ago, Vrin thought herself to be in control over me. But now, her life is in my hands and the sensation of power is far greater than anything I've ever felt before.

The moment I pull out the object, blood comes spraying out into a straight line. I must have hit an artery.

She stumbles backward until she hits the back wall of her office, leaving a blood stain that resembles one stroke of a paintbrush. With bloody teeth, she smiles at me. "Even... Even dead... I'm twice the leader... y-y-you'll ever be..."

Shouting as loud as I can, I pull the metal object out of her throat and stab it right back in. Her eyes bulge out before she collapses to the ground. As she falls, I follow her to the ground and force my way on top of her, taking several light punches to the face. But she's so weak that it feels like I'm being hit by a child.

Finally, I manage to slip my arms through her swings, straddling over her stomach. I tear the metal letter opener out of her neck, and blood spews out. It stains my white overcoat and sprinkles across my cheek. She stares up at me, life slowly fading from her eyes. But it isn't enough—I need to hurt her more.

I raise the weapon above my head, and then, fueled by pent-up rage, stab the sharp point straight into her chest.

She kicks the air and I bounce up, but I don't lose

my grip. She has a lot of fight, but it won't last long. Blood pools out of her mouth, and she takes another swing at my face. This time, I hear a crack, but I don't feel anything.

"Die," I hiss. "Fucking die."

Her punches have transformed into gentle taps. Her face is now white and she wraps her hands around her neck in a desperate attempt to stop the bleeding.

But it's useless.

Vibrant red spills through the cracks of her fingers. Pushing the entire weight of my body into my hands, I crush her throat.

She gargles with wide, terrified eyes, and taps my hands as if begging for mercy.

"What's wrong, Vrin? Cat got your tongue?" I can't help but laugh. "You think you're so smart, don't you? No one will know what happened to their precious little leader. If APHRODITE's down, cameras aren't working."

I hate her.

I fucking hate her.

She finally stops slapping my arms but I don't let go—I'm in control and she's helpless and that's precisely what I want.

"Stupid bitch," I mutter. "How dare you—"

In an instant, a faint humming sound fills the room and the sound of doors unlatching echoes in the distance. I pull away and stare at what can only be described as a bloodbath. She's so still, her blue eyes empty and her lips parted slightly as if all she wanted was to release a few final words.

Multiple stab wounds make her neck look like a minefield. Her chest, too, is covered in puncture marks.

How many times did I strike?

Why can't I remember?

Staring at her, reality begins to set in.

What the fuck have you done, Eve? No one will follow you now.

I jump up and begin pacing back and forth in her office.

She deserved it.

But no one can know about this.

No one.

I catch a glimpse of my reflection in her office window—a crooked posture I've come to recognize as someone other than myself—and I step toward it.

"Everyone will follow me," I say aloud. "Without Vrin, they'll turn to me."

You fool. You'll pay for what you've done. There are cameras everywhere.

Fuck.

The cameras. They're back on. Shit. My heart skips a beat and I swallow hard. Although I should be petrified to be caught and trialed for what I've done, legal consequences are the last thing on my mind. What I fear more than anything is being viewed in a certain light. The women won't follow me if they know what I've done.

Fuck. Fuck. Fuck.

I search the room and then the ceiling to ensure no cameras are installed inside her office. In that regard, I'm safe. Still, the moment I step outside, I'll be caught leaving the scene of the crime.

How am I supposed to get out of this?

As I stare at my hunched figure with messy hair, everything comes into place; I know exactly who to pin this on.

CHAPTER 32 – GABRIEL

Freyda's probably getting pretty pissed by now.

I told her I'd meet her in the courtyard at three. It's almost four. But I had to get a change of clothes for the training and I couldn't even get into my room. I rush down my corridor and make my way to the elevators. They weren't working earlier, either, but they seem to be fine now.

After our time together, the last thing I want to do is upset Freyda.

We're doing good. Really good.

The moment the elevator reaches the Hub, I run toward the courtyard. Women stare and point—they must not be used to seeing someone run in Elysium. Then, men in black BIO-8 Skins and large guns across their chests glare at me. One of them points a finger and shouts, "No running!"

What the fuck is this? Church?

The last thing I need is to get arrested, so I do what I'm told.

I walk fast instead, fantasizing about punching one of them in the face. After everything that's happened, I guess I'm pretty fed up with authority figures. I'm especially fed up with military men.

The moment I step outside, Freyda throws two arms into the air and runs toward me.

Shit. I pissed her off.

"Where were you?" she shouts. She runs closer and wipes a line of sweat from her eyebrow. "Jesus, Gabriel, you had me worried. The training's over. Lucy and Emily already went back inside."

Worried? So, she isn't upset with me? I feel like an ass for missing out on training with those kids. Freyda told me she knows them and that it would mean a lot if I helped her train them.

"Sorry," I say. "I had to get a quick word in with Vrin, and then I went—"

But I stop talking when screams start echoing behind me from inside the hallway. The doors open with a swoosh and out come the same two guys with guns who told me to stop running.

What the hell do they want? They're searching everywhere with scowls on their faces. Like they're pissed off about something. Either that or something's wrong.

Behind them, the screaming gets louder. Something's definitely wrong.

Without thinking, I run toward them. I can't let all my years of service go to waste. I may not be a guard here in Elysium, but I can help fight if that's what they need.

"What's going on?" I ask. "Let me help."

The guy on the right, a young blond man with a nasty scar cutting through part of his nostril, looks at me, wide-eyed. It's like he wasn't expecting me to appear in front of him. The surprise doesn't last long.

Maybe a second. Now, he's glaring at me with so much hatred that I take a step back.

"It's him!" growls the other one.

He loads his gun and aims it at my face. "On your fucking knees!"

I raise both hands and slowly kneel. What the fuck is this about? What did I do now? Did I have another episode that I can't remember?

"What is this?" Freyda asks, running toward me.

The blond guard aims the gun at her. "Step back!"

"Hey!" I shout, wanting to protect Freyda, but all this does is piss him off more.

He kicks me in the chest and I fall to my side.

Suddenly, another dozen guards come running outside and women scatter in every direction.

"That's him!"

"Son of a bitch!"

Two solid hands yank at my wrists and I find myself eating grass. I turn my head from side to side to try to see what's going on. To my left, the guards are circling me while one of them ties my wrists together with handcuffs.

To my right, women are moving closer looking as confused as I am.

Someone yanks me up and I find myself face-to-face with a dark-haired, red-faced man. His beard reaches his massive neck, where squiggly veins pop out like he's about to start convulsing.

He stares at me dead in the eyes, so close to my face that I can hear his teeth grinding.

"You're under arrest for the murder of Vrin Lykson, you fucking piece of shit."

CHAPTER 33 – LUCY

My mom used to say it a lot. Car crash syndrome, I think it was.

She'd told me it was when something terrible would happen and people couldn't stop staring even though the sight was disturbing.

That's what's happening right now, for everyone, I think.

Eve doesn't even look like Eve anymore. Her white overcoat is splattered in so much blood it looks like buckets of red paint were spilled on her. She sits on the solid white floor in the middle of the Hub with blood smudged all around her. With trembling hands, she pulls at her clothing and at her hair, probably having a nervous breakdown.

"I tried… I tried…" she keeps repeating.

Women gather closer, but not too close.

"Is it true?" someone whispers.

Weeping and shouting spreads across the Hub.

What happened? Why is everyone so upset?

"I tried to save her…" Eve says. "There… There was so much blood."

Tears stream down her face, slipping through the blood smears and forming little beige lines on her cheeks. Every time she opens her mouth to talk, slimy saliva sticks to the corners of her mouth like she hasn't had a drink in days.

"Out of the way!" comes a man's gruff voice.

He rushes through the crowd and kneels by Eve's side. "Come on, let's get you out of here."

"I tried..." she keeps repeating.

He tries to help her by scooping her underneath the arms but she pulls away violently. "Get your fucking man hands off of me!"

Everyone takes a step back.

With hands still trembling, she wipes her face, though all it does is smudge more blood on it.

"Don't you all see?" she says, eyeing the crowd that's formed around her. "History is repeating itself." She rolls her hateful eyes toward the man who tried to help her up. He looks pretty shaken, too, with both hands by his face. Obviously, he wasn't trying to upset her. He only wanted to help. "Vrin's allowed men to carry weapons... She's allowed men as much freedom as us inside these walls, and look at what's happened. A man killed her. A *man!*"

She sounds broken.

Then, she lets out a maniacal laugh.

"This *man* wasn't even armed!" Her voice carries across the Hub and all the way up the walls. "Is that how you want to live? In fear?"

Slowly, more guards approach, both men and women. The women seem to be keeping their distance from the male guards now, almost as if they're carrying some infectious disease.

"Oh my God," comes a familiar voice. Two solid

hands grip me by the shoulders and I know it's Nola before I even see her face. I turn around and hug her tight.

"Are you all right, sweetheart? I saw Vrin come into the Medical Unit. It was... It was awful—" She doesn't go into any more detail. She must be afraid to scare me. "She was pronounced dead the moment she got there. Is it true? Was it this Gabriel man?"

Women around her start chiming in.

"It was the man."

"Yeah, that guy who jumped on Stacey and the others when he first got here."

"He was unstable."

Someone scoffs.

"Unstable is putting it lightly. The guy's a fucking lunatic."

I'm so confused, so I don't join in. How could Gabriel do something like this? I don't know the guy, but I've seen the way he acts around people. He seems too nice and gentle. I've also seen the way he cares for his dog. How can a guy who kisses his dog murder someone so violently?

Nola doesn't have to give me the details about how violent it was; I already know. Everyone around me has been talking about what happened. They've been arguing about the murder weapon, and most people seem to think it was a letter opener. And as for the stab wounds, well, no one seems to know, but I've heard the number twelve thrown around a lot. It's an estimate, but it's enough to make me sick to my stomach.

If it was Gabriel, he's a complete psychopath.

Then, someone with a calm voice enters the room and everyone goes quiet.

"Enough," the voice says, and Nayma surfaces from the crowd wearing her famous blue-rimmed glasses and beige khaki pants. A tight bun sits atop her head and her shoulders are drawn back.

She isn't smiling, which makes her look like an entirely different person.

"Come with me, Eve," she says. "Let's get you cleaned up."

She pulls Eve up onto her feet and Eve doesn't put up a fight.

"Who's taking over?" someone yells.

"We'll deal with that later," Nayma says.

A man wearing black pants and a black padded shirt steps forward. His boots, which are as black as his clothing and his skin, are shinier than the floor. He isn't overly large—maybe Eve's height—but he's stocky with a thick neck. The sides of his head are shaved and the top covered with a short layer of fuzz that matches his beard—something so dark that it masks half of his face.

With a calm, gravelly voice, he says, "I'm second in command to Vrin."

"Zander's right," says the guard standing next to him. "By default, he becomes the new leader."

At first, no one responds. Maybe they aren't sure how to. There's always a second in command in the event something happens to the original leader, right? How can anyone argue that?

Eve, however, isn't afraid to speak up.

She lets out a forced laugh and rolls her eyes. It

looks like she isn't trembling at all anymore. Maybe she's calmed down. Though that's a big change out of nowhere.

"You think that after what's happened, the women of Elysium will allow a *man* to take charge?"

The women around her start shouting overtop one another and pointing fingers at Zander.

"I understand your concern," Zander says calmly. "This, however, isn't up for a vote. Vrin made it clear that should anything happen to her—"

"Do you hear that, ladies?" Eve says. She's so angry it looks like she's about to laugh again, which freaks me out. I've known Eve long enough to know what her angry smile looks like. "A *man* is telling us what to do. Doesn't this sound familiar to you? Don't you see what's going on? This was certainly orchestrated. Kill off the female leader so that men can rule over Elysium."

She starts pacing in the Hub, leaving bloody prints on the floor.

Some of the male guards are gripping their guns and eyeing the raging crowd.

"This isn't America anymore!" Eve shouts and everyone goes quiet. "There's no president, and your opinions matter. So why don't we do this the way it's been done for hundreds of years?" She smirks, brushes a few strands of hair out of her face, and plants a hand on her waist. "Let's put it up to a vote."

CHAPTER 34 – EVE

The male guards appear on edge.

Some of them tighten their grips around their massive guns while others scan the crowd with large fearful eyes like helpless zoo animals.

Zander, the second in command who only moments ago believed he should be in power, crosses both arms over his muscular chest and glowers at me.

What's wrong? I want to say. *Feeling outnumbered?*

"I nominate Eve to be leader!" someone shouts from the crowd.

Similar words spread throughout the Hub and hundreds of women nod in agreement. Most men remain silent, which is precisely what they should be doing. If they've heard of me—which, surely, they have—they know not to piss me off. They know that I prefer to run things without the presence of males at all.

The truth is that Zander is the best choice for the men—slowly, he will turn things around and allow men to have all the power as it's always been.

What confuses me is that the unarmed men—the ones in basic cotton clothing standing among the women—aren't joining in. In fact, they aren't participating in the chaos at all. Instead, they turn to their wives, mothers, or daughters, and wait for them to make a decision.

Only a handful of men with guns step forward, chests heaved and shoulders drawn back.

"Zander is the rightful leader!" one of them growls.

A few other men throw balled fists into the air and cheer, but for the most part, the men in the Hub remain quiet.

Why is that? I tilt my head and stare at them, trying to understand. Why not support their own sex? That's what men do, isn't it? Team up against women? Why stand there like a bunch of silent fools and allow women to take charge? These men must care more for their loved ones than they do power. I don't understand it, but I don't bother wasting any more energy trying to figure it out.

All I care about is regaining my rightful place as leader.

"Eve!"

"Eve!"

"Eve!"

The voices become so loud that I feel the vibrations underneath my feet and through the tips of my fingers. Elated, I draw my shoulders back and stare at the growing crowd before me—at my people.

Zander's dark brows come together and his lips are pursed in anger. Within seconds, I managed to take away all of his power, or at least, the power he deluded himself into believing he had.

I stare back at him, fighting the urge to smile.

"The people have spoken!" Nayma shouts over everyone. She removes her blue-rimmed glasses, tucks them into her shirt pocket, and reaches for my wrist. When she pulls it up over my head, I see the bloodstains on my sleeve. "Eve Malum, ruler of Elysium!"

The room fills with so many voices that I can't determine who is saying what. If the walls weren't so thick, I'd believe them to be shaking. I stare up toward the ceiling, which looks to be a mile high, and on each floor, a few people stare down through the glass.

Everyone's eyes are on me.

This is yours, Eve. This place is yours.

The moment I raise an open palm into the air, the crowd becomes silent and all that can be heard is everyone's rapid breathing.

"Given recent events," I say, my voice carrying over their heads, "men are no longer to be armed." I gaze toward the crowd of armed men. "Lay down your weapons."

"That's ridiculous!" Zander shouts.

Now, I see his true colors. He appeared calm and levelheaded seconds ago, but now he stands before me with his angry, twisted face inches away from mine. He breathes loudly through his nostrils and tries to tower over me even though we're the same height.

He's behaving like any other man, trying to make himself look big to intimidate me.

It doesn't work. I'm not afraid of him, nor any man here in Elysium.

The sound of guns powering on fills the space

behind me and a group of armed women circles in front of me with their energy rifles pointed at Zander's face.

Smirking at him, I elevate my chin.

A few armed men retaliate by pointing their guns at me, creating a standoff. That's when every single woman carrying a gun steps forward, eyes gazing down the sights of their guns.

"Lower your weapons," I repeat to the men.

Then, to everyone's surprise, something spectacular happens.

The men and women of Elysium—the civilians in blue cotton clothes—step forward with fists clenched, prepared to fight. I stare at Zander again, this time, from head to toe, and wait for him to command his dogs to lower their guns.

"You heard Eve!" shouts one of the female guards. "Put down the fucking weapons or this gets ugly!"

Several armed men farther back of the Hub have already set their guns down.

With an elevated chin and a hateful smirk on his face, Zander slowly sets his gun to the ground. It makes a soft ticking noise the moment it hits the floor, and he straightens his posture, his hands outstretched.

It doesn't truly look like he's submitting to me. He's staring at me as if visualizing how he's going to make his way back on top—how he's going to take me out.

"Arrest Zander," I say, and several gasps fill the space around me.

"You have no fucking right!" he snaps, but he

doesn't have the time to come after me.

Two female guards grab him and pull his arms behind his back.

"You disobeyed a direct order," I say. "In fact, you endangered the lives of my people by continuing to hold a dangerous weapon when advised to do otherwise."

He breathes hard, his flared nostrils doubling in size.

"You won't get away with this," he growls.

* * * * * *

"You won't get away with this!" the old man shouts.

He trembles with his long, crooked finger pointed at me as if he possesses the ability to judge me in the afterlife.

I don't have time to argue with a *man*.

Stepping over a dead carcass, I gaze back toward the crowd of women following me.

"Ignore the hatred," I shout. "Where we're going, there's no room for men like him."

"There's no room for men at all, right?" a woman shouts, her voice quivering.

Right now, most women look like her. They're petrified of what's to come, but it's apparent they're all in agreement over one thing: men are not welcome.

I smile at her. She, along with every other woman following me, understands what they're getting themselves into. "That's right," I say.

Then, to my surprise, comes a woman's shrill voice.

"You can't do this!"

Next to her are two young boys, most likely around the ages of five and eight. She pulls them close to her with her hands on their foreheads as if protecting them from an evil force. Her lips, dry and cracked, are slanted on one side as if she's suffered from a stroke. I should feel sorry for her, but I don't—all I feel is hatred for men, and all I see when I look at those boys are future weapons.

Her eyes dart from side to side as if hoping someone will come to her aid, but no one comes.

"You can't make me choose between life and my boys," she cries, pulling them even closer. "I'll always choose my boys!"

"I'm not making you do anything," I say. "You have free will. Your best option is to join Vrin."

The frightened look on her face quickly transforms into loathing. She clenches her teeth, grabs her two sons by the wrists, and turns around, heading back into the devastation of a once-astounding Washington, D.C.

Ash covers the streets and carcasses lie everywhere. Most people have returned to their homes for safety, while others fight over supplies.

The old man who shouted at me a short time ago shakes his head and goes on to help an injured woman on the ground.

"Get your hands off me!" she shouts.

Two other women come rushing to her aid, pushing the old man back. He trips over a car's bumper and smashes his skull against the sidewalk. A loud cracking sound pierces the air, and although I should feel bad, I don't.

Why is he trying to help us? Where was he when President Price took away women's rights? Men like him are nothing but cowards. Blood spills from his head, forming a dark pool around his cheeks and neck, and I turn away.

Lucy grabs my hand—a cool, fragile touch that reminds me that her mother's blood is stained on my skin. But I don't pull away. Instead, I squeeze it and smile down at her.

"Everything's going to be fine."

* * * * * *

As the guards pull Zander out of my sight, I get the feeling I'm being watched, and not in an admiring way, either.

I follow my sense to a woman mixed in the crowd. She has curly brown hair that looks as though it hasn't been washed in months. On either side of her, two teenage boys tower over her, having obviously gone through a growth spurt with their awkwardly lanky limbs.

But what catches my eye isn't the hateful glare she's throwing my way—rather, it's her disfigurement; her lips droop as if she's recently suffered from a stroke. The two boys must be her sons—the ones I refused to allow her to bring along to Eden.

Behind her, a few other women whose faces I recognize from Eden are staring at me with arms crossed over their chests.

Wonderful. I already have enemies.

I offer them a smile, but no one smiles back.

You don't need them, Eve. Look around.

One by one, the men and women of Elysium begin

lowering themselves onto one knee. I catch a glimpse of Lucy and Nola at the far back, their eyes darting from side to side. Their bodies, however, mimic the movements of everyone else as they lower themselves into bowing positions.

I draw my shoulders back, feeling Vrin's dry blood crack apart on the skin of my face.

You did it, Eve.

I smile at everyone before me.

The road ahead won't be easy—I have a lot of trust to earn back—but very soon they will see that I, Eve Malum, have always been the one true leader capable of rebuilding America.

CHAPTER 35 – GABRIEL

She's looking at me like I'm a stranger, so I look away.

I didn't do anything wrong, but I feel ashamed. Ashamed of what she's probably thinking of me.

"I didn't do it," I mutter, staring at the metal floor.

I'm sitting behind a glass wall like a caged zoo animal. Inside my cell is a shitty bed, a toilet, and plain white walls. Why didn't they banish me? Eve wanted this, didn't she? She wants me to suffer.

Freyda's helped the guards place me in confinement. That's the only reason she's here. But it killed me. She looked at me like I was the biggest piece of shit she'd ever seen.

Why's she staring at me like that? And why isn't she saying anything?

A loud clicking noise echoes behind her and she turns her head to look.

When she realizes the last guard's left the room, she sticks her face against the glass of my cell. A small window is open, right in the middle, so I can hear her.

"What happened, Gabriel? Tell me everything. Where was Eve when this happened? I need details. If you want me to get you out of here, I need to know—"

"Get me out of here?" I ask. "So you believe me? You know it wasn't me?"

She sighs. "I know it wasn't you, Gabriel. Someone's framed you and I won't stop until I find out who it is."

CHAPTER 36 – LUCY

"Isn't it a bit weird? I mean... It happened pretty fast. And conveniently, if you ask me." Abigail jabs her fork into her pile of hot buttered peas. "And why's your food so much better than ours?"

She's referring to the sixth floor, where she was assigned by Nayma when we first got here.

"They're always feeding us potatoes. And rice. I guess a lot of carbs, now that I think about it. Maybe they're trying to fatten us up." She makes her eyes go big, and her freckles seem to enlarge with them. "Hey. I should ask Eve to change up the menu. You think anyone can go up there and talk to her? Does she let kids into her office?"

Emily rolls her eyes at me as if to say, *Thank God she wasn't put on the fifth floor with us.*

"Maybe I can even get her to reassign me here, with you guys!"

My fork scratches my plate. "You wouldn't like it here... It's a lot of the original people from Eden. Isn't it cooler to meet new friends?"

She sighs and rests her chin on her fist while chewing her peas. "Yeah... Yeah, I guess."

"I don't know what Eve allows or doesn't allow,"

Emily says. "All I know is that she doesn't put up with bullshit." She shrugs. "I kind of like her."

I stare at Emily. Does she mean that?

"Look," she says, possibly reading my mind, "Eve had some pretty weird methods in Eden, but ever since she's been put in charge here, all she's done is disarm men. Nothing else." She shrugs again while taking a bite of lamb. "If you ask me, I'd say she's the kind of leader we need. Her top priority is women. Vrin didn't seem to have the same idea."

"I think Vrin's top priority was survival and comfort," I say, a bit peeved off that Emily would ever side with Eve.

"Well, I think—" Abigail starts, but a foghorn-like voice fills the eating lounge.

"Attention, everyone."

It's Adimmer, our Facilitator. His beard, smooth and perfectly trimmed and attached to long sideburns, makes him look younger. He tugs on his canary yellow overcoat—something I've seen him wear every day since being here—and smiles at everyone, waiting for a few to swallow their bites of food.

"In ten minutes' time, anyone interested in participating in a movie night is welcome to join us in room 502."

"Movie night!" shouts a teenage boy.

An angelic voice follows. "W-what'th a movie?"

She must be no older than four years old, which means she's never experienced a movie before. How is that even possible? How could Vrin have built such an advanced society and not offered movies? I'm automatically reminded of Lucas and the television program we watched together.

We'd sat there in the darkness of the basement as if what we were doing was top secret.

Why?

A chair screeches loudly against the floor and a middle-aged woman stands up. "What's the meaning of this, Adimmer? We were told by Vrin that Elysium didn't have any movies... That television wasn't an option for us."

Adimmer raises his hands, palms up as if to say, *I'm just the messenger.*

"What movie?" someone exclaims.

The voices louden and people start getting up from their chairs.

Abigail throws her fork onto her plate and it makes a clanging noise. "I wanna go. You guys coming?"

Emily looks at me, almost as if for permission. Either that, or she doesn't want to go without me.

"I haven't seen a movie in... God. I don't even know how long," she says.

I smirk at her. Although I'm not in the mood to be surrounded by screaming kids, I can't say no. It would be nice to sit back and be entertained for an hour or so. The only entertainment I get is reading fiction, and even that is extremely limited. I wonder if that's been Vrin's plan all along—promote education over entertainment.

Sliding my chair back, I jump to my feet.

"Whoa."

I swing around to find Lucas standing behind me

with two hands firmly planted on my chair.

"Oh, sorry," I say. "I, um. We're going to see the movie. You coming?" I ask, staring at his freshly shaven face. His hair, too, was recently washed. A droplet of water drips from his forehead and glides along his combed eyebrow.

He smirks and I catch a scent of something— either cologne or body wash. It's fresh and crisp and it makes me feel weak in the knees.

"That depends," he says.

I stare at him. "On what?"

"Are *you* going?" he asks.

I giggle and feel like a total loser. Why'd my laugh come out like that? He seems to have liked it, though. He tilts his head to one side and watches me make a fool of myself.

"Well, yeah," I say. "I mean, *duh*. Why else would I have asked you?"

Why can't I stop staring at his lips? Does he notice? The second I look up, I catch him staring at mine.

"All right, Lucy," Emily says impatiently. "I'll see you in there."

She and Abigail walk away whispering and chuckling, no doubt making fun of how I'm acting around Lucas.

"How've you been?" he asks.

"Good," I say, not knowing how else to respond. I haven't seen Lucas in over a week which led me to assume he was either busy working on his inventions or outright trying to ignore me. With the way he's smiling, though, it's obvious he wasn't trying to ignore me.

"It's weird, isn't it?" he asks.

"What?"

"Vrin," he says, and for the first time, he looks sad. "She was good for this place."

"What do you think of Eve?" I ask.

He tightens his lips. "Honestly, I don't know her well enough yet. But she's obviously way more lenient than Vrin. I mean, this whole movie night was her idea."

I'm stunned.

Why would Eve allow everyone a movie night? Why would she want us to have *fun*?

"Vrin would've never allowed that," he adds.

"Why not?"

He scratches the back of my chair with this thumbnail. "She believed that mindless entertainment rotted the brain. Why do you think the Library barely has any fiction? She wants kids focused on studying or being physical outside... Not sitting on a chair and staring at a screen or letting their imaginations run wild." He forces a laugh. "You should see the pile of movies we have downstairs—" Yet when he undoubtedly realizes he's said too much, he clears his throat. "Um, that's between you and me only, Lucy."

"Your secret's safe," I say. "Besides, it makes sense that Vrin would focus more on studying."

"Yes and no. I agree that studying is important, but so is having fun. I don't know. I think Eve's doing something right. The whole disarming thing was a bit sudden, but I get where she's coming from. Especially after..." He rubs his forehead. "I can't believe someone would do that to Vrin."

I bow my head, sick to my stomach.

"Sorry," he says. "I didn't mean to get all dark."

The room feels eerily quiet.

"Did everyone already leave for the movie?" I ask.

"Looks that way. Here." He reaches behind him and pulls from his belt my H-Cap.

"Oh my God!" I throw both hands into the air and snatch it from him. "Is it fixed?" I press the power button and it turns on with a soft beep. "I-I can't believe it. Lucas! You did it. You fixed my H-Cap!"

He grins at me with shiny narrowed eyes. It's as if he's enjoying my reaction more than anything in the world.

"Thank you," I say. "Thank you so much. You have no idea—"

And he plants his thick, warm lips against mine. The short stubble of his shaved beard tickles my chin, but I don't mind. His hand, strong and firm, holds me tight at my lower back, pressing me into him.

After everything I've seen, I should be afraid, but I'm not. In his arms, I feel safer than I've ever felt before. His fresh cool scent enters my nostrils and I breathe it in without removing my lips from his.

Right now, this is the best feeling in the world.

Slowly, our lips separate but our eyes remain locked.

"I... I'm sorry," he says. "I didn't mean to—"

I clear my throat. "N-no... Please don't apologize. You didn't do anything wrong."

"I should have asked—"

"No," I say, my legs wobbly. "It was perfect."

His canine tooth makes an appearance.

"I, um," I try. "Do you mind if I meet you in the movie room? I'd like to take a look at my H-Cap, but I'd like to—"

"You need your space," he says sweetly. "I get it, trust me. I'll save you a seat."

As he walks away, he grabs my hand and allows it to slip out of his.

Is this what a crush feels like? I need to talk to Nola. I've never felt this before. Every part of me is tingling and all I want to do is shout or dance. I'm so excited I feel like I could burst. Clutching the H-Cap against my chest, I rush to my room, unable to wipe the grin off my face.

I throw myself onto my bed, imagining it to be a floating cloud.

God, I could live with this feeling forever.

But I'm pulled back to reality when I remember what I'm holding—my H-Cap... memories of my mother. I scrunch my pillow underneath my neck and bend my knees. With the H-Cap resting on my thighs, I turn it on.

A small green light appears at its rounded tip and all of my old pictures are projected into the air in front of me.

I'm about to start enlarging them when I see something else. At the top right-hand corner of the projection is a flashing exclamation mark. It sits directly beside my Messages folder, which has always been empty.

A new message? How is that even possible?

I touch the icon with the tip of my finger and a

new screen appears with a video frame. It's blurry, and I can't quite tell what it is. Underneath, it's written: July 19, 2064.

July 19? How? That's the day Aunt Eve came back for me. That's the day the war ended.

Hesitant, I allow my finger to float up to the video frame. Although afraid of what I might see, I have to play it. The screen flickers and suddenly, my mom's face appears.

"Is this thing working? Come on. Come on."

She toys with the screen and taps at it. I'm not sure what device she's on, but obviously, it isn't hers.

"L-Lucy, honey," she says, now staring right into the camera.

Where is she? It looks like a fancy office.

"If this works, honey, you should receive a message to your H-Cap. Listen, things are getting out of hand, and Mommy wants you to know she loves you so much, okay? Whatever happens, promise me you'll find someone good... Someone honest... to take care of you."

Tears are streaming down her face and with the back of her hand, she wipes them.

My throat swells watching her. She looks beyond terrified. It's like she knows something awful is coming. I watch in horror, wanting to turn it off. But I can't—I need to know what happens.

"I..." She turns her head sideways to a bunch of frenzied voices in the background. "Shit."

She hits a button on the device, trying to turn it off, but nothing happens. Instead, I'm left staring at a beige and white wall and part of the American flag.

"Put that down!" someone yells.

Holy shit. That voice. It's President Price. What's Mom doing with the president? Where is she? Where's Aunt Eve? They left together. Are they both there? My palms slip against the metal of my H-Cap, but I don't let go.

"You're not a murderer. Let this go," my mom says.

My heart's beating so hard it feels like a hammer's stuck inside my chest.

A bunch of shuffling and grunting fills the air. Then, something cracks, and the president whimpers.

"What're you going to do?" he sneers. "Beat me to death?"

Oh God, I wish the camera would turn. I need to know what's happening.

"Stop it!" comes my mom's voice. "You don't need to do this!"

There's more shuffling and it sounds like she's fighting someone.

"It's not loaded, you dumb bl—" says the president.

But then, he goes quiet. The next thing I hear is gargling.

What happened?

Oh God, what happened?

"You don't deserve a bullet, you motherfucking—"

My stomach sinks—I know that voice.

It's Eve.

Then, a loud noise follows. It sounds like cartilage being crushed or smashed by a hard object. I'm assuming it's President Price's face.

"Oh God, what did you do?" my mom says.

She sounds so frantic.

"This is for all the women whose lives you've ruined," Eve growls.

It sounds like she's beating him, but he isn't making a sound. Is he dead? There's so much noise going on, I can't tell what's happening. I almost wish the video would end, but it doesn't. Instead, I see something I wish I hadn't.

Into the camera's view comes my mom, clasping at her throat. Blood comes pouring out through the cracks of her fingers.

She drops to her knees.

"O... Jesus Christ, Ophelia. Please, no. No, no, no," Eve sobs. She steps into the camera's view and grabs my mom with one arm, falling down with her. In her other hand is a huge rifle with a bloody bayonet attached at its tip.

"Come on, we have to go," comes another familiar voice.

Vrin.

Vrin knew about this?

My mind is racing a mile a minute.

My mom gargles one last time before her head falls back, revealing a large open gash at the base of her throat. I turn away and grind my teeth.

"I'm so sorry," Eve cries.

I squeeze my H-Cap so tight that the frame cracks out of place and the image distorts.

Eve always warned us about not letting snakes into our garden, when this whole time, she was the fucking snake.

Visit **www.shadeowens.com** for more works by Shade Owens, including **Elysium**, the fourth book in the Garden of Evil series.